And She Lived

And She Lived

Camile Jené

Formatting by:
Love Wins Publishing
www.lovewinspub.com
Redlands, California

Printed in the United States of America

First Printing, November 2020

To CeeCee and The Boy,
I love you with my whole heart.
May you see that anything is possible
and never lose your faith and belief in God.
You are excellence personified and I eagerly
await what you will create for this world.

Prologue

Jasmine age 89

"Thank you, Papa! Thank you so much!"

Isabella stuffed the money in her pocket and hurried inside. Surely, she was headed to send text messages to her friends about the brag-worthy amount she scored for their movie night.

Jasmine stifled her giggle with a fist.

"Oh Izzy, you didn't stand a chance," she said shaking her head.

"Hmm?"

"You're always putty in that child's hands just like you were in her mother's hands sixty-two years ago," Jasmine chuckled as she spoke of her nineteen-year-old granddaughter, Isabella.

Israel tried to strike the seriousness from his face, but laughter won as he chuckled at the side-eye from his wife of sixty-five years. Jasmine was right, and Israel could not deny it. Anything Isabella asked, her Papa would grant without too much thought. He lived to take care of his family, but he took particular delight in spoiling his grands.

"Jax, leave me alone now. Don't start nothin', won't be nothin'."

"Mmmm hmm," Jasmine hummed contentedly, the blue yarn flowing through her fingers.

She knitted as often as she could to keep her hands active and the range of motion healthy. At one point in her life, she wondered if she would live long enough to use her hands. The weakness in them from disease plagued her daily activities. But even in her old age, they were strong now. A reminder of God's healing promise.

Her hands reared a house full of beautiful children into adulthood. They kept a home inviting, tidy, and a safe space for all who dawned the doors. And cooked nutritious meals which kept bellies full, souls satisfied, and promoted a love of healthy cuisine that now spanned generations. Jasmine's hands caught the firstborn of her firstborn during an impromptu home birth. Her hands lovingly now stitched a blanket for her 1st great-grandchild, slated for arrival next month – the firstborn to her only son's son. Her hands healed as they touched. Jasmine's hands brought so many people joy throughout the years.

With each stitch, the sense of joy built as she thought of the miracles her life manifested. The manifestation of the promises of God, prosperity, and legacy that her family represented elicited an urge to run or shout. Family and friends voiced concerns in the early years. Would she live long enough to see her children into adulthood? Her lips spread wide as Jasmine glanced upward and caught a glimpse of her granddaughter Carmen marching down the street toward their porch. She beamed. Adult children and grandchildren? And now a great-grand on the way. Remarkable. The perfect word. Jasmine, healthy and spry at 89 years old was a walking miracle. Victoriously overcoming the battle for her health when life looked bleak at one point to even Jasmine. Actually, a few times, with scars and life-altering changes before she hit a stride. If Jasmine were honest with herself, at times, it seemed impossible to survive. The thought now brought tears. What a dark and low place, imagining her life ending way too soon had she given in to doubt and manifested her improper destiny. And her health was not the only would-be casualty. Jasmine's marriage barely survived the bumpy road. But God! The tears that brimmed now did not hold sadness, they shined with triumph, thanksgiving, and she couldn't keep them back as they began to flow.

Israel, ever watching, ever-present, his silent strength always a comfort, patted her hand softly. He tapped her twice and shook his head up and down. He knew. And she found comfort in his validation. What those two had witnessed... Some of it – most of it – was just between them and God. No words needed to be exchanged.

Jasmine blotted her tears with a handkerchief she kept handy and smiled so big her cheeks began to throb, that familiar feeling of unspeakable joy warming her heart.

"Nonnie!" Carmen ran up to the porch and stomped up both steps. Tears streaked her contorted face.

The youngest grandchild of the bunch at only five years old (until her great-grandson Martin the Third made his arrival), she was used to getting her way. As the baby of Israel and Jasmine's youngest daughter Courtney, she got her spoiled honest. Jasmine's older children Carleigh, Mariah, and Martin often reminded Courtney that Carmen was her righteous payback for the terror she reigned on them as the young tyrant princess Israel and Jasmine allowed her to be (of course they denied it). As the oops baby that came when Jasmine was 42 years old, she took the whole family by surprise. And by storm.

"What's wrong with Nonnie's favorite 7-year-old grand-girl?"

"They are *not* sharing," she said as she let a fresh set of tears fall.

Her hands dropped to her sides slumping down as her shoulders heaved. Her head shook with disappointment.

"Who isn't sharing with my baby?"

"Those other kids next door. I was *so* nice to them. I gave them my winning smile exactly how you taught me, but they treated me mean. They were *so* mean!"

"Now, now, sweetie. Come to Nonnie."

Jasmine allowed Carmen to lay down in her lap as she rubbed her head full of soft two-strand twists.

"Nonnie, it's not fair! Chelsea and Moises have fun over there, but I never do!" She said, referring to her two older siblings.

"I asked them to bring me home!"

"Baby, some people just aren't your people. If they don't want to share, it looks like they will miss out on the best playing partner this side of town."

"They are Nonnie?"

"Oh yes," Nonnie said, reassuring Carmen with a look. Israel chuckled softly.

"Then why is Papa laughing."

"He is displaying agreement laughter. Huh, Izzy?" Jasmine looked at him pleadingly.

At her mature age of eighty-nine, inconsolable toddler tears were no longer her specialty. She needed peace and quick!

"Oh, yes, babe. Agreement laughter. Carmen, you're the best, like your Nonnie said."

"Well, why don't they want to play with me then?"

"Baby, do you remember what I told you a while back about people?"

"Nonnie, you tell me a lot of things. Which one?"

Carmen asked with her nose scrunched up.

"Everyone won't be kind or have a sweet disposition as yourself. But never let others change you. Never let this world take your joy."

"Oh yes, Nonnie, I remember that one. I'm not going to be mean to them even if they are mean to me."

"Yes, honey. You have the right idea," Jasmine said as she remembered having these conversations with her own children.

Her mind decided to go back further to the conversations she had with her mother. Jasmine affectionately called her mother Anita, "Mommy." Anita always spoke of Jasmine's joy and unrelenting smile. One day Anita sat Jasmine down for a chat. At six years old, she was still young but she hung on to her mother's words because her seriousness alarmed Jasmine. She thought she was in trouble. She remembered the words clearly.

"Never stop smiling baby. Don't let the world steal your joy."

Anita would catch her smiling so hard that her cheeks would hurt. Anita saw the freedom Jasmine basked in daily and how her joy lit up a room. Anita also understood how determined the world would be to snuff out Jasmine's light. She wanted to warn Jasmine against the imminent attacks. She wanted Jasmine to know it was okay to still be kind and never mimic the darkness.

Jasmine stared solemnly into the sky. She remembered that conversation and Anita's reminders throughout life. Jasmine took the words to heart. Of course, there were several times in life where she found it hard to follow Anita's advice. When she forgot how to smile and was too hurt, exhausted, and stressed to carry joy. She remembered when she had let trials overtake her and almost lost her smile, and her life, for good.

Chapter 1

He has clearly *lost* it. My dear, sweet, husband. I rolled my eyes as far back into their sockets as they would go. I attempted to muster feelings of admiration as I thought of how hard Israel worked for our family. Nope. Still, *so* annoyed. With eyes slit, I stared at my phone, mouth agape. I blinked and read it again.

8:32 PM: Hey. Long day. Need a break. Going out.

The exhaustion threatened to involuntarily cause my eyes to shut as I bowed my head, causing my curls to cascade into my face. I've been at this house with our lovely children all day. A sunny, breezy, Southern California Saturday that should have been spent frolicking in the grass at Hamilton Park or strolling gingerly through the sand as the children skipped rocks at Leo Carrillo Beach's bay. Family day, the original plan, swirled down the drain with the last remnants of mouthwash as Israel made his way out of the bathroom and hurriedly threw on khakis and a loose-fitting SnackJoys button-up for a "quick meeting." My chest rose quickly and caved with a sharp breath as I let the familiar words fall to the ground with a thud. Quick meetings, or any business transaction for that matter, were a mirage when it came to Israel and his true love, SnackJoys, the company he built from the ground up. Israel founded his company a few years into our marriage around the time I quit my teaching job. At first, I was elated to help build his business but it quickly turned into the focal point of our entire existence. Nothing trumped SnackJoys. Not our kids, and certainly not me.

As he prepared to leave, my "Have a good meeting," was less than halfhearted. If he noticed, he made no indication. He hurried out the door and only returned to feather-light peck my cheek after I sharply whispered, "Well, have a good day!"

When you marry an ambitious entrepreneur, off days, don't really exist. Somehow, I thought today was different. He told the kids. That's like cardinal rule number seven of parenting. *Neve*r tell the kids about an outing until the seatbelts and car seat stage of the plan comes into play. You think a nagging spouse is annoying? *Nothing* agitates a last nerve better than a child who knows you're going somewhere. The endless questions feel like assault. I knew better, though. With the unpredictability of his operation, things could change momentarily. Still, my annoyance remained. And resentment flared. Left with the responsibility to break the news to the kids, my shoulders slumped. Why weren't they up as usual at the crack of dawn so *he* could tell them of our broken plans? Then again, I had tossed and turned all night leaving me stiff and unrested so I chose to relish the snippet of quiet time.

The day hadn't been awful. There was no way I could take the kids to the park or beach alone with the level of tired I woke up feeling so we did our usual; played in the backyard with bikes, trucks, and kinetic sand, and as a salve for their father's absence, I let the kids break out the paint. I loathed painting with my youngest. The paint somehow always ended up somewhere other than the carefully placed contact paper meant to catch any drippings. But she surprised me today with her cleanliness. And I became downright flabbergasted when she willingly took a nap! That's rare for a child in our home. Thank God for small victories. But as the sun set, and we began to wind down, that sleep I didn't really get the previous night came for me with gusto and I just knew that at any moment Israel would walk through that door to relieve me. When he hadn't returned by lunchtime, I knew he would most likely stay the whole day at work but here it was well past family dinner time, and instead of coming home, he decided to go out? And the worst part, his little text message had been his first communication to me the entire day. No, "Sorry babe, the meeting ran over." Silence. I didn't sign up for this. And in the famous words of a little church boy forced to perform his Easter speech, "I'm tired of this church."

8:42 PM: Israel, you do you.

I pressed send and cast my phone to the side. I still had kids to bathe, dishes to wash, and I hadn't eaten dinner myself. Typical night in our home.

"Mooooomy," I heard my eldest daughter Carleigh.

Her sweet voice snapped me out of my thoughts causing my heart to slow and my tense muscles to relax. A welcome reprieve.

"Why yes, my love?"

"Since we didn't go to the beach or the park or Disneyland," she yelled as her eyes shown with wonder, "and I mostly did a small amount of jumping, how about I skip my bath *just* for tonight. Me, you, and Mariah all get in your bed. Snuggle up to a good movie…Maybe eat a little popcorn…"

With hands on my hips and head cocked I barely held my giggle. "Oh, so you have it all figured out, little miss."

"Mom, you need breaks too!"

She scrunched her face in an attempt at firmness. The laughter burst from my lips as I listened to my child regurgitate the refrain that had clearly become my mantra in the last year. My chest heaved as we both dissolved into a fit of chuckles. And it felt good, and so did the tears that slipped out. I quickly wiped them as not to alarm Carleigh. Something had to give.

Happily, ever after is what I thought we'd share, but our current situation? B-movie at best. You know the films that go straight to video, not even a consideration for the theater. I thought my marriage would be an Oscar-nominated film type awesome. I expected a hot, passionate romance complete with spontaneous sexual encounters on island vacations or the local beach and forever dates learning and introducing each other to emerging interests with a side of parenting and money-making with a few shots of hard times just for good measure. It just had not come together as I planned, and each year, the collective disappointment of failed goals and unmet expectations caused us to drift further apart.

Married but essentially, alone. That was my present predicament. I went to church alone, because Israel had to work. I attended family events, friend's parties, and appointments all alone because Israel had to work and prioritized it as the main responsibility for us all to endure.

He'd say, "This house and all these toys and gymnastics lessons cost! I have to work. And you don't work so, it all falls on me."

When I'd correct him and remind him that I worked just as many hours as him *inside* the home, he'd halfheartedly acknowledge my "work" but remained steadfast that any familial obligation could be postponed or canceled due to work. So, it was just the girls and I most times. I mean, it hurt to admit it but for the last few years, I truly felt like I was in a marriage by myself. The more I reached out to Israel for deeper intimacy, invitations to counseling, to do any of the work that would better our marriage and help us dig out of our rut, he pulled away even more. And it was heartbreaking to experience and even to think about it so I didn't. Instead, I dug in deeper with motherhood.

Don't get me wrong. My husband is an amazing man. And I appreciate how hard he works to provide, but I expected a bit more balance. I thought we'd rise and grow together but the partnership I thought we were building feels lopsided. The appreciation and admiration I thought I would receive from my husband just isn't there. Instead, he treats me like a hefty bill – like a student loan! You're going to pay your loan bill so your credit stays credible. But you don't necessarily want to. You needed or wanted that loan. You wouldn't be where you were if you hadn't used the loan to accomplish your agenda. But now, the loan payments are a burden. Painful even. What a lousy vibe to receive from your spouse. And it hurt. Deeply. The hurt from the lack of accountability to me and consideration for me felt palpable.

The phone chimed with Israel's personal ring tone. *Dang it!* I forgot to turn my ringer off so I could effectively ignore him.

8:51 PM: I will.

His response caused bitter laughter to bubble up. Before I could respond, "You always do," I see the familiar text message indicator dots.

8:52 PM: We need to talk…

Chapter 2

Jasmine age 18

"You're never going to get married if you don't have sex."

"Mom!"

"What? I'm just saying, Jasmine. Men want sex."

"But you told me you were proud of me that I made it to 18 without having sex," Jasmine said, confused. "That was last week! You said that last week, Mommy!"

"Girl, I just wanted you to make it through high school without having sex and clouding your mind. But you're talking about marriage and relationships in *college* with grown *men*. Men want sex!"

"Dang Mommy...you're not making me feel hopeful. I've been learning at church we should wait until marriage…"

Jasmine and Anita were having this "pep talk" just three weeks before Jasmine was set to leave for college. She tried to hide it but her feelings were not only hurt, but she was also a little shocked by Anita's words. Anita wasn't into the church like Jasmine but she seemed on board with Jasmine's commitment to wait until marriage.

"Wait. I don't know, Jasmine," Anita said with a shrug.

"I didn't take that route, but I think it can work for you. I don't want to discourage you. You can do it if that's what you truly desire."

"Thanks, Mommy," Jasmine said flatly, her face matching her deflated mood.

Jasmine was not entirely convinced her mother believed it would work out for her. She assumed Anita's first thoughts were her actual feelings, but Anita realized the sting of those words, tried to clean it up. Regardless, Jasmine felt defeated.

Jasmine replayed that conversation after excusing herself to go declutter and begin packing for her dorm. *Men want sex.* With her mother in her head as she sat on her bed, completing nothing, Jasmine thought about boys. Or lack thereof their presence in her life. She wanted a boyfriend. No. She wanted a husband. Jasmine wanted a husband since the age of ten. Even though she was only 18, marriage and family had been on her heart since she could remember. Love stories and chick flicks were definitely her brands of entertainment. She loved love, and not having it was making her feel sad and a little resentful. But she had her convictions. She wasn't willing to be out there busting it wide just so she could say she had a man.

Jasmine was already nervous about how her views about dating and not having sex until she got married would bode in a college setting anyway, so that conversation didn't help.

Staying a virgin was mostly unheard of at her age. All around her, people were getting it all the way in. And in a college known as the party school? She knew people thought she was crazy to even try. She also knew luck was not at all what she needed to stay committed to her goal. She needed a prayer life, like-minded individuals, and a guy who had the same goal. She had survived high school without two of the three, but she had a feeling that wouldn't work in college.

In high school, she had made it out as one of the only virgins in her group of friends. As she watched each of her girls bite the dust one by one, her journey to remain sex-free until marriage became fueled by her friend's encounters.

Early on, her mother explained to her the power of a woman's special place. She said, "it has no face. Men just want it. They don't care who it's from." And Jasmine saw this play out in her friend's relationships. The guy they were so excited about would show so much interest initially. He'd call and be sweet and talk on the phone for hours. Then the friend would report that they had sex. Next thing you know, the guy vanished. They referred to this phenomenon as "hit it and quit it." Jasmine's friends would be devastated after the guy stopped speaking to them and got what they wanted, and Jasmine was devastated for her friends. She committed to herself that she would not be that girl. Nope! She declared that no man would be able to just take sex from her and leave, after she was what she heard some of the guys her age refer to as "damaged goods."

Jasmine wasn't into church much then. She was about 15 years old when she made the decision to not have sex with any ole stankie boy. But later that year, Jasmine had an encounter with God. Through a mentorship program, she started going to church. She loved it! She saw kids who cared about reading their bibles, worshipping, and having a genuine connection with Jesus. She learned about saving yourself for marriage because of God's purpose for sex inside a marriage and how not waiting could lead you down a path of heartache. Soul ties with multiple partners, pregnancies with men she wouldn't get a commitment from, and diseases were all roads Jasmine did not want to travel. Besides, seeing her friends play the hit it and quit it shuffleboard bingo was a great reminder. She had watched her own parents engage in the dance as well. They divorced when she was only six years old.

A forever family, with a mother and father, and children who could have both parents together, loving one another and joyfully participating in life – the activities, functions, celebrations, creating traditions and all the other familial things. That is what Jasmine wanted but had yet to experience, and at 15 years old, she made the decision to take steps to create that forever family by waiting to have sex and choosing one person who she'd give herself to. It seemed easy enough back then. Guys are just silly and awkward at 15 years old. And where is one having sex at that age? Her mother was an absolute gangster and had put the fear of God, man, woman, and beast in her at an early age. It wasn't even a thought to sneak a boy in. And she'd die of cardiac arrest if she were caught having sex in the stairwell like some of the other frisky teens. She'd heard of teens having sex at lock-ins at church and in broom closets too. These children were getting it in. None of this sounded appealing to Jasmine. Thinking of the germs involved gave her a stiff pause. She made it to 18 without having sex, to the utter joy of her mother. But with college came a whole new set of obstacles for the virgin chronicles.

Chapter 3

Jasmine age 18

In the beginning, boys and a relationship were nowhere on Jasmine's radar. Jasmine was in a new environment where her self-esteem, identity, and coping skills were truly tested and shaped during those first weeks of school and of course, throughout her college experience.

Jasmine arrived at her apartment-style dorm and looked around. She was a little anxious after having to console her sobbing mother, who cried as if she were leaving her child six states away.

"Mom. Don't cry. I'm close by," Jasmine said of her sixty-minute (with traffic) commute.

It was shorter without traffic. She wanted to laugh a little. No, her mother wouldn't be driving the forty-five minutes daily to see her, but she could! It wasn't too far but far enough for Jasmine to feel independent and to be stuck not having a car. Far enough for her to do her own thing, have an excuse to live in the dorms and be close enough to come home if she needed a hug.

"I know, Nonnie. I know. But I'm going to miss not seeing you every day. I'm so proud of you. You do everything you set your mind to. You said you were going to a university even though we don't have all the money to fund it, and you did."

"Thank you, Mommy," Jasmine said, feeling joy that her mother saw her commitment to be the first college graduate in her family.

"I mean it, Nonnie. I love you, and I know you're not far, but I'm going to miss seeing you daily. I can cry. Stop looking at me like that," she said, swatting at Jasmine playfully.

Jasmine ducked having an all too familiar flashback of one of those famous, quick, get you together pops up the back of the head. They both laughed, embraced, and Anita cried some more tears. Jasmine tried not to roll her eyes, but her mother was really downing her mood.

When she finally made it into her room, she was excited and relieved! The set up was just like the apartment she had grown up in with her mother and older sister Anise. She was bummed Anise wasn't there to see her off, but she *was* serving her country in the Air Force, so she got a pass.

Jasmine was the first one there out of the four ladies assigned to apartment 210. She wondered who her roommate would be, but she was too excited that she made it first and was able to pick the side of the room she wanted to set up.

Jasmine walked through and thought the setup was not so bad. She'd seen some sparse looking dorm rooms on "Sister, Sister," "A Different World," and "Moesha." The only dorm room she remembered having a kitchen was "Saved by the Bell: College Edition." Jasmine was thrilled.

She entered the door and immediately saw the

kitchen to the left. Not only did her dorm have a kitchen, but it also had its own bathroom with a separate door for the showers and toilet so the double sink could always be free. Now it wasn't The Ritz, but she'd take it any day over a community floor bathroom and hot plate setup. She admired the full-size refrigerator, stove-oven combo, and a dishwasher. She grew up in a classic Black household that frowned upon using dishwashers even if they were in perfect working order so she had some plans for that beauty in her dorm! She walked to the living room-den areas and noticed the modest wooden table with four blue cushioned chairs for dining. She sat on the blue couch just to test it out. It was surprisingly cushy. She envisioned having friends sitting on the accompanying loveseat studying as they ate snacks from the well-worn wooden coffee table.

In Jasmine's room, there were two wooden bed frames with mattresses, two dressers, two wooden desks, and two chairs. Jasmine chose the bed by the window. The window had a built-in wall bookcase that she thought would make a perfect spot for her trinkets.

It took Jasmine all of twenty minutes to unpack. Her mother had convinced her she just needed the basics. Beside her toiletries, she had clothes for a couple of weeks, two pairs of shoes, a CD player, some money for food, bedding, and a few trinkets to remind her of home. She unpacked everything, made up her bed, and sat down to get comfy and...do nothing. School wouldn't start for another four days. She knew no one, not even her roommate. She sat there looking around, feeling alone, and began to cry. She missed her mom. She missed her bed. She missed her room, all her stuff, and she needed another hug from her mother. *Oh, but she was downing your mood a second ago* she internally chided herself. She picked up her cellphone, flipped it open, and speed-dialed her mother.

“Mommy,” she said with the tears in her voice.

“Jasmine? Girl, what's wrong with you?”

“I'm sad.”

“What's wrong?”

“Come back, Mommy.”

“Girl, no! I'm already too far.”

“I don't have enough stuff. You said only bring a little. I'm gonna be bored here.”

“Girl...you better study! That's what you're there for.”

“I know, but I need other stuff too like a trash can, and a pot so I can cook, and a bath rug. And cleaning supplies,” she said as fresh tears started to fall.

“Okay, Nonnie. Calm down. We can get you that stuff. Your sister will be home next weekend on leave. We can get those things and come back down.”

“Okay,” Jasmine said, sniffing and feeling some comfort.

“I love you. You will be fine.”

“Okay. Love you, Mommy.” I said feeling some relief. “Mommy?” I asked sweetly.

““‘Yes Jasmine?”

“What you doing?”

“Girl, get off my phone!” Anita said, laughing as she hung up.

Jasmine got off the phone with her mother and dried her tears. She would have to make do for a week.

Chapter 4

Jasmine age 18

Jasmine couldn't utilize the kitchen yet, so she decided to go find food. She used her dorm map to make it to the food hall. Jasmine let in a deep breath as she took in the scene and made a note of the student help office. The staff was waving and passing out waters to the students. She had made it to a university and could not help the sense of awe and accomplishment she felt. Anita's words hit her then. Her mother was proud, but Jasmine was pleased too. College was the first step in Jasmine's life plan. It was not optional. Still, it felt surreal. Jasmine felt like she had indeed accomplished a goal that would benefit her life in the long run.

Jasmine made it to the food hall and realized the building wasn't just a cafeteria; it was quite interactive. She saw a computer lab, a game room complete with air hockey and a pool table, lounge chairs and tables, signage pointing to study rooms for individuals and groups, stairs

"You there, Jax?"

"Oh, sorry, girl. I got caught up in my thoughts."

"Did Israel tell you he was going somewhere with John?"

"We sent some quick text messages. He just said 'out.' I assumed it was with John. And you know what that does."

"I know that's right, girl," she laughed.

"Alright, girl. Let me get in this bath and relax my muscles."

"Love you. Goodnight."

"Goodnight."

I had to get off the phone with Deb and collect my thoughts. Israel wasn't a "go out," often type of guy, and when he did go out, Deb's husband John was usually his counterpart. He had a handful of close friends who he'd go out with. I wanted to text him to investigate, but my pride paused me.

I let the warmth of the water melt away the tension, even if for a few minutes escape. How had we ended up here? Silent, sullen, lacking intimacy, and connection. Terse kisses on the lips or cheek with a goodbye and an occasional quickie pretty much summed up our intimacy and sex life. I missed his arms around me. I missed his body against mine. Married but we felt more like acquaintances. Conversation about kids and bills. No laughter. Was there love left? And when had it gotten to this point? I think I remember how love felt, and I think it wasn't this way. We've had several outside forces hit us throughout our eleven years of marriage, but I thought we were handling them together. But this latest test is showing me all the cracks in what I thought was a sturdy foundation. At the least, I thought we'd be friends. But the stoic demeanor I have received lately from Israel feels like I'm walking through enemy territory. And as I stay home daily with the kids, no adult interaction besides chatting with another friend with screaming kids, I missed our connection increasingly with each passing day. Oh, how I missed my friend.

Chapter 6

Jasmine age 18

Just as Jasmine thought to get up to answer the door, a petite Black girl entered the bedroom. She had two suitcases, one in each hand. Her thick black hair was slicked into a bun at the top of her head. Her tight acid-washed jeans and letterman jacket gave her a preppy look. Jasmine noticed how sleek and put together she was. She even had bracelets and a nice gold chain to match her earrings. Jasmine looked down at her plain clothes and made a silent comparison.

"Hi...I'm Shayna. This was my room last year too. I had that side...." she said pointing to Jasmine's bed as she let her voice trail off.

"Oh okay...." Jasmine spoke carefully. She wondered, what the girl was alluding to? *Wait! I know she doesn't think I'm giving her my side of the room. She should have gotten here earlier.* "That's cool… that you're returning. I chose this side so I could be by the window.

and an elevator that led to more meeting rooms, conference rooms, and a boardroom. The place was huge!

She felt electricity running through her. What an honor to have such a great facility at her fingertips. A little girl from the 'hood? This was huge for Jasmine and her family.

The sudden jolt of her stomach growling catapulted her from her euphoric state. She remembered what she'd come for. Food! She looked off to the left and saw a snack shop, but the way her hunger and her body were set up, snacks weren't going to cut it.

She did buy a bag of chips and a soda for later, but Jasmine needed a meal. At 220 pounds standing at 5'7 and wearing a size 16, she was no small woman. And Jasmine loved to eat because food was her number one comfort. Food was life. If she were honest with herself, Jasmine knew she used food to cover up and feed her emotions, good or bad, and she needed a fix with how uncertain, vulnerable, and uncovered she felt while being alone in her dorm room.

Food had always been her thing. She wasn't a hoarder or binger (mostly – there was that one time at Hometown Buffet where she was too stuffed to drive home), but a chocolate sundae after a hard day, check. A chocolate sundae after an "A" on a test, check! A chocolate sundae because they taste bomb even if you already ate, check! Food was always there for Jasmine. Men, they let her down. People, in general, let her down. But the food never did.

As she paused for a moment, she thought of how food and her pudgy body played a role in her lack of dating life. Though she wasn't having sex, she still wanted to date. But she lacked self-confidence for the most part, and she was always "the friend." She had only had one boyfriend in high school, and he wasn't worth mentioning. He just wanted sex, of course. She wasn't budging, and he kept trying, and she wasn't there for it, so it ended. But it seemed like the skinnier, prettier girls got more prospects. Jasmine felt herself getting sad over it. She needed to find that cafeteria quick!

Jasmine looked to the left and found the arrow to the golden egg, lunch! The sign read "Hamburger and fries $4.99 or 1 meal point." She thought for a moment, she had one hundred dollars for the week and had already spent three dollars on her midnight snack. If she spent five dollars a meal, three times a day, for the next five days until she went home, there would be less than twenty dollars left for the books and supplies she needed for class.

Jasmine asked the cashier about lunch points, and the disgruntled worker silently pointed at the finance clerk. Jasmine wondered how one could be disgruntled on the very first day of receiving students, but chose to let it go and see what those points were about.

"Hello. I'd like to sign up for the lunch points? How do I go about that?" Jasmine asked nervously.

"Hello, young lady," the elderly gentleman greeted. He put Jasmine at ease with his warm demeanor as he beamed fatherly. "Do you have financial aid?"

"Yes. I do."

"Great! Let me get your student ID number, please."

"Okay."

Jasmine fumbled with her lanyard to get her student ID out. She hadn't memorized the number yet.

"Take your time, darling."

Jasmine was grateful for his calming tone. She took a deep breath and got herself together.

Calm down, Jasmine. She spoke to herself to calm her nerves. This adulting and conducting financial business stuff was new to her. She didn't have formal training. Heck, she didn't have casual training. She had a bank account that had one hundred bucks in it and a debit card.

Jasmine produced her student ID and slid it across the counter. As the man typed and drug his mouse back and forth, Jasmine stood there looking like a deer caught in headlights while her stomach grumbled like a bear. She prayed silently that the man didn't hear it. She punched her belly out of his view to try and quiet the noise to no avail.

"Okay, Ms. Wesley, you do not have enough financial aid right now to cover a meal plan. Everything is still pending, but you can get a loan for the dorm meal plan since you're a resident here, and it will be under your financial aid once everything processes. I will print the paperwork out. But you do need to go to the financial aid office and check on everything and sign your loan entrance exam paperwork."

Jasmine felt her heart beating fast. *How can I get a loan?* Panic flashed over her. This adulting stuff was no joke.

But Jasmine had to eat. Right? But a loan? How would she pay it back? Financial aid pending? She had no idea what it even meant.

"Ms. Wesley. Calm down." He must have seen Jasmine about to spiral. "It's okay. Many kids do this. If you need to, you can call your parent to discuss it or call financial aid to see all your options."

But Jasmine was hungry now and she'd already spoken to her mother. And she for *sure* did not want to go to the financial aid office. The line was hideous. Before she could process all her thoughts, she heard herself say, "I'll take the loan." She blinked and the paperwork was in front of her.

She skimmed it not really understanding it completely.

"You can choose 3 meals a day. For eighteen hundred. You can eat here or on campus. One meal, one drink per swipe. If you get two meal items at once that will take two swipes. You're allowed to do that but it won't reset until the next day."

"Okay," Jasmine spoke on autopilot.

"If you don't need it that much and it will just be an accompaniment to your cooking, you can do the flex pay where you get a stipend a week or 2 meals a day. That's twelve hundred."

She quickly made the choice to get the 3 meals a day. She could eat on campus and in the dorms? Sounded good to her! She'd figure the financial aid system out later. She signed, posed for her picture, waited for her card to print out, thanked the finance clerk, and raced to the food line.

Her eyes danced and her stomach did too when she saw that it was buffet style. She thought she would lose her mind. Southern-style macaroni and cheese, grilled salmon, *fried* chicken, burritos, pizza, a full salad bar, soups, all the sodas! It was truly a stress-eating big girl's dream. And they had to-go boxes! Jasmine filled her plate, swiped her meal card and made it back to her dorm to chow down! She ate so much she was just a tad bit uncomfortable. She knew she'd overdone it but promised herself to watch it next time.

In the six weeks between high school ending and college beginning, Jasmine had already gained ten pounds back from the thirty pounds she lost for her prom. The flashback to that day made her smile. She was smaller than she'd ever been in high school and when she dropped the weight, she started getting all the attention at school from guys who'd previously friend-zoned her. She felt amazing and loved the new attention back then but she also felt resentment to those guys who never paid her any mind during the three and a half other years of high school. She couldn't believe guys were that shallow. So yes, she was bummed over gaining the weight back but she also felt comfortable finally *not* counting calories. She decided she would utilize the salad bar included in her meal plan at least once a day. She'd start tomorrow.

I got a loan today, Jasmine thought. She was being faced with challenges she didn't think were involved with college but she had just overcome an obstacle. And made an important financial decision. This adulting thing was proving to be quite the adventure.

Ding The doorbell jolted Jasmine to reality. She felt nervous and excited all at once. She wondered which of her three roommates this would be. But then it dawned on her. A roommate most likely would have used a key. Was there a visitor?

Chapter 5

What does he want to talk about? Great! So, this long day is just going to refuse to end. I, for sure, can't go to sleep with a text like that from Israel ponging around my brain. He is a traditional, typical man. "Needing to talk," is just not a thing for him. And most men. Men *flee* from needing to talk like the plague. They treat it like babies treat mushed peas or how toddlers treat nap-time.

Prepare yourself. I jumped! I heard that loud and clear, but it wasn't *me.* I mean, it was in my brain, and it was my thought, I guess. I mean, I *thought* it? It was in my thoughts…but I didn't *think* it?

Steady yourself. Whoa. I heard it again. I must really need that vacation I've been begging for. And a psychiatrist. I can't deal with the voices.

I decided to take a bath and call my friend Deb while I let the tub fill. She's a fellow stay at home, mommy. She gets me. She doesn't mind staying on the phone while my wild things run rampant in the background. It's remarkable how kids will be quiet, building a replica of the statue of liberty, working together, concentrating, sharing, etcetera, etcetera. But as *soon* as a mother gets on the phone, they sense it. They instantly need a snack, water, to potty, can't share, got stuck, and the list goes on endlessly. They get reaaaally loud, and it just makes talking on the phone a sport. I get it, but every caller can't deal with it sounding like war in your background so I cherished calls with Deb.

"What up, Big Bird!" She greeted me with our familiar hello.

"Big Bird! Nothing. Chilllliiin'," I respond in my "Martin," voice.

"Girl…I just got my last tiny terror – I mean lovely, sweet, God-given blessing of a child down. How about you?"

"Thank God my son missed his nap, or you know he'd be up right now."

"See! You were mad when he missed the nap, huh?"

"Yes, girl," we both laughed.

"And what you thought was a loss has turned into a win!"

"Yessssuh! And now I'm sitting here just taking a moment to breathe."

"Same girl. Same," her voice trailed off. We sat there, breathing for a moment enjoying the quiet alone time in our respective homes. Enjoying not being needed. Even for just a moment. "Where's your husband?"

"Somewhere having fun with yours, I presume."

"John is right here fast asleep. Came home talking about he was sick. Girl, I gave him the deepest internal eye roll while holding a sweet face," she laughed and was waiting for me to join in.

I wanted to. I was trying to, but the information she'd just shared had me on pause.

Allergies," Jasmine said, sniffing for effect.

Shayna looked like she was going to try and plead her case but had an internal dialogue and realized it wasn't worth it.

"What's your name?"

"Jasmine. I'm a freshman."

"Nice to meet you. I won't be here a lot anyway but let me know if you have any questions. We can walk to campus and I can show you where your classes are too. Just let me know."

Jasmine was relieved that Shayna presented herself as an ally instead of being angry and petty for not getting her original side of the room back. She was also relieved Shayna hurriedly, and haphazardly, unpacked her things and left out just as quickly as she'd popped in. She could get used to a roommate who was barely around.

The next few days were hard for Jasmine. She met her other roommates. They were nice enough. She'd gone to campus a few times to map out her schedule and was beginning to feel acclimated to the environment but her visit to the financial aid office had been a major blow on top of her homesickness and she was already wondering if she'd made the right decision by not going to community college first. She was broke. I mean this wasn't a new revelation. They had never been rich. As a single mother, Anita somehow made magic happen daily. They had all they needed and most of what they wanted. Anita worked hard to supply all her daughters' desires and she made it look effortless. Jasmine shuddered at the times she'd been ungrateful wondering why her requests for more were met with a mournful and sometimes irate response from her mother. She was asking her mother to squeeze blood from a turnip as the old southern folk say.

Jasmine felt deflated. Broke. No money. Financial aid still pending. Before admittance, she'd turned in all the documentation. She went to a workshop to learn how to fill out the paperwork. And it took. For. Ever. She had to get tax information and receipts. It was mentally exhausting, frankly. She wondered who created the torture device that was known as FAFSA. The pages seemed endless. The information they were asking so invasive. But Jasmine had done it all. She felt so relieved to submit those documents. But now it seemed like she hadn't done enough. In reality, she had done all she could. She hadn't understood that financial aid could take time with an influx of new students. And her class had been the largest to enter the school in years. The counselor had mentioned both of those facts briefly but it went over Jasmine's head.

All she heard was, she wouldn't have enough money for her books. Though she had saved some money and vowed not to spend any more until it was time to purchase books, she knew the chump change she carried would not be enough to buy more than one textbook. She'd used textbooks all her life but had never purchased one. She cringed as she flashed back to high school seeing herself carelessly toss her textbooks. She'd have to treat these college textbooks like newborns so she could re-sale them. Her trip to the bookstore prior to arriving at the financial aid office was a very rude awakening. They didn't have a t-shirt in that place that wasn't at least twenty-five dollars. The books were on average sixty-five dollars. Although many books fell under that range, many of the books she fingered as she walked through the aisles were over one hundred bucks. And paperback no less! She fingered the seventy-ish dollars in her pocket as she perused. She then hightailed it out of there so the sticker shock wouldn't cause her to faint and marched to the financial aid office.

No money. That blared in her mind. She didn't know what she was going to do for class in just two days. She had a couple of notebooks and pens and a cute backpack but as for college materials, she had no idea how she was going to start her assignments. Her teachers were obviously going to expect her to have the books already. She didn't know that. She found it out randomly while checking her email in the dorm computer lab. That place had become her second home. She wasn't even looking for an email from a teacher. She was checking on news about her financial aid. She received an email from her teacher amending a book on the syllabus and apologizing for the inconvenience of having to return a book.

The teacher said she wanted them to get an early notice so they could have the books ready for the first day of class assignments. Jasmine's heart beat fast as she read. She didn't know how any of this worked and as she was finding out that she was not at all excited about any of it. This revelation is what prompted her to go to the bookstore and then financial aid anyway. As she came to the conclusion that college really was different than high school, she felt that sinking feeling in the pit of her stomach. No, the first day would not be a free day. These teachers were ready, and expected her to be. How was she going to perform and be ready with no money and no books? She was finding it hard to smile. Hard to feel joy and hard to see the good. Why wasn't she more prepared than this?

Chapter 7

Jasmine age 18

Jasmine did what she always did when feeling overwhelmed. Instantly, the tears came, and begrudgingly fell. She hated her frustration tears because what did they help? But she couldn't help them from falling. "God, help me," slipped from her lips. "Give me direction, please. Amen."

She heard the familiar refrain from Anita in her mind, *God takes care of babies and fools, and I ain't no baby…*

"Mommy!" Her best friend! She had to call her.

It seemed like for the twentieth time since she had been dropped off, she was calling her mother. But her mother was indeed a friend and had established herself as Jasmine's safe space. She knew that even if her mother couldn't, or wouldn't, fix it, she'd guide her in the right direction.

"Mommy..." Jasmine was barely able to get out

before the dam of tears broke through.

Jasmine explained what was going on through her tears. She was the first four-year university student in her entire family. This was new to her and her mother.

Anita calmed Jasmine down and assured her everything would be all right. She said she would work to get some things together and get back to her.

"Nonnie, you're there now. So, make the best of it. Don't let this ruin your experience. Keep your smile."

And there it was. The magic words. Anita had been preaching that since Jasmine was a little girl. Never let the world, people, or your current circumstances, steal your joy.

Jasmine instantly began to smile. It wasn't her beaming, cheek-hurting smile, but it was a hopeful smile that things would be okay.

Gingerly, Jasmine walked back to her dorm. She was in no rush. She was actually looking forward to class so she could get a homework assignment or something to occupy her time. No cable - no television at all. No friends. Just a few books and a handheld CD player. Not even a radio where she could be free from her mesh-covered headphones in the Southern California valley heat. Thank God for air conditioning in her dorm, but still. She wasn't looking forward to being bored and alone. She kicked herself again for having listened to her sister's minimalist packing advice!

As she walked and took in her surroundings, counting the leaves on the ground, she thought she heard her name. Jasmine stopped, looked around, noticed no one, and kept going. She must have been dehydrated or something because no one knew her there. None of her friends had chosen the college she'd chosen.

She was almost to the end of the library steps when she heard her name again. She was sure this time. She turned to see who it was. Had her mother been waiting in the raptures ready to come scoop her like a mama eagle? She laughed at the thought.

"Jasmine," she heard again and saw a familiar face from high school waving at her as she turned to investigate.

She instantly felt exhilarated and ran to Angel. At that moment, her name was indeed a perfect representation of the feelings she invoked in Jasmine. This was ironic because Angel could not stand Jasmine in ninth grade homeroom. Angel was what you'd call an old soul. Jasmine's silly and at times, boisterous demeanor was too much for the reserved and always, even at 14 years old, put together Angel. Through their high school years, they had remained in the same homeroom each year, and somehow, Jasmine had won Angel over. She couldn't remember if it was the end of tenth grade or the beginning of the eleventh, but they had actually become cordial. Maybe not friends but definitely friendly. But as the two girls ran to embrace one another, Angel's qualms about being seen as boisterous and loud were put to the side, and they were friends that day. An instant bond was formed.

The two hugged and swayed like two long lost sisters meeting after years of separation.

"It's so good to see a familiar face," Angel said excitedly.

"I know! I have been so alone. I haven't met anyone yet. And my roommate is never there."

"Ooh! Come to my dorm. Meet my roommate. Her name is Annie, and I love her! I'm about to cook dinner. You can have some. And we can go explore the dorms!"

"I would love that! I didn't even know anyone else from our class came here. I thought I was alone."

"I decided at the last minute. I was going to go closer to home but decided a change of scenery was in order. I was on campus, purchasing the rest of my books. I have most of them already. Just needed a couple more."

Jasmine felt so embarrassed. Angel had it together, as usual. Jasmine had some learning to do and fast!

"Oh cool," Jasmine stated nervously. Well, I'd love to come to your dorm. I'm starving!"

The two walked side by side, chatting away. You could see hands flying and then randomly stopping to recover from laughter as they trekked in the valley heat. Jasmine met Annie, and she was, indeed, remarkable. She felt like an instant friend. They ate, talked, sang, went around the dorms meeting and talking to people, and had more fun than Jasmine could ever remember having. She was so grateful for the turn of her first dreary days of dorm life. Jasmine was experiencing the enjoyable college experience she had imagined and she was grateful.

Chapter 8

I sat there listening to her talk, mesmerized. I could not take my eyes off her attire. Her dress cinched perfectly at the waist and flowed seemingly endlessly. The top buttoned up and softly opened at the top to reveal a moderate, but sexy glimpse of cleavage. The fabric was a fire red but it looked soft and like it would caress the skin. She was killing her look. As usual. I followed her on social media for over nine years. And this is why. Though her fashion had evolved over the years, she stayed relevant. Her posts always brought me fashion inspiration but she brought much more to the table. Her marriage seemed so solid. She painted such a happy picture. I wanted that fairytale.

"Yes. You can ask me anything. We will start the 'Ask Kim' Live Q&A portion in just one minute. And you all can ask your questions in the comments too."

She shifted her gaze from the crowd and spoke directly into the camera that her assistant or event coordinator held in front of her face. She let us know at the beginning of the meet and greet that her live viewers paid a ticket fee for the live-stream and she would involve them as much as she could. The whole event was exciting and intriguing. I was so glad I found a last-minute in-audience ticket and got Deb to watch the kids. For some odd reason, Israel was unavailable *on* his day off but we can discuss the frustration of that later.

"We're ready in five, four, three…"

"Okay ladies *and gentlemen,"* she said acknowledging the few men sprinkled about.

I was tickled to see them but was surprised I hadn't spotted her husband. He was usually at every event.

"Don't be shy! You know me. I won't answer it if you're in my business too much but don't let that scare you," she joked.

We all laughed. A young lady sitting toward the middle raised her hand and waited to be acknowledged.

"Where's your hubby and how has being in the spotlight affected your marriage?"

"Okay, you went straight there, honey! Well, let's get into it. I am no longer married to my *ex*-husband but I'm sure that won't last long," she said, her voice sounding like a love song.

Her laughter felt soul-fulfilling. You could see the glow all over her. I wanted to be sad for her divorce but it was hard to with the way she beamed.

"My new man has placed and kept a smile on my face."

Prepare yourself. That voice again…

"Will we be able to meet this new guy?"

"I wouldn't usually share because we have a few things to clear up but hey, I'm too happy and so is he! So yes, I'd like to present to you my guy, Izzy. Wave a hand babe."

Steady yourself. That dang voice!

I looked with the rest of the audience to the

direction she pointed. I blinked and tried to unsee the man I was seeing. My face dropped at the recognition and felt like it shattered into a million pieces. No wait, that was my heart. I could hear it pounding in my ears. I tried my best to steady myself but I was losing it.

That was *my* husband. She was calling him Izzy. *He* was putting that smile on her face? I wanted to get up. I wanted to slap that smile off her face. I wanted to smack that stupid grin off his. THEY HAD ME MESSED UP!

Do not engage. I heard the voice so clear. I wanted to react and cause a scene. *Focus on you.* Focus on me. The instruction was plain. At that moment I realized I wasn't going crazy. That was God speaking directly to me. But how was I supposed to focus on me? The humiliation of finding out your marriage is over while in public as your spouse is introduced as someone else's love interest? It's too much!

As I sat there processing, all the emotions flooded in. So, I wasn't mistaken. I felt that we were lacking connection. The intimacy was off and on. But the extra cool vibe I had been feeling from Israel over the last few months was this? He had always presented himself as a man with such integrity. But here he had started a whole relationship while he left me at home from sun up, to sundown watching after his children. He just bought a new car. A luxury car, while I sat home with the bare minimum. He said he needed the car for work and to elevate his career but he needed it for *her!* All the revelation flooded in as the dots connected in my mind. The million pieces of my heart broke into a million more.

I feel my phone vibrate. It startled me because I know my phone is on "do not disturb." I see a text from Angel that's marked urgent. *The kids!* Wait, Deb had the kids. Angel doesn't know I'm here. What could she want?

6:47 PM Check social media now!

I log on and check my profile. I receive a notification to update my relationship status. Confused, I go directly to Israel's page. He has changed his social media status from married to me to in a relationship with Kim! I feel myself about to explode, and tear up this meet and greet with my rage. Before I can stop myself, I run for Kim at full speed like a bull a-

I gasp as my eyes pop open and I bolt upright and fling the covers off. My chest rose up and down rapidly. I used my hand to steady it. I immediately grab my phone, log into my social media, and use my index finger to scroll. It still lists Israel and I as married to one another but I am still fuming! That dream felt too real. My hands and heart are indicators. I take in a slow ragged breath. The coughing begins. Lung disease. Hands trembling, I fumble for the water bottle. And then I pause. Slowly my head turns left to see his side of the bed still neatly made. I glance at the nightstand and as I suspect, it's well past 3 am.

"You have reached Israel with SnackJoys Vending and -"

I clicked off before the voice mail greeting could finish. Leaving a message was not a great idea I decided. My chest continued to pound.

3:42 AM: Where are you?

The audio version of Kim Cash Tate's latest novel *When I am Tempted*, should have lulled me to sleep or calmed me down. It accomplished neither as I waited for Israel's text, shifting my body from left to right in an attempt to find comfort and relief from the pounding. The sweat that began to form on my brow alarmed me. I'm no sweater. I know it's just a dream but we never stay out late without so much as a call. This new level of disrespect…

I jump as Israel's special tone chimes. I'm relieved he text messaged back so fast but pissed he chose to text message me back instead of call. The strikes against him continue to add up.

4:03 AM: Out.

4:04 AM: With whom? What's her name, Israel?

My phone rings immediately. *Oh,* now *you can call,* I think with disgust.

"What are you talking about now? You know I'm out with the guys."

"Actually, I know nothing. Except that you aren't out with John. He's home sleep with his *family!* You gave me no information. Nor did you ask how I feel or if I had something planned after I've been in the house with the-"

"I'll be home shortly. We definitely need to talk."

"Why wait? Let's talk now Israel!"

"That's what you do! It's already tense, and you push! I said we will talk when I get home."

He disconnected the call before I could respond. I chucked my phone across the room and almost gave my own self time-out after the loud thud hitting the wall resulted in a whimper from one of the children. The last thing I needed was a child waking up. I needed both of us to be present for this conversation.

Chapter 9

Jasmine age 18

The first day of school came and Jasmine was so excited and nervous she thought she'd pass out. Or throw up. She made it to her Introduction to African Studies course. She was so proud to take the class. When she first decided she wanted to attend college, an HBCU was definitely her plan but due to circumstances, that didn't happen. She was super excited to apply to Howard University. She applied to Hampton as well but was not really feeling her dream school's rival. She never heard back from Howard during decision time. She was accepted to Hampton but her heart was not into attending. It was Howard or home. She committed to the university in her home state only to hear from Howard a couple weeks before school was to start. Somehow, her application had gotten "lost in the mail," they explained, and they never processed it.

They wanted to process her application for the

spring. It was bittersweet for Jasmine. On one hand she felt relieved she had not in fact been rejected from the school she fantasized about as a kid while watching episodes of "A Different World." On the other hand, she felt disappointed her money had been wasted on an application fee and she'd already done so much preparation, enrolling, and making her peace with staying at home. Ultimately, she decided to just stay home. But she also decided she'd take as many Black studies courses as she could, join the choir, join the Black Student Union, find a Black Church and create her own little ethnic experience while attending the diverse PWI. So, as she sat in her first Black studies course, she beamed with delight.

Mrs. Williams was intriguing to say the least. She was vanilla as Anita would say, short statured but on the plus side, she wore her salt and mostly pepper hair in a short press and curl, thick glasses at the tip of her nose, and walked elegantly but oddly enough with a slew footed gait. She was married for the second time but lived in a separate home from her spouse. They ate dinner and spent time and then went to their respective homes. She had degrees on top of degrees and Jasmine felt as if she could listen to her speak and tell her stories of rich and empowering African American history all day long. Not only was Mrs. Williams elegant, she was so well spoken and wise. Jasmine hadn't known what to expect about her courses but with this class, she was delighted!

Mrs. Williams asked for a volunteer. She wanted to know what the class knew about their own personal history. On a whim, Jasmine got up in front of the class. She felt energized at seeing all the Black and brown faces. She was also feeling cute that day so she didn't mind showing her outfit.

Mrs. Williams asked a series of questions. Jasmine answered as best she could. When Jasmine was asked, what her goals for the course were, she was eager to respond.

"I want to learn all I can about Blacks in America. I learned so much during high school but our history is so deep. This history is mines so I want to know all I can."

"Mine."

Jasmine was confused by Mrs. Williams response to her and awkwardly and involuntarily said, "Hunh?" She was immediately embarrassed.

"You said mines," Mrs. Williams said softly. "That is incorrect. No need for the 'S' on the end. Mine is plural."

"Okay...thank you," Jasmine said as she rushed to her seat, her face surely red with the embarrassment she felt.

Mrs. Williams thanked her for sharing and moved on as if everything was great. Jasmine sat there mortified. She had been corrected in front of the entire class on the first day of college. No, Mrs. Williams was not rude. Her tone was in fact kind and helpful but that correction in front of the class made Jasmine feel so small inside. She already felt like she shouldn't be there and this incident shook her confidence even more.

Jasmine's week did not get any better. As a first timer, she just chose the classes that were available from her list of required courses for general education. She was unaware of these classes' proximity to one another. So, on the third day of school when she found out she would have fifteen minutes each Monday, Wednesday, and Friday to make a twenty-minute walk clear across her massive campus, she felt disrespected by her own self for putting herself in such an impossible situation. She would definitely look at a campus map when creating her class schedule from that day forward. Why hadn't she known to check the distance between buildings? She was tired just thinking about running and making it to class in a sweaty mess. Every Monday, Wednesday, and Friday. Asthma had been kicking her butt since childhood and it would make these power walking stints interesting to say the least.

Jasmine's bad week turned into a bad month. Her financial aid was still mixed up. Somehow paperwork was not filled in correctly and her financial aid package had to be redone.

Her mother had come through with money for a few books and her aunt Diana bought two but with five classes with multiple books for some, it was pretty tough to get assignments done without all she needed. Eventually the money came in but not before Jasmine fell drastically behind, racking up unfinished chapters and segments of reading she needed to complete in order to be prepared for quizzes and midterms. She felt defeated before she could get a good head start and this feeling bled into the whole semester.

Each day wasn't terrible. Jasmine was making friends; she had joined the Gospel Choir as planned and found an amazing church. The social aspect was amazing and all she imagined but her academics were severely lacking.

Academically, her confidence was shaken to the core and ultimately, she let the feeling steal her focus. She was often late to class and missed assignments too. When she received her first set of grades, she wasn't even surprised at what she read on the screen: A, B, C-, D, F. Jasmine managed to receive one of each grade a person could get on an academic scale. If it weren't so terrible it would have been funny to her.

Receiving an "F" caused her heart to feel heavy. She couldn't bring those grades to her mother. And she wouldn't. That was the best thing about college, the independence. No report card was being sent home. It was also the most difficult to navigate. No one was getting after her to get things done. She realized she no longer *had* to share grades with her mother, but she also had to understand the responsibility that came with independence. *She* signed those loan documents. She was paying for school. She didn't understand how an eighteen-year-old could so easily get thousands of dollars but she rolled with it. College was growing her up in ways she hadn't expected. Independence could be fun but she was learning it could also take you to uncharted territory.

Chapter 10

Jasmine age 19

Academic probation? Jasmine thought as she read the letter. Her hand trembled slightly. She had eagerly thumbed through the mail looking for her new Old Navy credit card. She could envision herself strutting across campus in her new jeggings and preppy sweater. Yes, her first year of college had caused her to stress eat the rest of her thirty-pound weight loss back on as she trudged through the academic portion of college, but socially, she was blooming and having a blast. She loved meeting up with her friends, having lunches, "study" sessions (more laughing and talking went on than anything else), dorm parties, and trotting. Trotting included but was not limited to wearing your best clothing and walking around the dorm community scoping out and talking to cute boys. The freedom of it all.

"Academic probation?!" she said aloud now, jolting herself from thoughts of clearly the wrong thing.

Anita would literally take her hands and ring Jasmine's neck if she discovered that Jasmine would be kicked out of school if she didn't pull her grades up asap. She would not embarrass her mother in that manner. She quickly stuffed the letter in her purse as she heard the tapping of Anita's shoes from behind.

"You ready," Anita asked as she looked down adjusting her top.

"Yes," Jasmine spoke, the brightness in her voice noticeably dim.

"What's wrong?"

Jasmine had rarely successfully lied to her mother. She wasn't going to start now. Anita would be able to sniff the lie like a bloodhound. But Jasmine was no fool. She could not confess about academic probation.

"My Old Navy card didn't come in so I won't be able to get the outfits I wanted."

Her mother didn't need to know there was a deeper disappointment.

"Aw man Nonnie. Well, I can get a couple things for you so it will still be a fun day."

Six hours later the pair trudged in the house with over ten bags between them. The mall, grocery store, and fabric barn, had collected all their collective coins. They shopped and snacked and laughed at people to their heart's content.

Jasmine placed the ground turkey, taco seasoning, and vegetable oil on the counter and refrigerated the rest of the groceries. She began browning the meat as her mother sorted yarn and assembled her supplies. They each worked at their task while chatting and laughing about various topics.

Jasmine beamed at her mother. Though the lady could be a firecracker, Jasmine cherished the moments they were able to spend together.

"Mommy?"

"Yes?

"I've been thinking about what you said about sex and I want to wait until marriage. I really believe I can find someone who cares like me and wants to wait and honor God and our marriage."

"Okay, Jasmine. I think you can do it. You do anything you put your mind to. You said you were going to go to college at a university and not community college, and you did. You said you were going to go to a magnet high school, and you did! I'm so proud of you."

Jasmine's heart beat fast. She averted her eyes and begged the tears not to come. The first tear trickled down her cheek and within minutes her entire face was drenched.

"Mommy you're not going to be proud of me if I get kicked out."

"Huh? Kicked out? Jasmine?"

Jasmine covered her face with her hands and let out a deep sigh as she prepared to tell her mother the truth.

"Mommy. I'm on academic probation. I have one semester to pull my grades up or I will have to leave, go to a community college, and hopefully transfer back."

Jasmine released the tension in her shoulders and sat back able to take a deep breath for the first time that day.

With the next breath she braced herself for the pensive words her other would use to scold her. Yes, she was grown. Technically. But what is grown to a Black mama?

"Aw man Nonnie. I know your semester was rough but you gotta pull those grades up."

Jasmine turned from left to right and scrunched her eyebrows.

"What?" Anita said, surprise in her voice.

"I was looking for my real mama. I was waiting on you to pop me!"

“Shut up Jasmine,” Anita said as she playfully swung at Jasmine’s head and they both dissolved into a fit of laughter.

Jasmine hadn't realized how burdened she’d been. Her mother’s encouragement was just what she needed. Instead of the fussing and cussing Jasmine thought she would receive, her mother empathized and helped come up with a plan.

Jasmine returned for her third semester of school with a new computer, books pre-purchased for each class, the minimum number of units for full-time status, and a solid determination to succeed. She created a study schedule for each class after reviewing, highlighting, and organizing her various syllabi. She was ready. She decided her focus would be school and passing each class with an “A.” Choir, bible study, and the social aspects would have to take a back seat. She wouldn't totally quit those activities but they would be limited.

Jasmine was finishing up some reading on the geographical location of puffer fish. Marine biology was turning out to be a good decision. Part of the reason Jasmine had lacked focus was due to poor class choice which was due to her financial aid being late and her having to choose what was left instead of what truly interested her. This semester, everything was different. She was prepared financially, she felt supported, and her mindset had shifted.

Suddenly Jasmine heard rapid knocking. It sounded as if horses were beating their hooves across the door. She continued reading trying to ignore her unwanted guests. Jasmine did not have time.

“Jax! We know you’re in there!”

Jasmine jumped off her bed as her book flew in the air. Angel and Annie had left her door and come around to her window successfully scaring her. Jasmine angrily looked out as the two held their stomachs bent over with laughter. Jasmine could not hold her laughter in and joined them begrudgingly at first but soon was in full rolling giggles.

She invited the two in but they declined.

"No Jax. We are not coming in your dorm. You need to get out."

"Not today y'all. I feel a cold coming on and I need to rest before class tomorrow. I finished my reading early just so I could go to bed *on* time."

"Annie has to go to work and I need to go to Building A to meet a guy I've been talking to in my Black Entrepreneurship class. I need a buffer. Please don't make me go alone Jax."

Jasmine's eyes rolled to the top and she let out a brief sigh. She was not supposed to be trotting this semester. That's how she got in this mess in the first place.

"I don't know," she said, her eyes darting to her books and her hand moving longingly across the pages.

"Come outside friend. It will be fun and we will only be gone an hour. Two tops."

"I don't know guys."

"They have food there!"

With those magic words Jasmine shut her window quickly and pulled on her softest sweatpants and thickest hoodie. She did not care to look cute. She was going for moral support. It seemed like it took forever to make it to Building A. Angel was talking nonstop about some boy named Javier and Jasmine was feeling sicker as she trekked along. She felt her throat being engulfed in the flames of common cold glory. She let out a sneeze and had to use the back of her hoodie's left hand to get the snot. So gross. Angel looked at her face and stopped talking abruptly.

"What?" Jasmine said wondering why Angel's eyes

looked so big.

"Uh...Jax...I didn't realize you were *sick* sick. You are looking a little zombie-ish."

"Girl shut up and let's go meet this boy."

Angel laughed, "You're going to scare him! Stop looking mean!"

"I don't feel good. I can't even help it."

As they arrived to Javier's dorm, the smell of warm tortillas, pico de gallo, refried beans, and fajita steak greeted them. Jasmine thought the food smelled lovely but her stomach did not greet her with its familiar rumble.

Building A was different than her building which was much more reserved. This building was like she'd imagine a dorm at an HBCU. People had their doors open, walking in and out of each other's spaces with shareable side dishes of Mac and cheese, garlic bread, chicken wings, and French fries. Angel and Jasmine were greeted with smiles as they walked in. It was a beautiful sight to behold. Jasmine felt so welcomed. She resented the fact that the cold had decided to manifest rapidly at this very moment.

Introductions were made and Angel was whisked away to make a plate. Jasmine sat down and tried to get comfortable but she really just wanted her bed.

Someone handed her a plate filled with the Mexican feast. She tried to eat it but was unable to get more than a few bites down.

As the night progressed, Angel's promise of an hour came and went. Jasmine got up to leave and get some fresh air. She wasn't going to leave her girl but she definitely needed a moment.

She started walking down the hall and felt faint. She didn't know what made her do it but she knocked on the half open door of one of the guys who had been in the party. She noticed him because he had said hello when they arrived.

He came to the door with a beaming smile. She took notice of his deep brown skin. It was flawless. His glasses and fresh fade gave him that preppy chic look.

"Hey…"

"Hi. I'm Jasmine."

"Jasmine. Nice! I'm Harold."

"Hi Harold. I know this is totally random but do you have some cold medicine? I'm feeling awful! I didn't know I would feel like this when I came over here. It just came on me."

"Uh...let me check. Do you want to come in and sit down?"

Jasmine was instantly nervous. She had never been alone with a guy in his dorm. She did not know Harold from Adam. But as the wave of heat came over her and the aches in her legs throbbed, she realized she was much sicker than she thought. She needed to sit down.

She plopped on the couch and sat there trying to keep her eyes open. Harold came back with a cough drop after what seemed like an eternity.

"Thank you so much," she croaked. Her throat feeling as if it had been rubbed with sand paper now prevented her from speaking in her normal tone. "I can't believe I'm this sick. Like I was literally just a little sniffly a few hours ago. Now I'm miserable. I'm so sorry I'm here getting you sick."

"It's okay. I hope you feel better soon," Harold said. His voice was so calm and Jasmine felt so exhausted. Before she could even help herself, she rested her head on his shoulder and drifted into a peaceful sleep.

Chapter 11

Jasmine age 19

Jasmine was abruptly awakened by shrieks and a bright light flashing in her eyes. Angel and Annie began inspecting her by holding up her arms and checking her eyes with a flashlight. She barely understood where she was and immediately began struggling against their inspection.

"Girl! We were looking for you. Annie came from work because I couldn't find you. I thought you went back home! Are you okay?"

She looked around and saw Harold sitting on the love seat wide-eyed.

"Y'all. Harold didn't do anything to me. I just dozed off. I told y'all I didn't feel good and was sleepy. Thanks for checking on me and being concerned though."

"We were *so* worried. You just ghosted. You think you grown?"

They all laughed.

"Can y'all stop hemming Harold up in his own dorm?"

"Alright *Harry*! You're off the hook. *This* time…But I have you on my radar."

Annie walked around his chair sizing him up. The trio laughed as they walked Annie back to her work station in Building J.

"Annie, I love you girl. You are the real MVP. I don't have to worry about someone getting my butt-ginity when you're around."

"We gotta stick together chica," she quipped in her saucy Latina accent.

Jasmine and Angel continued walking as they chatted about the guys. Jasmine had never been alone with a guy in his place. She felt somehow more grown than she ever had falling asleep in his dorm but she also felt weird. What made her trust that this dude wouldn't try anything?

"So, you think Harold is cute?"

"Yeah. But he seems so nice. Like, just a friend. He was so nice to me. He saw me looking and feeling miserable and let me lay on his shoulder. It was really nothing more than that."

"Okay. If you say so. But um, did you eat that food? It was *so* bomb!"

"The few bites I tried to eat were delicious. I know that food was good. You gotta keep Javier around. I'm ready for the next taco Tuesday when my taste buds and throat aren't waging war against my stomach."

"I can def keep him in the rotation."

Though Jasmine enjoyed that night, she continued to keep fun on a low priority, as needed basis. Jasmine remained steadfast and diligent in her studies. She was committed to succeeding but she was drawn to Harold too. Her mind was so conflicted as she received text messages checking on her and offers to come study together. No guy had done this so far. She kept it cordial at first and blocked all his invitations for one-on-one interaction but ultimately gave in to his requests to come study.

Her encounters with him were strictly friendship based at first but eventually he tried to kiss her. It was awkward. And it never got un-awkward. His breath smelled bad and she could not move past it. One particular evening while in her dorm, he decided to go for it. He began touching her body, caressing her breasts and waist and it was not enjoyable. Jasmine tensed up and closed her eyes and braced herself. For what, she was unsure. Harold stopped. She slowly opened a corner of one eye. Harold was staring at her blankly.

"You want me to stop?"

"Yeah," she said as relief washed over her. She hadn't even realized she was holding her breath. He probably thought she was crazy as they both watched her chest rise and fall rapidly.

She was just not feeling Harold romantically. All through high school she wanted a *real* boyfriend. A guy who would dote on her and send her a valentine's day flower-gram to class and make her feel special. She had seen other girls receive that treatment and she wanted it for herself. And here she was with Harold laying it on thick. But no, Harold was not it.

Harold packed up his study materials hurriedly and left without another word. She hoped she hadn't hurt his feelings too bad but she needed to focus on school. She wasn't saying that a boyfriend was completely off the table but she didn't want to focus on a guy she wasn't really feeling in that way. And he was trying to have intimate relations before even taking her on a real date. That hit her like a ton of bricks as she sat with her thoughts. Jasmine felt so conflicted about how she didn't voice that she was saving herself until marriage. There really wasn't time though. It happened so fast. He just started roaming her body. And she let him roam her body. It was her first encounter but she vowed to be prepared the next time she came in contact with a guy in this manner. Next time she would make her stance known. Establish some boundaries. Next time she would stop before it got too serious.

To her credit, she hadn't known Harold would try anything. He said he wanted to study. So, from then on, she planned to have mixed company study sessions only. And her decision paid off. She finished the semester strong and made it on the Dean's list.

Relief was an understatement. She also felt validated and like she could overcome any obstacle that was put before her. She would have multiple opportunities to test this theory.

Chapter 12

The familiar rumble of the garage door introduced his arrival. Instantly my face turned red and my temples throbbed in sync with the pulsing headache that developed as I lay there exhausted but unable to truly rest. I had just calmed myself but the ragged breathing and perspiration returned. His very presence vexed my spirit. The under-appreciation, lack of emotional availability, and his terse disposition toward me had taken its toll. Staying home with children all day, coupled with having no adult outlet and a spouse who holds themselves from you emotionally and physically, can break a person's mental resolve. I was not afraid to admit I was there. Broken, confused, and fed up. Yes, we did indeed need to talk! I refused to go another day like this.

With each noise he made indicating his close proximity to our bedroom, my breathing intensified. I knew if I didn't calm myself down, I was going to scream or have a panic attack. Since the passing of my mother, anxiety in the form of paralyzing panic attacks had become my norm. Feeling like you'll suffocate as the rapid breathing takes over is not my idea of fun so I tried to avoid the experience by staying calm when stressed but I could feel my resolve unraveling. But I didn't want to scream or have a panic attack. I wanted to come off as strong and firm. I know my tears won't move him. They will just make *me* feel vulnerable. That's not what I wanted to project.

I decided I would be the first to speak. He needed to hear me loud and clear.

He had one foot through the threshold when I said, "Let's not drag this out, Israel," I said as I stood from the bed. "You have been treating me like crap!"

"Jasmine, I want a divorce."

I felt like he knocked the wind out of me. *A divorce?* The words reverberated in my mind. *No. No! We said we would* never *get a divorce. Wait…*

"We said we would never get a divorce." The words came out of my mouth in such a small voice.

The vigor and energy I had riled for this conversation had shriveled like scared prey.

"Yeah, we've said a *lot* of things."

"So, you're just going to give up on all we have. You don't want to fight for our marriage? Eleven years Israel?"

"Fight for what? Eleven more years of what? You complaining? What do we have?"

His words felt like a slap, the type that leaves a hand-print. And it stung.

"Israel, all of it? All of it was trash for you?" I asked in a voice so small I didn't recognize where it came from.

How could he say that and mean it? About our marriage? About our little family? There had been many ups and downs but the factors were mostly outside contributors like my health and financial issues. And while those times where things would flare were uncomfortable, we always pulled through because we kept moving forward. Yes, it was hard and we made each other angry at times but we always made it through. Together.

“What do we have?! *Eleven* years of marriage? Two children and we’re building a life and a legacy. Seriously? It’s been all bad to you? We’ve had tough times and obstacles, but that’s normal. We’ve also had some pretty amazing times.”

“Yeah, it seems like the bad outweighs the good.”

His words made my eyes sting with tears I refused to release. Furrowed brows and balled fists expressed his frustration. Something had shifted. He didn't just seem like what had become his usual disposition of detached and jaded. Today he projected bitterness and anger. His stance caused me to shrink back. Was he just mad in this exchange, or was he refusing to filter his words because he was hurt and wanted to hurt me? The fact that I couldn't tell the difference startled me. I really didn't know the man standing in front of me, and that thought crushed me. It took my air away. I sat back down.

“No, it doesn’t Israel,” I whispered not sure I believed the words myself. “Well, um,” I kicked myself for stammering. “Maybe right now, but not *all* eleven years.”

“There’s always an issue Jasmine. Nothing is ever good enough. And the way you treat me when things get hectic, I don’t like it. I’ve told you that for *years!* And you continue to do it. Just like right now. Coming at me all strong. I hate that! The disrespect!”

I could not believe the words coming from his mouth. My heart beat so fast I could hear it in my ears. *Duh dump. Duh Dump. Duh dump.*

“We are both upset. I don’t get to feel? And have emotions? I have been asking you if we could go to counseling *for* years now to iron some of this out. And just talk. You don't talk to me. You're never *here* to even talk to me. So, then we just have these explosive moments."

"I don't really want to get into all that."

"*No!* You can NOT say you want a divorce and say you don't want to talk about it. That's wrong." My voice cracked. I wanted him to know how I felt but I still wanted him. Divorce was not the answer.

"See! There you go Jasmine. You're *so* disrespectful. You talking to me all forceful like you a man! You cannot tell me what I can and cannot say or do!" He bald up his fists and took steps toward me. my heart lurched. Who was this man in front of me?

"How? Israel, I am upset." I tried to calm my tone to deescalate. But I was too amped up. "You're speaking about ending things. I get to have feelings about that. And express them when I'm angry! Or let down? Or disappointed by another one of your empty promises?"

"And that's what I'm talking about." He let his hands fly through the air in exasperation. "'One of your empty promises.' It's disrespectful. It's a slight at all I do for this family. I BUST MY BUTT! And I get a snarky remark. WHERE'S THE SUPPORT?!" He exploded.

"I do a lot for this family too! My whole *life* is this family. My career, dreams, ME! I'm on hold while you live your dreams because I'm here holding it down. I bust my butt as well. I have Carleigh and Mariah day and night while you work. I'm in the trenches with you. You do the business well but you leave *me* Izzy. You've left *me* baby. And our marriage. You're here but you're not *here.* That's what I've been screaming for you to see. Not meaning to disrespect or discount your work. But this marriage takes work too. And I've been working on it alone for years now."

"I've prospered in my business despite your complaints that it hasn't happened how and when you wanted it. I've prospered in my social circles and have supplied every need for this family. Yeah, I've missed some date nights and birthday parties but that's what it takes to provide the life you want. The medical care you need. So, don't start with me on that. That's no excuse for how you make me feel like it's never enough. I provide for this family and then you want me to come home and help you too?"

"I tell you what I need from you emotionally and in our home, and you bring it right back to work. Your true love. And the things *I* want? I never asked for luxury cars and mini-mansions. That was YOU. I want you. Your ear and for you to care that I'm suffocating. And I NEED the healthcare and you knew that before you said 'I do' and you want to throw it up in my freaking face?!"

"I'm not throwing up anything in your face. I'm just *telling you how I feel*," he said mockingly, scoffing at my failed attempt to get him to connect with me on an emotional level. "Bottom line, I provide for this family and then you want me to come home and help you too? Mad when I don't have time to go to every little party and event you want to throw for the girls. I'm over it."

"Israel. It's called being a family and making memories. You can't just provide financially. That's not the totality of your responsibility."

"I'm tired Jasmine! TIRED of the lack of support. I don't want this anymore!"

"Are you freaking kidding me?! I've been right here going through the ups and downs. You hold everything in and don't make me privy to all the info and when I react, I'm not supportive? You've shut me out! Financially *and* emotionally! When I was the one who started this whole thing with you. My blood, sweat, and tears run all through SnackJoys! I have supported you. We spent the money my mother left after she died to get SnackJoys out of the raw deal you made last year. The money my mother left me is gone! And I didn't even blink.

I just signed the check because I support you."

"Look! Jasmine we are both unhappy. This isn't working. I don't want to live eleven more years like this. I don't want to fight anymore! I won't live another year like *this!* I WANT-"

"Please!" I hissed. "Stop yelling so you don't wake the children."

He rolled his eyes before finishing his sentence.

"A divorce. I want... A divorce."

Everything paused. I felt my heartbeat reverberate through my ears.

"I...I can't believe this," I stuttered.

"I tried to support you Izzy. You have kept things from me. And our communi-"

"I don't really want to argue... Or discuss any more in a long-drawn-out way."

"So that's just it? No reasoning with you? Can we go to counseling?"

"I do not need to go to counseling for anybody to tell me *anything*. No."

"Israel. I cannot believe you are sitting here, saying we have nothing. We have issues that can be worked on but haven't been because we have both been overwhelmed. This is worth saving."

"I'm tired. I'm done trying to fix it."

"How could you be done when we haven't done the work? Can you say in your heart of hearts that we've identified the issues and worked on them? Or have we just been surviving after reeling from one thing to the next?"

"Jasmine...I don't want to discuss it."

"I get a discussion! I GET to talk about this. I have been here in this house alone! Not talking. Hoping it would get better. Hoping you would *see* me."

"Jasmine, I'm not arguing."

"Israel, is there someone else?! I find it hard to believe you just came to this conclusion out of the blue!"

"There's no one else. I'm just done with this. Can I not just be over my relationship with *you*?"

Those words stung more than any he'd spoken so far.

"Wow," was all I could muster.

"I will take care of the kids, and I would never just leave you high and dry. You know because you're sick and all," he said with such pity in his eyes. "That's why it's been so hard to make this decision."

I felt as if a slap with a scalding hot hand had smacked the other side of my face. And the pieces of my broken heart continued to crumble into dust. Divorced, alone, and sick. What a life this was shaping up to be.

God help me, I prayed silently. I took a deep breath to keep the tears at bay. He would *not* get my tears!

"Oh, okay. You've stayed, so you don't look bad, leaving the sick girl. Not because of all the ways I've helped you elevate your life?"

I was floored by his gall. Bitter laughter flowed up from my feet and reverberated through my body as it burst out of my mouth. It was deep but held no joy. Israel looked at me with concerned eyes. He was concerned for my sanity judging by his expression. We shared the same concern.

The coughing spasm came on strong as I continued to laugh and shake my head from left to right. These coughing spasms were normal for me now after years of dealing with lung disease. I stopped laughing to try and calm myself. I quickly realized something was off as my breath refused to catch. As I reached for my bottle of water, I suddenly experienced an unrelenting pressure close to my left breast. Hand over my chest, I gasped for air. Israel's alarmed face was the last thing I saw before…

Chapter 13

Jasmine age 20

Jasmine finally found her stride in college. She was doing well in her classes and studying came easy now. She even had a part-time job to save up for a car. She felt like she was doing pretty good and wanted to try her hand at finding love. She felt ready to balance dating on top of her full social calendar. Online dating was definitely a thing but people were embarrassed to let others know they had found love online. So even though people frowned upon online dating, she thought it would be fun. Besides, the guys she was interested in on campus were either taken or not interested in Black girls. She wanted to graduate with a degree and an engagement ring and she spent 80% of her time seeing the same people so online dating seemed like an exciting way to meet new people. Even though she had a small concern about meeting a serial killer, she decided to put that on the back burner and jump in to the virtual dating pool.

She definitely met some weirdos. There was Joshua, the overly religious guy who would ask her to stay on the phone with him while he sang and prayed. She had nothing against worship sessions but did not consider that a great way to get to know someone before a first physical date. Blocked!

Then there was the Nasty Bennie. He kept sending her thang pics! She was so mad and startled when she scrolled down that first time. Before sending the thang pics, he had been the most normal and the most promising of the bunch. He had quickly taken her number, moving from the inbox and would send her funny messages and check on her. She thought Nasty Bennie was *so* sweet. He ruined any chance when he sent the unwanted pics of his nether regions and requested nudes from Jasmine. Blocked!

Next, there was Anthony. Anthony seemed so sweet. He mentioned to Jasmine how he was waiting for marriage to have sex. She was so caught off guard because she hadn't mentioned any of that to him. She quickly learned to keep that information to herself until the right time because guys were either scared off by it or took it as a challenge. And she rarely found a guy committed to saving himself for marriage. He was saying and doing all the right things. They even discussed their favorite gospel artists. She found out he went to the neighboring college and actually felt safe setting up a meeting. But Jasmine wasn't dumb. She would have Angel go with her. She showed Angel his picture as she dreamily described how amazing he was. The cackle Angel let out.

"Siiiiiiisssssss. No!"

"What," Jasmine said confused.

Angel laughed to tears! Jasmine was so confused. She cleared her throat and crossed her arms waiting for

Angel to explain.

"He told you he was waiting until marriage to do what? Cuz baby boy is busting them DOWN across TOWN! Haha get it? Down, across town, at the other college?" she said while cracking her sides with laughter.

"What are you talking about?"

"Jax. You know I be knowing. I don't just trot here. I TROT! The whole area. For a time such as *this*, baby! I have your back. And Mr. Anthony is no virgin. In fact, he has a baby on the way. And that's facts."

"What?"

"Just let it go sis. Try someone else because he ain't the one. He's definitely known."

Jasmine hated to believe it but one thing Angel was not was a liar, and one thing she was, was informed. Always. She always knew the business. So, Jasmine was done! With him and online dating. It was fun while it lasted but she was 3 for 3 and online dating was clearly not her thing. Anthony, blocked!

Jasmine headed to the mall to do some shopping for her new walking shoes. She stepped into the shoe store with laser focus. She had a budget and she was sticking to it. She noticed the cute associate but she wasn't worried about his flirty grin. He just wanted a sale.

"Hello beautiful."

"Hi," she responded flatly.

"Let me guess, you're here to get some sandals to showcase those pretty feet and those beautiful, thick legs?"

Jasmine swallowed a bit trying to act like the compliment didn't make her want to grin from ear to ear. "Uh. I just need some walking shoes.

"Well how about I help you find the perfect shoes and as a gift to me you honor me with your digits. I'd love to get to know you."

"Now how many women did that work on today?" Jasmine asked with pursed lips that she couldn't help from turning into a smile. She hated that she was letting this dude charm her but he was so inviting. He seemed so cool.

"Nah. I love a Black queen. Not many of "us" are out here. I mean I have dated the rainbow but my heart is with the sistas and seeing one of y'all is rare out here. So, no ma'am. I'm not 'spitting game'."

Jasmine took Joey up on his offer to get to know her. He was funny and pretty charming. He was a broke college student like her so she didn't expect him to wine and dine her. She enjoyed just getting to know one another and feeling googly about his calls.

One day, Jasmine casually mentioned she braided hair on the side. He wore his hair in two cornrows. She did his hair for free as a one-time courtesy. He knew she used her braiding skills as a way to gain extra income but he became relentless in pursuit of her free services. Their conversations of getting to know you and jokes quickly turned into inquiries about his hair only. He kept trying to come to her dorm so she could braid his hair. Jasmine did not feel comfortable and kicked herself for allowing him to know where she lived. She probably wouldn't have minded but he wanted it done for free and he was too forceful. She felt so uncomfortable with him asking for free services repeatedly. She felt used and duped. She thought they were off to a really good start and he was actually interested in her. So, she had to do the only thing she could from preventing Joey from calling and text messaging her. Blocked!

Jasmine was over dating online and in person. But then, Nathan changed all that. Nathan was like a breath of fresh air. He was so handsome to Jasmine from what she could see on his thumbnail. He slid into her social media inbox one fall morning and it was a wrap. Chocolate – the really milky kind – strong jaw line, clean shaven and big beautiful eyes. From their interactions, Jasmine discovered he was over six feet-four inches tall. He played the piano and he made her laugh. He had so many good qualities. His conversation was refreshing. He was well spoken, no typos in his text messages, and he had a great job. With further conversation, they discovered they shared a hometown and some of their cousins attended the same church growing up. And not only did Nathan have a good grown-up job, he was a minister! This excited Jasmine because she felt safe and like her no sex before marriage goals would be safe with him. She also liked that though he was a minister, he was funny and down to earth. Best of both worlds. That took down Jasmine's defenses immediately. He was most likely who he said he would be in her mind.

Within a few days of chatting online, Nathan requested an in-person meeting. He asked her what she was most comfortable with. This further chipped at the guard she had lifted. He was such a gentleman.

Jasmine had no vehicle. She didn't want to bus it at night and she also didn't want any of her friends who usually gave her rides to know she was meeting up with a guy she'd never met. She knew she was wrong for being sneaky and she should always let someone know when she was meeting a potential serial killer. But she didn't want Angel spoiling it. She knew she was wrong. She had preached this to all her friends but here she was planning a rendezvous behind the scenes.

Nathan agreed to meet her at her dorm for dessert and movies. She figured the dorm wasn't her *real* home so she was safe. She would make the dessert and he would bring the movies. Sounded simple enough. Jasmine cleaned all day in anticipation of his visit. She cleaned the bathroom twice and dusted the table until it started squeaking. She jolted herself with the fresh air as she opened the balcony to sweep.

Jasmine. Get it together girl! There's nothing left to clean. He's going to like you or he's not. Either way, you'll be fine!

She straightened her beige A-line skirt and black top that let out just enough church girl cleavage. She didn't need the minister thinking she was fast. At the last minute she decided it'd be smart to reach out to Angel anyway. She quickly sent Angel a text informing her that she had an internet date coming over and to call 911 if she didn't hear from her by the morning.

She took in a shaky breath as she heard her phone chime indicate an incoming call.

"Hello?"

"Hello beautiful. I will be there in five."

"Okay," Jasmine tried to say confidently. But she could hear the nervousness in her own voice. She hoped she didn't come off as crazy.

Jasmine almost gasped when she opened the door for Nathan and looked up at his very tall and very lean body. She immediately felt insecure. *We will look straight like the number ten. I definitely have to stick to my diet if I'm going to date him.*

"Hello beautiful," he said as he bent for a hug before entering. He presented her with the choices of romantic comedy or action film before even walking through the door. They both laughed. She let him in and then told him that as her guest, he should decide. He chose romantic comedy. Another point for him.

Jasmine set out a plate of homemade chocolate chip cookies and fresh cut strawberries, put the movie in, and sat down by Nathan on the couch leaving a little room between them. The movie started off with a laugh which lightened the mood. Nathan cracked jokes the whole time and Jasmine laughed so hard she cried. It felt nice.

The movie ended and instead of awkward silence the two flowed into easy conversation. They talked about everything. They compared stories of their childhoods, connected over their favorite musical artists, and laughed at the shenanigans of her cousins that went to his church. Jasmine was pleased with her decision to meet Nathan. His confidence and deep voice were quite attractive to her and he was so respectful. He didn't try to kiss her or touch her inappropriately. The entire experience received a ten in her book.

"Well, I definitely have work in the morning. But I would love to see you again this weekend...that is, if you will have my company again my lady," he drawled in a terrible British accent as he bowed at the waist.

Jasmine covered her mouth as the giggle escaped. *Girl stop. You're giggling like a schoolgirl. Be grown up! This is a* real *man.*

"I would love to your grace," she said in an equally terrible accent as she curtsied.

He kissed her lightly on the cheek as he made his exit. Jasmine closed the door and rested her back on it as she stared dreamily at the ceiling. He was such a good guy! And she felt so comfortable with him.

BOOM! BOOM! BOOM! Jasmine jumped off the door and hit the floor. She *knew* he was crazy. He was coming back to kill her! *BOOM! BOOM! BOOM*!

Wait...Were those gunshots? Her inner-city upbringing taught her to drop first and ask questions later.

"Jasmine! Open! This! Door! You all right?!"

"Angel!" Jasmine mumbled to herself. "What is she even doing here?" Jasmine's fingers fumbled with the locks as her heart beat wildly. She swung the door open as quickly as she could. "Girl! You're gonna get me a noise complaint. I know it's after 10! Get in here," Jasmine said as she yanked Angel by the arm and pulled her across the threshold.

"After 10? Try 2 am! And I've been text messaging you since 8:30 P-M when YOU first messaged ME!"

A wave of recognition flashed over Jasmine as she realized that she silenced her phone once Nathan arrived so the chiming wouldn't ruin the mood. She was so wrapped up in her date that her phone had long been forgotten. Jasmine went and got her phone and scrolled through Angel's messages.

> **8:30 PM: What? Online dating again huh? Well, be safe and check in. Okay?**
>
> **9:15 PM: When he gets there, let me know. And when he leaves.**
>
> **10:20 PM: Send an S.O.S., pigeon, smoker signal. Something!**
>
> **11:15 PM: Jax?!**
>
> **1:00 AM: Ma'am! I'm about to come over there if I don't hear from you ASAP.**

Jasmine looked up and tried to keep a straight face but reading those urgent messages and seeing Angel stand there, with a bonnet on, hands on hips, lingerie pajama teddy top, baggy sweats and fuzzy slippers, was a sight to behold. Angel's eyes flashed with anger but she couldn't hold it as she saw the tears of laughter slip from Jasmine's eyes. Angel swatted at her and joined in laughing.

"So? You're alive. He's gone I assume. He betta not be in yo' bed!"

Jasmine rolled her eyes toward the ceiling before saying, "Girl…" and shaking her head. "Now, you know!"

"CLANK! CLANK!" They said in unison referencing a Madea line from one of Tyler Perry's plays before dissolving into a fit of giggles.

"Okay, so the honey pot was not compromised. Well? How was it?"

Jasmine sighed contentedly. “It was great. He’s such a nice guy. And he didn’t try anything. He was a total gentleman Angel.”

“Good! Well, you’ll have to give me the full rundown tomorrow. I have work in the morning.”

“Me too,” Jasmine said dreamily.

She was sure she’d be stopping herself from floating while at her desk with how giddy she felt. Cloud 9. Nathan had her head in the clouds for sure.

Chapter 14

"Jasmine, both the ablation and the blood transfusion went well. Your levels immediately stabilized after the procedures but it was touch and go. Said plainly, your heart almost gave out from pumping too rapidly for too long. You coded twice."

"What's an ablation?"

"The short, they went through your groin into your heart to fix a faulty blood vessel."

"That sounds scary. And the ablation saved me? from – um – passing away?" I gulped.

"You *coded* because enough oxygen was not getting to your heart due to critically low iron. The transfusion saved you. The ablation was needed once the transfusion was complete because leaving the arrythmia untreated could possibly aggravate your overtaxed heart. But interestingly enough, the two aren't related. The arrythmia was pre-existing."

I'm sure the confusion on my face caused her to

pause. It was all too much to take in.

"Please explain."

"The critically low iron was a direct side effect of your new lung medication. But the need for the ablation is not new. The state of the vessel they catheterized was not congruent with sudden cardiac arrest. Did you feel your heart beating rapidly earlier today or any time in the last few months?"

Sincere concern etched her brow.

"Dr. Melbourne, honestly, I've been feeling the rapid heartbeats off and on for a while. I mentioned it to my rheumatologist…almost a year ago."

"A year Jasmine," she gave me that familiar warning look filled with concern.

"It would go away, with rest. So… I just thought nothing of it." I shook my head. "I guess I would have eventually brought it back up. I thought I had time." I attempted a smile. It did not reach my eyes. "I'm still in shock. I just blacked out. I felt like I was suffocating before I fainted. It was *so* scary."

"I know it was. And you're out of the woods for now. We need to keep you a few days to monitor you. And honestly, I've seen these types of blood vessel issues return with high stress. So do your best to keep all stress down."

Dr. Melbourne patted my hand. It was a comfort to hear my first name and receive the prognosis from my long-time primary care physician. Laying in this bed, unaware of what really took place, and the nonstop visits from nurses and multiple specialists – strangers – who used the formal "Mrs. Ford" in monotone as they casually spouted doctor jargon I couldn't decipher, the familiarity soothed my nerves.

"Okay Dr. Melbourne. What does this all mean? I almost…died? I cannot believe that."

Her glance at the floor confirmed my words.

"You got here at the right time. You're so lucky."

"Thank you," I mumbled. Unsure I believed her.

"If you're unaware your iron is that low, it can turn for the worst fast. But I will be honest with you. We are a little stumped with your case. We switched you to the liquid version of Borcept so you could get the higher dose quicker for your lung health. An ingredient in the liquid version has interacted with your other medications and supplements. We can switch you back to pill form, but now you have a whole new layer of challenges we will need to work through and heal. I wish your rheumatologist had caught the fact that the ingredients with the two medications could interact. Or the pharmacist. Somewhere, someone dropped the ball. I'm so sorry."

Her glassy eyes alarmed me. The doctor isn't supposed to cry. But I understood. We had history. She had been so sweet throughout the years. We had been pregnant together twice growing our families while she grew her practice and I helped grow SnackJoys and Dr. Melbourne had literally walked this health journey with me. She wanted me well just as much as I did.

"Well, that's good to hear. You're switching me back to the pill form of the medicine for my lungs?"

"Eventually. But we are at a wait and watch stage. That new medicine was not only leeching the effectiveness of your iron but all your vitamins; Vitamin D, folate, magnesium. Your entire body took a hit. We need to make sure your organs are rebounding and can take the Borcept."

"Wow Dr. Melbourne. I'm shocked." I now understood why while upon waking my body felt like it endured a Hulk slam. "I felt tired but I'm always tired so I just pushed through."

"I understand. Well now is the perfect time to get some rest. Hubby has the kids. So, you get rest! I hope to see him when he comes to visit. We will discuss next steps after more test results come in. And remember. Stress free. As much as you can."

Stress free. Hmph! That felt impossible. If she only knew...

My eyelids felt like bricks. I could barely keep them open but my racing mind refused to allow me to drift off to sleep. What I thought was anxiety or a heart attack had been my body frantically working to produce more blood. I shuttered now, replaying the doctor's words. I had almost died right in my home. With my kids in the next room. Right after my husband asked for a divorce.

As I sat there, alone in the hospital, letting the beep of the machine lull me, the tears fell as the rush of emotion hit me. What had I done to deserve all this? Instinctively I dialed Israel, the only number I knew without the help of my smartphone's contacts app.

"Hello," he rushed the greeting.

"Hey…"

"Hi," he stated flatly. No warmth detected. I don't know what I expected.

"I just spoke to Dr. Melbourne. She asked about you. Wondered if she would see you when you came up here."

His silence was deafening. I heard the kids laughing in the background. Then Carleigh yelling at Mariah. Tears ensued.

"Y'all have to sit down to eat," he stated firmly to the kids.

"Israel…"

"Yes Jasmine," he said annoyed.

"So, are you coming? Not sure how long I will be here."

"I didn't know it was that serious, where you'd need to stay for an extended time. I need to get back to SnackJoys. I don't know if I will have time to bring the kids."

"I almost died Israel. Life is so fragile. Can we please stop all this and just hash it out and work out our differences?"

"Jasmine, don't. Nothing has changed. You going to the hospital changes nothing and these kids won't watch themselves. I gotta go."

He disconnected the call. Tears flowed down my cheeks.

"Really?" I yelled toward the ceiling, grateful for the private room. I'm sure it did not contain the sound. I couldn't care less. "I've had *nonstop* trial," I clapped my hands for emphasis, "NON! STOP! And now I have to lose my marriage too!? Why is this happening to me?!" I sobbed. "Why is this *happening?"* I sighed in defeat.

Heartache consumed me as I settled into the disappointment and hurt I felt over my current situation. Israel was my reassurance. He was an answered prayer. He was my peace and sounding board. And now…*Now what?*

Our last conversation replayed like a broken record in my mind. *WHERE'S THE SUPPORT?!* His words boomed through my thoughts.

Where had I gone wrong? He said I didn't support him and I was disrespectful. Those were the aspects of wifehood I worked on the *most.* But I missed the mark, in his eyes, and I knew I couldn't discount his perception. Sitting with the revelation that I hurt him stung. All the scriptures and marital advice books, blogs, and articles I read over the years and still I failed. Here I thought I was hitting Proverbs thirty-one-woman marks, but instead my marriage had crumbled around my feet.

And now I'm left alone in this hospital after almost dying. Israel got me in the ambulance but of course he had to stay behind with the kids. But he wasn't getting a babysitter and then coming to see about me. It's literally too much to process. My life. This is my life?

Chapter 15

Jasmine age 20

Jasmine was living her best life! She went from struggle meals and stalking bible studies and campus meet and greets for free food, to ordering expensive cuts of steak and perfectly cooked lobster tails at restaurants she hadn't heard of prior to dating Nathan. She admired and photographed beautiful artifacts at museums, she let the wind flow over her face as they rode up the coast sightseeing, and she window shopped and shopped-shopped at the promenades, all on Nathan's dime. He spoiled her. She was living *the* life.

Jasmine and Nathan saw each other every few days. It had been a little over 3 months, and they had seen each other dozens of times. This is the dating experience Jasmine saw on television and hoped she'd have one day but was doubtful it would happen with any of the financially struggling college guys she often came in contact with. Nathan was a bit older and already had a great job and lived rent-free in his parent's pool house. Nathan literally had the best of both worlds; privacy and access to all his cash. And he freely spent it on Jasmine. He would roll up to the drive-thru ATM, cash a check and just hand her the money. Granted, these were smaller gig checks, not whole paychecks, but it was enough for Jasmine to get her hair done or buy a new dress. He was literally a dream come true.

Jasmine loved their dates, but the most special time she had with him was their church dates. She enjoyed watching him play the piano. She felt odd to admit it, but that's when he looked the most attractive to her. His long fingers curled effortlessly over those black and white keys. He made that instrument sing, and it set the church on fire Sunday after Sunday. He truly helped the spirit move freely as he played the music on his heart and guided the worship leader to sing songs that ignited the fire of worship over the entire congregation. Jasmine loved bonding with him over their love of God. She was new to faith and learning the Bible so these times growing her faith with the man she admired, she cherished.

One afternoon Jasmine received a call from the hospital regarding her mother. Anita had suffered a mild heart attack and was rushed to the ER. Jasmine immediately caught the train to the hospital. She had to see about her mother. She was there all day and into the night. She only left because Anita was stable, awake, and insisted she go home and get some rest.

She felt her phone vibrating as she sat looking absentmindedly at the television. It was definitely watching her. She hoped it was not the hospital again. No news was definitely good news.

She tried to sound calm as she spoke to Nathan but

he instantly picked up the heaviness in her voice. Within the hour he arrived with chocolate chip cookie dough, two DVDs, and an overnight bag.

Jasmine and Nathan ate and talked over his latest project at work. They baked the cookies, watched the movies, and even played a few games of speed. He did everything to keep Jasmine's mind off of Anita's health scare.

As it grew later into the night, Jasmine could feel herself getting nervous. She glanced at his overnight bag, nervously.

"Let's sleep out here. We don't have to go in your room," Nathan breathed into Jasmine's ear as his hands massaged her scalp.

Her shoulders began to ease down at his touch. She hadn't even realized how tight she was wound up. That made Jasmine a little more comfortable. She made a thick pallet on the floor with blankets so they could relax while watching more movies.

It started with a kiss. They had kissed before. Even swapped a little tongue. It was fun. Jasmine was discovering that she loved kissing. But this was different. She could feel his passion. He moved to her neck and began undressing her. Here she was *again.* And while with Harold she was able to disconnect and make her body flop like a stiff noodle deterring Harold from continuing, she actually cared for Nathan and enjoyed his touch. She only wanted him to stop because she knew she would want more.

That night they did not make it past kissing and a semi-unclothed massage but Jasmine felt so guilty when she woke the next morning. They were Christians. She felt like they should be saving the intimacy for commitment. She felt convicted. She knew he felt the same and was ready for a discussion when he woke up. He was the veteran Christian.

"Hey beautiful," he said reaching over for a kiss.

"Good morning," Jasmine said offering her cheek.

"Oh, I know. Morning breath!" he laughed but her face showed her concern.

He reached for her as he asked, "Is it bad news with your mom."

"Oh no Nathan. She's better. She can come home in the next few days. I just spoke with her. But I…" she couldn't find the words to say.

"What's wrong?"

"About last night...like...am I the only one who feels a certain way about our um...interaction."

Nathan was taken aback by her statement much to Jasmine's surprise. *He* was the minister. He didn't feel as convicted as she did?

He bowed his head and chuckled, disarmed by her furrowed brows. "Come here baby," he said guiding her to sit on his lap which made them both laugh because he was so thin and her plus size frame was not light. "Are you uncomfortable with our interaction?"

"I mean…"

"Look. We didn't have sex. We are Christians and there are lines that need to be drawn yes, but we can still have fun. I don't feel bad about what happened last night."

"Okay," she said unsure.

"We don't have to do anything like that again. It's what you are comfortable with baby."

"Okay," she said more sure. "I'm okay."

"Good. I enjoy our time together."

"Me too."

Jasmine let it go that day. She hoped she had the courage to stop herself from going any further in the future. Kissing and massages. If he was good with it and agreed to stop there, so was she. And she would follow his lead. She enjoyed her time with Nathan and the idea of a relationship with him. So many new experiences. She didn't want to mess it up by being too immature. She would just trust he'd walk in his maturity and mandate as a man of the cloth. And God would help them both.

Chapter 16

Jasmine age 21

Jasmine laid across Anita's couch haphazardly as she contemplated the ins and outs of her and Nathan's relationship. Kissing and massages of course turned into more. They weren't intimate beyond Jasmine's comfort level often, but eventually it happened a second time, they crossed the line even further than before. They discussed it again and Nathan assured her that if as a minister, he had no issue with it, they were good. Naturally, it continued to happen until the lines became blurred.

She tried to retrace her steps. Where had she gone wrong this time? That first night he slept over. She said she was "okay," and then went on about their day. She should have set the boundary in that moment instead of trusting his convictions and adopting them as her own.

Jasmine had given things and done things with Nathan she knew that she only wanted to do with her husband. They hadn't gone *all the* way but the way their interactions made Jasmine feel, she felt as if she might as well had gone there. But that wasn't the worst part.

Three months ago, when they first broke up, she was hurt. But honestly, she felt they would rebound. At first, Nathan hadn't technically broken up with her. He said he wanted to see other people. She was fine with it. They would still date each other but keep their options open. But when she discovered he was taking someone else to the wedding they were supposed to attend together, just one week after they decided to slow things down, she was pissed and she was hurt. Voicing her concerns led to an argument.

"You know what, I don't want to date other people. We were already together. We told everyone we were boyfriend and girlfriend. We can just break up officially," Jasmine said with mild disgust in her tone.

"That's fine with me. We can be done, done."

"Oh, it's that easy? A few weeks ago you were sending me engagement ring photos. Now it's just whatever?"

"Stuff happens baby. That's just how this cookie is going to crumble," he said lacking warmth in his tone.

"Who are you right now? Where's the sweet guy from our first dates? There's been an imposter these last few weeks. Sarcastic. *Arrogant.* Mean!"

"Oh, there's no imposter. That other guy was just my representative."

Jasmine was shocked. This is how the minister chose to act? She felt so betrayed. The worst part is she felt like she let God down and that He couldn't trust her. But she also felt like she had missed God. She was trusting the God in Nathan, and that backfired miserably.

Jasmine and Nathan's last intimate interaction, which had been the most intense, would be their last interaction. He immediately began acting different. He called her less that week. And then he called needing to "talk." She felt the change coming. What she had dreaded since high school happened to her. A guy got what he wanted physically, felt like she no longer had value, and was ready to bounce. She felt so played. They had discussed marriage and the future. She was so sprung and he was done. Already planning dates with the next woman.

Jasmine felt sad but she wasn't devastated. He turned out to be a jerk, so she easily moved on. She focused on her coursework even more. She lost weight due to her new workout regimen, and she started attending her own church again where she felt she was able to receive some healing and biblical teaching tailor made for her situation. She was doing well until curiosity got the best of her.

Today is the day she thought, as Jasmine decided she was ready to see Nathan again. She felt over him in the three months they'd been apart and she knew she was looking good, down fifteen pounds. She was even mobile now; having bought her first car and she was feeling her independent vibe. Jasmine wanted to rub his terrible decision in his face. A visit to Nathan's church was in order.

Jasmine got dressed in a form fitting floral wrap dress that accentuated her curves, put on her highest heels, and made sure each strand of her shiny flat-ironed hair was in place. Her intentions were to look so cute that he would miss what he once had and maybe he'd ask her out again.

But God clearly had other plans. As usual. The pastor had them worshipping and crying out to God with the sermon he taught on identity and the blessing and access to resources a person has with God as your father. Jasmine could not even help the tears that streamed down her face. She worshipped like she hadn't ever before. By the time Nathan saw her, she was puffy and her make up washed out. As she tried hurriedly to wipe the mascara and smooth down her hair, Nathan brushed past her and barely said hello. Before Jasmine could recover, Nathan's friend came up to her and gave her a sympathetic hug.

"I'm so glad you came today. We missed you. I know it may be odd coming to church when his fiancée is here but she doesn't come every Sunday but even when she is here, it doesn't matter. Any time *you* want to visit you are welcome, welcome, welcome!"

Jasmine felt like she would pass out at first and then all of a sudden, she felt hot. *Fiancée? Fiancée!*

It hadn't been three months and Nathan had chosen a bride? No wonder he gave her the cold shoulder. She felt like someone ripped her heart out, put nails on it and jumped up and down to make sure they went all the way through. She hadn't even gone on another date and she had shut down her dating profiles and here Nathan was, getting married!

Even though Nathan had treated her like a jerk when they ended things, she knew he could be sweet and deep down she wondered if her and Nathan could strike something up again. She was so ashamed to admit it. As fresh tears streamed down her puffy face, she realized this was her first heartbreak and she did not like this feeling. And the tears that flowed as she made it to her car had been falling for hours as she realized their time together was officially over. She never wanted another heartbreak again.

Exhausted by the events of the day, she decided to go to Anita's house instead of making the drive to her dorm. She needed cookies, ice cream and free premium cable, the college student's dream. This fresh crack to her heart was getting all the cookies.

Anita walked in with a bag of wings from their favorite hole in the wall spot. Jasmine heard her stomach rumble.

"Hi Nonnie. I didn't know you'd be here. I know you have school tomorrow. You heading out soon?"

"Eh. I don't know Mom. I was going to just chill. I had a rough day."

"Well get chu some of these wings. It may hit the spot and we can talk about it if you want."

"What flavor?"

"Good ole B-B-Q! And some garlic pama-john," Anita drawled in her exaggerated inner-city girl tone.

"Pama-john," Jasmine repeated letting out her first laugh of the day.

They dug into the food with vigor, smacking, cleaning bones, and dipping the tender wings in the thick blue cheese dipping sauce. There was no room for discussion as they chowed down.

"Whew…" Anita said as she sat resting her hands on her satisfied stomach. "A good meal will turn that frown upside down."

Jasmine had to admit she felt better. And now she was ready to talk about it. Or so she thought. As soon as the words were at the tip of her tongue, fresh tears began to fall.

"Nathan is engaged. To the girl he went to that wedding with when he said he wanted to, 'See other people,'" Jasmine scoffed as she threw up air quotes.

"Aw man Nonnie. I'm sorry to hear that."

"Mommy, I'm angry and I'm hurt because I really liked him. I thought maybe I even loved him? He sent me rings like the week before we parted. To start seeing the style of ring I wanted. And now just a few months later he has completely moved on. That hurts!"

Anita listened as Jasmine poured her heart out. She didn't have much advice but a listening ear was definitely welcomed.

"Well Nonnie, you know what I've said from the time you were a little girl. This too shall pass. Don't let it steal your joy. And he is the one missing out. I know you don't want to hear it but it's true.

It was true. Jasmine did not want to hear it. She couldn't receive it. All she felt was hurt. As she sat there processing, she realized that she wasn't so hurt that he moved on but that he was getting married, the very thing she desired since she was a little girl. She knew she wanted marriage before she even chose a career.

"A family mommy. That's what I want. I want a marriage. I want a family that stays together."

"I know honey. It's what you've wanted since you were a little girl."

The mood was somber. Jasmine did not want to hurt her mother's feelings.

"Mommy I know your marriage with daddy didn't work out. But I thank you for the family unit you created for us. You always made sure we were taken care of. I just want to have a chance at marriage too though."

"Jasmine, I totally understand. Don't worry about me. I'm not offended. You can want a traditional family and a marriage even though mine didn't work out. And I want that for you. I pray you have a wonderful marriage."

"Thank you, mommy. Me too!"

"So cheer up! Nathan is not it. Girl he was too skinny anyway. Y'all was walking around looking like the number ten."

"Mommy! Dannng," Jasmine said as she cocked her head to the side. They both laughed.

"What?"

"I asked you if I was too fat for him when you first met him."

"Girl you didn't have a car then. He brought you to the hospital. I wasn't about to insult him."

"You get on my nerves Mommy!"

"Love you too. Now let me finish teaching you how to crochet this scarf. But first, let's get some of this good ole ice cream and peach cobbler I made."

"Okay," Jasmine said beating Anita to the kitchen.

Chapter 17

Jasmine age 5

Jasmine and her older sister Anise laid in their beds. They could hear screaming and slamming of doors but could not decipher the exact words. Something shattered. They heard bumping and as if something heavy was crashing. They knew not to cry out or move from their beds. Fear kept them still.

"Jaxie it's okay. Don't cry."

They spoke in hushed tones.

"Okay Nisie. I won't."

"I wish they would stop."

"Me too."

And like an answered prayer after one more loud boom, the arguing stopped. Jasmine drifted off to sleep despite the feelings of uncertainty and she woke up to the same uneasiness. She apprehensively tipped out of her room to survey the atmosphere. When she walked out of her room, her parent's door greeted her. It was off the hinges and rested on the wall in the hallway. She slowly walked into her mother's room to find her cleaning up the broken pieces of glass from a mirror.

"Mommy...what happened?"

"Nonnie…"

"How did that happen to the door?"

"It was an accident."

"How did the mirror break?"

"Something was thrown and it got pushed over. Be careful. Don't step in this glass," Anita said.

She looked so sad to Jasmine. But it was more than sad. Remorseful and haggard was a better description.

"Where's Anise?"

"Your Dad took her to school. You're staying home with me."

Jasmine was happy for this news. She did not like the daycare much anyway. As a big five-year-old she longed for kindergarten. She longed to read books and learn but due to a late birthday, she had to stay in daycare one more year.

"Do you need help mommy?"

"No. Go brush your teeth and get dressed. Then I will make you breakfast."

Jasmine and Anita made it to the kitchen at the same time. They both looked up at the same time at the metal fork stuck in the ceiling. Anita knew the question was coming so she braced herself.

"Mommy...why is that fork in the ceiling?"

"It was an accident."

Jasmine knew better than to continue her questioning. But she had so many. Her parents arguing was nothing new but her young mind wondered why they had to yell. She was told not to yell. When she got angry or frustrated, she was told to stay calm and use her inside voice at daycare. But adults yelled. And apparently, threw things.

Jasmine's father returned. She watched her parents move awkwardly about. They were so nervous around one another but they hugged. She hoped they could just keep hugging.

A few months later Jasmine remembered packing boxes for their new place. Just the three ladies. Daddy would be living in his own but would be sure to visit.

And shortly after Jasmine remembered her mother receiving mail that immediately sent her into a cursing fit.

"Oh, you want to serve me here?! Where I live? While the kids are here?!" Anita screamed at the papers.

"What mommy? What is it?"

"Your dad wants a divorce Jasmine. Those are the papers."

Something in Jasmine broke. She immediately began crying. She knew what divorce was. She had just turned six and people thought she was still a baby but she knew things. And she was devastated. Her dad was gone but she always thought he'd return. These papers made everything feel so final.

"Noooo!" The scream came from the depths of her soul. Anita was shocked. Anise came from her room with a bewildered expression questioning what was going on.

"Jasmine," Anita croaked as tears fell and she reached for her daughter.

"No!" Jasmine screamed as she ran from the living room and locked herself in her bedroom.

She cried and screamed into her pillow until she couldn't cry anymore. She wanted her family. She didn't want to live apart from her father. She didn't want to live in a stupid apartment. She didn't want to have to visit her dad on the weekends. A family, even if they argued sometimes, meant so much to her and losing her family as she'd known it had devastated her soul.

Chapter 18

On a mission, I hopped in my car and headed to Angel's house. I needed laughter and good food. She provided both. As I pulled up, I couldn't help but marvel at her home. She lived in a modern, two-story, mini-mansion. Well, everything was modern except for her front door. I sat there admiring the sunburst-stained glass centered in her antique front door. The tree of life, multicolor design was so beautiful in contrast with the teal painted wooden door. The vibrant colors always invoked a sense of joy. And the antique feel felt welcoming. Angel's home was inviting and right now, she was one of the only things that felt like home. But something wouldn't let me turn the car off and walk to her door. She knew me too well and I knew I would be spilling my guts. I wasn't sure I was ready for all of that.

I gathered my nerve and my belongings and exited

my vehicle with a huff. It was now or never. As I opened the unlocked door and crossed the threshold, not needing to knock, as was her open-door policy, I immediately felt a sense of calm take over as I breathed in undertones of lavender and vanilla. Her home felt like a sanctuary. I needed to feel a sense of peace for my restless mind and weary heart.

We settled into easy conversation like good girlfriends effortlessly do.

"Girl! I was swinging like this," Angel's demonstration of prayer shadowboxing forced laughter I tried my best to stifle. I wanted to continue my wallowing. She made it impossible. "I said, 'You can't have my friend! You ugly scum bag!' I HATE the devil!"

"Angel!" I laughed shaking my head at her antics. Her demonstration of fighting and praying while I was at the hospital, was quite comical.

"I'm just glad you're on the mend. We need you girl. And you're looking good! It's only been what? Two weeks?"

And just like that, the dam broke. The tears rushed from my eyes as I almost screamed, "Yeah. Two weeks from hell!" And as usual, Angel was prepared. There was tissue in my hand before the first snot drip.

"Talk to me friend. Tell me what's going on."

"I'm so embarrassed." Angel squeezed my hands. Her eyes with no judgment urged me to continue. "Right before I fainted, Israel asked me for a divorce." The last word came out in a whisper. My breath caught as I barely finished the sentence.

"Wow…what? I'm sorry friend. That is a lot to handle."

"I'm scared Angel. I don't want a divorce. I knew we needed help but I thought we could go to counseling and fix it," the sobs felt like they would choke me.

"Calm down Jax. Calm down honey."

"He doesn't want me! He doesn't want our family! He's willing to just walk away. I HATE HIM!" Angel held me and consoled me as my mother would. I needed that feeling of love. It was ice cold at my own home and I was not doing well with the change.

Divorce. I knew it wasn't something that just snuck up on a couple. Some people are blindsided but most know the issues are going unattended. Maybe they saw the things that needed to be fixed but felt like they had time. But we all know time does not wait. You can't redeem time spent and worrying about regrets will waste more of it for sure. But I couldn't help but look back on my marriage and kick myself for not seeing the signs and being able to turn the tide sooner.

For better or worse. We'd been through it all. Anyone viewing our story would agree. I thought Israel and I could and would make it through even more but according to him, our forever had come to an end.

"Jax, you can talk and express yourself to me. But I need you to calm down. I do not want you to suffer a panic attack today. Nor do I want you passing out. I got insurance and all but a sister doesn't need the neighbors all in my business if we have to call the ambulance."

"Girl shut up," I jabbed her arm laughing through my tears. I closed my eyes and breathed as deep as I could. "Okay. I'm as calm as I can be right now. Thank you for being a safe space. I'm just so confused. And hurt. You know he didn't even visit me at the hospital. He even hung up on me when I asked him about visiting. And since I've been home, he barely says full sentences to me. It's like overnight, all the love he ever had for me is gone."

It was dry and depressing in the Ford home. All the pet names, attempts at loving gestures, and attempts to stay connected and get him to be more affectionate were squashed down by Israel. The few times I slipped and called him a pet name, the look on his face stopped me in my tracks. He wanted a divorce and he was serious. I somehow thought me almost *dying* would help him see how short life was and reconsider. No. I could tell by his actions he was done. And when I made it home from the hospital I thought if I cooked more of his favorites or was more wifely, he'd soften. Nope. Totally detached. I could barely get eye contact from him. He acted like the years of our marriage meant nothing.

As not to have the children in a toxic situation, I chose to be peaceful and put on a happy face but inside I felt like I was dying a slow death. After eleven years, he was done. My mind had been trying to process it while not zoning out. I still had the girls, the housework, the cooking…and managing very real health issues. But I felt like I was losing the battle to hold it together. I explained all if this to Angel.

"Overnight?" was Angel's one-word response.

I immediately felt annoyance.

"I mean…I know nothing happens overnight. I feel like I've been in a trance, like a zombie state just trying to survive and now I'm up and I see the world with new eyes and it sucks!"

"I can understand that. All I'm saying is nothing happens overnight. But you can't *do* anything to change his mind right now. He's hurt."

"*I'm* hurt! He hurt me and he's purposefully hurting me Angel! He's downright mean!"

"Hurt people, hurt people."

I scoffed. "Get that cliché bullsh-"

"Please Jax. Not in here." Angel said to my slip of profanity. Angel's tight lips and raised brow stopped me in my tracks. I would not disrespect her home.

"Okay. Well, I'm over talking about it right now. I'm over these tears," I lied as a fresh set rolled down my cheeks.

"I know." She said rubbing my shoulders. "But I

need you to hear something."

"Yes Angel," I let out in exasperation.

"I mentioned something about Israel and how he may be feeling and you immediately brought it back to you without sitting with it or even considering it. And you missed my entire point. I'm your friend and sister. I need you to hear me."

"Okay…"

"*Both* of y'all are hurt. Both of you did or didn't do certain things to lead to the current state of your marriage, right?"

"Well…I mean yes. But if he's saying he's tired of me then I need to fix it."

"Sweetie," she held my hands. "You can't fix this alone. And this isn't just on you."

"But if it's all my fault," I said as fresh tears fell, "I have to try. I can be better."

"Jax! Stop honey. You are an amazing freaking wife! And I'm not saying that because you are my friend. You have withstood a lot that many would have or could have not. And that is me speaking from the outside looking in. I won't let you blame yourself for this whole thing falling apart."

The tears stopped me from speaking as I held on to her words. But they were hard to believe. Good wives don't get left. Right?

"I want my marriage and my family so I will just suck it up and try to be the support that he wants and I will just stop bringing up the changes I want to see and-"

"And *what*? Pray more and continue to shrink back and be a watered-down version of Jasmine. And continue to pull all the weight at home and continue to have your health affected? Oh, and continue *not* pursuing your dreams and exercising the power and authority God gave you? That my dear, will lead to your demise."

Her statements made me sit back. "What?" I asked

confused.

"Jax. You walking around here half dead already, living like you're already somebody's corpse. Israel is not the end and the beginning of your life and him leaving wont crumble you, unless you let it. I'm not saying this to hurt you but I can't let you think you weren't a good wife and that him walking away is not his loss. There were things he didn't 'provide' and you know it. You can't see it now but it is true. And I have watched you deflate year by year in your marriage!"

"Why didn't you say anything?" She gave me a knowing look.

I looked down. Knowing.

"I tried in my little ways but you know you. You get an idea and you're loyal to that to a fault. I couldn't make you hear me so I prayed and provided support wherever I could."

"But I was supposed to be loyal to my marriage. I waited for him. I did everything 'right.' And now look at my wrecked life!" I said wiping my tears and rolling my eyes.

"I know. I know. It isn't right. But it will be okay. Can I pray for you?"

"Girl wait. Didn't you just scoff at prayer?

"Hush! Now you already know I don't play about the Lord. And you know what I meant. We will pray something to *death* when God already told us to move. That is unproductive and God is just looking like I already answered!"

"That's true."

"Or, we will feel disconnected from God and not pray at all…"

I knew she was hinting at me. I wouldn't give her the satisfaction of confirming or denying.

"Hmmm…Well. Sure…you can pray," I murmured.

But if she could see my internal eye roll, she'd jab me. We could pray if she wanted but I had prayed all the prayers. I was exhausted. And right now, I needed to borrow some of Angel's faith and belief in God because I wasn't afraid to admit I was lacking in that department.

Actually, I loved this piece of Angel. Her deep faith and spirituality. In college, she was known as the party girl, alcoholic beverage mixologist, master twerker, and all things ratchet but if I ever needed a friend to pray, she was my go-to. While she had put to rest most of her party girl ways, her spirituality had deepened and settled on her in a remarkable way. She had a gift to see past the situation and pray to the will of God. Her prayers were almost creepy with how God seemingly gave her a peek into your very situation. And you'd better record it because she never remembered. She was truly used by God.

But today, I didn't want to hear from God. I felt hopeless. I wasn't sure how her prayer could help, especially if she was on Israel's side. I steadied myself as she shifted on the luv seat toward me and grabbed my hands.

"Lord, I thank you for Jasmine and Israel. The attack on their marriage is from the pits of hell! We ask that you use this time to grow them both strong in You. They have both fallen off and out of relationship with You and as You pull to draw them near, the grace of following You will permeate and manifest every important relationship in their lives to fullness. Let them willingly be manifested by Your glory and the change You want to accomplish in and through them.

"Nurture them father as they heal. As You show each of them the areas where they need to be renewed and where they have wronged one another, show them how to be the spouse that You have called them to be.

"Thank You Father that Jasmine will heal – heart, mind, and body. I thank you that she will let go of her anger toward You for seemingly letting her down time and time again. I pray that she will allow You to be her one true God and her one true love. Show her how to remove Israel from that position. Guide her back to depending solely on You and seeing everything else as an extension of Your love and not a replacement.

"Rebuild Israel's confidence and identity in You. Heal him from his own broken heart. Break his walls down with Your love. Allow him to experience the tenderness of Your love and experience a forgiving grace that he can extend to himself and others.

"And Lord, protect their children from any fall out as You breakdown and rebuild their foundation. Allow them to see a healthy marriage and to enjoy the benefits of the renewing breath of fresh air You're breathing into their family. In Jesus name, amen."

After whispering amen, I sat there in silence too stunned to move. Mad at God? Angel said I was angry at Him in her prayer. The jolt of that revelation actually stung. In fact, I felt several jolts that could only be described as electricity, as she prayed. I began to feel uncovered but protected at the same time. Like a mask came off but God was right there to protect me. This had to be what the old church mothers described as the Holy Spirit coming upon you. As she prayed, I could clearly hear God speaking to me like never before!

"Jasmine?" I looked up at Angel. She snapped me from my trance like state. "You alright sis?"

"I…I don't know. What did you do to me?!"

"I didn't do anything! I just prayed."

"I heard Him! HIM!" I said pointing up to the ceiling.

Her eyes darkened with concern.

"Okay. Um. Stay calm sweetie. Let's get you-"

"No Angel. I heard God! Like I never have before," I belted. I felt energized now. I wanted to run.

"Okay, okay. I see. What did He say?!" She matched my excitement.

"He said…he said," I stammered the tears taking over, "That He wants ME! That I needed to get rid of what was blocking me from Him. And then you prayed it! It's like He came in my thoughts and whispered to me BEFORE you said what YOU said so I KNEW it was Him. My mind is completely blown," I got up and started pacing, ringing my hands and trying to stay calm.

I hadn't felt this much energy in years.

"Mine too! My mind is blown too!" Angel shimmied and clapped her hands with joy and then raised them above her head. "Come on God!"

"No Angel, you just don't understand," I sobbed and doubled over with tears. I tried but couldn't hold anything back. Angel was right there with me on the floor in an instant.

"I understand Jax. But let it out."

"God sees me. I've felt so forsaken. I cried out in the hospital. How could this be happening but what I meant is God, WHY WOULD YOU *LET* THIS HAPPEN?! And in this moment of prayer with you, He let me know He's here, He's *been here,* He sees me and He wants me back!"

Angel lifted her hands. "Yes God!"

I felt like a fool repeating myself but Angel wrapped her arms around me again and held on to me and urged me to keep going.

"I was ready to give up on Him. I didn't even really want you to pray." I said as we both laughed.

"I know."

She let me go and I could see her own tears. I shook my head with wonder.

"Sickness, my mother dying so young, and just my dissatisfaction with how life had turned out for me had me admittedly bitter and a little jaded toward God. But then this stuff with Israel was the last straw."

"Mad at God..." Angel stated quietly.

"It's so hard for me to admit. Religion tells us to just go on, no matter what, and God makes no mistakes and don't question God. But inside, you feel the anger and bitterness and you just fall away from anything to do with God. Or you fake it."

"That's so true friend," she sighed.

So many thoughts were bursting. "I needed this breakthrough."

"I'm glad you are here in this moment of revelation Jax. God already knows so you may as well take it to Him. So many walk away from Him because they don't understand. God is opening your understanding. Trust Him."

"Well, if I never truly believed that God knows before we even say it, I found out today. And ooh! He dropped a scripture in my spirit." I reached for my phone to open up my bible app. "Psalm one hundred and thirty-nine. Hold on. Let me look it u-"

"Search me, O God, and know my heart," Angel began before I could even unlock my screen. "Try me and know my anxious thoughts; And see if there be any hurtful way in me, and lead me in the everlasting way."

I sighed contentedly as I meditated on every word Angel was able to recite from memory.

"This is just the beginning Angel. I feel refreshed! I definitely need Him to search me and lead me. I don't want life to break me. I want him to show me how to do things fully His way. "

"Great plan. And remember to be easy with yourself. This is *not* your fault."

"That's not what Izzy thinks. He said I'm the reason we failed."

"Well, that's impossible. No one person is the blame."

"Right…"

"He will show you your next steps Jax. Do not forget this moment. When you get home, journal. And put away works because you won't change that man's mind. He is convinced. And working yourself to the bone won't change a thing. Let God handle this."

I rolled my eyes upward. "Girl. You think you know me *so* well."

"Um hmm," she quipped. "I'll repeat it so you can't say, 'Why didn't you tell me?'"

"Shut up," I said pushing her shoulder playfully. We both laughed.as she ducked.

"But seriously, you can't fix this. You can't fix your health by yourself nor your marriage. You need divine strategy. Ask God to posture your heart and actions toward Him. Yes, God wants *you.* Raw and uncut. Just like you were here today. And let Him instruct you on what to do next with your health and Israel. Whether he tells you to pray for reconciliation or just walk away."

"Walk away?!"

"Yes Jasmine. You can't make that man do anything."

"I know that. I know." I bowed my head as fresh tears fell. "But why wouldn't I pray for us to reconcile?"

"Hey, I don't know what you should pray. That's why you're going to go to God. How I did today, you do more of that! Pray. And not only read but speak aloud what you read in your word. That's where you let go of your pain and bitterness and receive healing. It's how you fight."

I hadn't come over here expecting to experience Angel's God thing. It was always interesting to watch her with others but it felt so creepy when she did it *to* me or maybe for me is the better word. Felt like she had access to private information I wasn't actually trying to share.

"Okay…" I conceded.

Smacking her hand away from my knee. I knew she was right.

"You are so silly. I love you *big* friend."

"I love you bigger." We embraced once more.

"Well…how long does your sister have the kids?"

"I told her a few hours."

"You hungry?"

"I could eat."

"Girl stop playin'! After getting slain like that in the Spirit I KNOW you're hungry," Angel chuckled.

She headed to the barstools set up at the kitchen's island. My gurgling stomach beckoned me to follow. Though health issues had caused me to stay on the slimmer side, my hunger and thick girl eating tendencies never left.

"Hush," I hissed swatting at the air.

The aroma of whatever Angel had in the oven wafted into my nostrils as soon as she opened the oven door.

"Ooh that smells BOMB! What ya got?"

"A seafood booooooo-illll," she said in her B-Love voice imitating our favorite Mukbanger.

I was still surprised at the way gluttony had morphed into a popular social media trend but the videos were fun to watch.

"Oh, so you slay me down with what 'thus sayeth the Lord,' then you drop my favorite food on me?"

"Yes ma'am!"

I was happy to share my heartfelt first laughs in what felt like months with Angel. As she prepared our plates, I clearly heard God say, *Live*!

"Live." I let the words roll off my lips softly. But wasn't I doing that?

Chapter 19

Jasmine age 23

"Nine, Nine, Nine! That's when I'm getting married."

"Okay girl. You better name it and claim it," they all laughed.

"I'm serious y'all. I want to get married. And that's the date I'm setting."

"All right now. I can feel that. You go girl."

Jasmine's women's discipleship group was the highlight of her week. As the women sat around the living room on comfy lounge pillows, couches, chairs, or laid across the floor, they bonded through sharing their goals, and breaking bread. Sharing her plans to be married in the future was not planned though. Jasmine kind of blurted it out when asked what she was expecting from God. September ninth, two thousand and nine. And there was no going back. Her palms tingled with excitement as the words left her mouth. And so what the date fell on a Wednesday. Her future husband would think she was low maintenance saving money by getting married on a weekday. Though the date was less than two years away, Jasmine felt that was plenty of time to meet an amazing man, fall in love, plan a wedding and get married and live happily ever after. She figured she had more than enough time to get her whole life together and be ready to serve as the wife she'd always wanted to be.

Two years since the breakup with Nathan, Jasmine was finally able to say she was happy being alone. That first year was sad. Her weight fluctuated and she was pretty detached from her friends. The second year she was bitter. She had to stop herself from looking at Nathan's wedding pictures. His bride was cute but she wasn't more beautiful than Jasmine in her opinion. She was thinner and her hair was longer. Jasmine kept comparing herself to Nathan's wife and getting angry. Yes, there were differences but ultimately, she was no better. No worse, but no better. And that revelation helped Jasmine move on. He just wasn't the guy for her.

In hindsight, Jasmine knew this. Even though he was a man of the cloth, he was as imperfect as they come. That was her biggest lesson. Just like she was flawed and asking God to help her walk a path pleasing to Him, so was Nathan. Seeing him as human, without the titles, helped the anger melt away.

She also recalled some of the statements he made about her body alluding to the fact that she was "the biggest he'd ever date," but it was "fine," and how he was glad she didn't have stretch marks everywhere and how she was "losing weight anyway," so she wouldn't be that big for much longer. These comments made her pause instead of stop and walk away. She should have run quickly away.

But two years later she was on a different path. She had in fact lost the weight. And kept it off this time. Because she decided to love herself exactly how and where she was. She had a come to Jesus talk with herself. As she looked in the mirror at her pudgy stomach she said, "Jasmine, you have thirty days to lose ten pounds. If you don't, you need to just be the flyest big girl you can be. Rock that plus size and make it your own."

She stashed all her "goal clothes," in a large chest (yes there were that many. Don't judge) and declared she would toss them if she didn't lose the ten pounds and keep up with the progress. She lost the ten pounds. And ten more after that. Loving herself exactly where she was had given her such a strong confidence and in turn had helped her reach her fitness goals.

It also gave her courage to embrace her singleness, stop comparing, and just live her life. And she in turn opened herself up to some remarkable people and experiences like this beautiful group of women who didn't laugh at and make fun of her declaration to get married but jotted it down on their prayer lists and encouraged her to enjoy her time dating and expanding her wardrobe. In fact, they were the reasons she was looking and feeling good in her cropped skinny jeans that accentuated each curve paired with a heather gray, form-fitting tunic now. They helped her shop and revamp her style and would surprise her with gifts and beautiful hand-me-downs. This group of women was truly a treasure.

"So, ladies. Anyone else want to share what they are looking forward to? What are you praying for and believing for?"

Marcella held the Daughters of Virtue meetings in her home once a month. The ladies would gather, bring dishes to share, worship, pray for one another, plan, cry, vent, and usually end with some sort of silliness. They always had an amazing time.

"Marcella, I am ready to go to the next level in my career," she said as she nervously shifted on the plush cushion. "I want to expand my business. I want to build my website. But I have no direction."

"Savannah, it's in this room honey," Delilah, one of the group facilitators said encouraging the young lady who had spoken. Savannah was new but had jumped right into the culture of the group and always had such a refreshing view on topics.

"Thank you for saying that. I wonder if anyone had experience to help me make it to the next step."

"Oh yes Honey," Delilah encouraged. "We have women in here who can do it all. That's what's so unique. I'm glad you made it known. Raise your hand if you have experience in building a website and are willing to guide our sister?"

Savannah smiled and her eyes shined with wonder at the three hands that shot up immediately. She let go of the pillow she had been clutching as she let her shoulders release the tension they'd been holding. Jasmine recognized that wonder. In this space, she had received workout buddies and diet encouragers. In this space she had received affirmation and courage to embrace herself fully. And in this space, she had grown the confidence to declare that she was ready for true love and would be getting married on a specific date.

Okay Lord. Nine, Nine, Nine. Let's make it happen?

Curled up in her own bed now, Jasmine cozied under a plush throw and wrote the date in her calendar. She took a moment to daydream before tucking the memory in her heart and before drifting off to sleep. For now, it would remain a dream because she still had a year of school left, she had to get a job and get settled into life as a true adult. She didn't have time to worry about anything besides finishing strong. She also had her mother Anita to tend to. She suffered from an autoimmune disease that would randomly flair.

She was amazing at managing the symptoms, but sometimes she needed Jasmine's help and Jasmine always wanted to be there for her mother. Jasmine was truly learning how to adult. She was coming into her own and it felt great.

Chapter 20

Jasmine age 23

"Run? I can't run! I have asthma."

"You can do anything through Christ that strengthens you!"

Jasmine rolled her eyes at her trainer Theo. They both laughed. She started working with him to take her fitness to the next level. She had lost a good amount on her own and now she wanted to tighten and tone a *little,* she told Theo. But as an Olympic trained athlete, he could not fathom the concept of a *"little"* workout. This was clear by how he pushed Jasmine to complete tasks she was unaware her body was capable of.

"Theo…you're not funny."

"And you're not incapable of running. You jogged parts of two laps last week. Usually you walk the whole thing. Let's go!"

Jasmine began her laps with a brisk walk. Though she initially felt a chill, she quickly warmed as her legs and arms pumped the blood through her veins. As her heart beat faster, her lungs began to feel the familiar tightness and tingling asthma brought on but Theo was right there with her asthma pump in his hand. "Let's go! You got this!" Jasmine rolled her eyes. Hard.

Jasmine's legs moved faster as she picked up the pace to a jog. As her foot hit the pavement with each stride, she could feel the adrenaline build. Her lungs hurt but she felt euphoric as she turned the corner beating her running distance from last session. The wind on her face felt too good as she dug deeper and pushed her body to go further.

"Let's go J! You got this. Keep it steady."

As she flopped on the ground after completing a mile, Theo jumped in the air ecstatic that she had shaved two minutes off her time from the week before.

"Wheeew J! That's what I'm talking about! Get up! Get up! Let's do some jumping jacks to celebrate." Theo pulled her to her feet and began counting.

"Aghhh," she fake cried as her hands flew up and down.

"Let's go Jax! You got this J."

"Are we done?"

"Almost! Now drop down and give me 20 sit ups. You GOT this!"

Jasmine took a deep breath before reaching for her feet. Up. Down. And again. And again.

Jasmine's heart rate began to regulate as she felt the adrenaline fade. The stretching was always last and she never wanted to do it but she was always glad she had. It ensured she wouldn't be that sore the next day.

Jasmine truly enjoyed her workouts. Her body was forming up like never before. She'd been able to lose some of the weight with just diet but pairing it with a guided workout plan helped her take it to the next level. And it gave her a sense of pride. As an asthmatic from birth, she'd never pushed the envelope when it came to physical activity. Theo was aware of her condition and told her to go until she couldn't anymore and bring her asthma pump in her backpack. He meant business. And Jasmine did just that. Today she proved to herself that she could push a little more when she felt she had nothing left. She was proud of the progress she'd made.

The two high-fived to celebrate another successful workout.

"You did that J. Shaved off another minute. You started at 20 minutes mainly walking and you've improved by a minute each week with increased running each time. That's dope!"

"Thanks Theo. You tryna kill me though."

"Pain is gain!"

"I guess..." they both laughed. "Thanks for helping me reach my fitness goals."

"You're welcome Jax. See you next week."

"God willing and the creek don't rise."

"You and your old negro spiritual sayings."

"Ha! My grandmother used to say that."

"Bye Jax!"

"Byyyyeeee!"

Next week did not come for Theo and Jax's workout session. Anita suffered a devastating work-related injury that landed her in the hospital. Jasmine was still very much involved on campus, and with just two semesters left of school, she had to keep focused on her classes and now her mother's care was added to her schedule. Everything else could wait.

Oddly enough, Jasmine found herself in need of checking in with her own health during the same week her mother was hospitalized. Since beginning to work out with Theo, she had noticed an odd feeling in her lungs. It wasn't asthma, she could tell the difference, but she wasn't sure what else it could be. It usually happened hours after her workouts. Pain meds helped, but the pain continuously returned. She'd gone to two separate doctors on campus. Bruised sternum was her diagnosis. She was told no heavy lifting, working out, and to take it easy. She thought, *good luck with that!* She was on the go and had so much left to experience ahead. She decided to hope for the best and focus on finishing college strong. She had no other choice but to tuck her feelings of worry and trudge on.

Chapter 21

"So, what brings you here this morning Jasmine?" my therapist Roberta asked.

"Um…I need more therapy?"

"Of course, Jasmine. I mean what would you like to focus on this go 'round?"

"OH! I got a little scared for a moment. Like did she change up her services on me? All these life coach, life style, my style, not style gurus. You're not into the fu-fu are you?"

We both laughed. Her laughter was pleasant. Mine, a nervous chuckle. I was not comfortable talking about the end…of my marriage.

"No. I'm still a family therapist."

"Well Doc, you helped me so much when my mother passed. I'm at another crossroads. And I need support to get through," -I took a deep breath- "…this."

"Take your time," She said.

I sat there trying to hold my tears at bay. Roberta handed me the box of tissue on her desk and just like that, the rivers of emotion began to flow from my heart through my eyes. I was *so* over the tears. But yet, they flowed endlessly.

"Jasmine. What are you thinking right now?"

"My marriage. It's in deep trouble. My husband wants to end things. He said he is going to file for divorce."

"I'm sorry to hear that. How is all of this making you feel?"

"Well…I feel everything."

"That's ok. Let's put some names to these emotions. Can you give me three?"

"Yes. I feel upset! *Incredibly* sad…and…angry! I'm *so* incredibly angry!"

"Did you see how you paused there? We will come back to the others but let's explore your anger. Why are you angry? With whom are you angry?"

"I am angry at my husband because I feel betrayed by him. I trusted him and tried as best I could to follow him. Follow his lead and submit like a good *Christian* wife," I scoffed. As I spoke, I could feel the anger bubble up. It was beginning to cease as I prayed and journaled but it was still very present. "I know I'm not perfect. I came from a single parent. I didn't learn how to be a wife from getting to watch my mother with my father. I learned how to be a nurturer and how to be great at taking care of people. And that is what I tried to do with him. I trusted him to honor our vows. I trusted him to work through any problems with me. And he is saying none of it matters. He doesn't even want to try. Won't do couple's counseling. So, I'm pissed! I *never* wanted to be a single mother. I wanted and want a marriage and unbroken family."

"Are you only mad at him?"

Her question was simple but landed heavy on my chest. Ever since Angel prayed the other day, I had been processing all my emotions. Anger was the most palpable.

If I stayed still too long, I could feel it pounding at my temples. I knew it wasn't a coincidence Roberta chose to focus on it. Neither was her pressing for me to admit with whom else I had anger.

"Well, if you would have asked me last week, I would have said no one. But that would have been a lie. I was mad at God and scared to admit it. I felt let down by Him. But I've been praying and reading my bible and I'm actually beginning to feel close to Him again. And with the closeness has come this unignorable, nagging honesty, and truthfully, I'm mad at myself."

"Let's sit with that." She let the silence give room for me to reflect. Little had she known; I'd been beating myself up as the honest truth rolled out. "Why are you mad at yourself?"

"I see my part in messing up my own marriage. I thought I was doing okay but I knew there were areas I could work on. I would start, then see my husband *not* working on his areas *I* felt needed work and I would focus on that. Then my mom died and my health got worse and there was just always *something.* It became a cycle and here we are in disarray. And I could have shown more gratefulness and complained less when things weren't perfect. But I just keep getting stuck at His wrong and God keeps directing me back to me."

"I like that. You only have control of you. But some things you don't have control of. And I really believe some grace and understanding of where your mind could have been is needed on your part."

"I can see that. That's what my best friend said."

"Great advice. I have a question. PPD. Do you know what that is?"

"Yes. Postpartum right? Yeah, I don't think I had that with either child."

"I wouldn't rule that out Jasmine. Your mother died the same day you had a baby. That's traumatic. Have you ever sat with how traumatic that is? And the affect it could have on your ability to be a wife, mother, and feel like yourself?"

"Uh no. I was being a wife, mother, and trying to feel like myself," I laughed. "I didn't really have time to dwell. Mostly, I just felt like I was drowning and now, when it's all failing, I'm looking at all the things I could have done different. But I felt so stuck."

"You're rehashing all you feel you did wrong?"

"Yeah, what fun," I sighed. "Looking at yourself and rehashing all your wrong. Whew-hoo," I fake a smile and tossed my hands up in mock celebration.

"While I do believe it's beneficial to see what didn't work in order to fix it, you Mrs. Jasmine need to give yourself some grace."

"I know. I just…" I hesitated.

"Release the words. This is a safe space."

"My heart is broken Roberta. I'm exhausted by the tragedy in my life. It has been thing after thing and now this? I thought *Israel* was my safe space. I thought I would have him forever. Even though all this happened to me," I said as I pointed to my body weakened by disease, "I still had my husband. And now he wants to bounce too. It all feels so unfair. I know that's a juvenile thing to say. But it's *so* unfair. And it hurts. And I'm angry!"

I let an expletive fly and it felt great. Roberta remained quiet. I appreciated her for letting me sit with my unrestrained feelings. Silence allowed for reflection. And moments for God to speak. Desperately, I needed to continue hearing God speak.

"You've been dealt some very tough blows. We have discussed many of them before in our brief time together after your mother's passing."

"I so wish I could have continued coming to you." SnackJoys was in a financial bind which hindered me from continuing any "extras" and sadly therapy had to go.

"I'm glad you're here now to continue your work. Your feelings are valid. You get to be angry. But you do not have to rehash your wrong. Especially not every day."

"Thank you," I whispered.

"You have endured trauma."

She let us sit with the weight of that statement. I closed my eyes and exhaled. I let my shoulders loosen and my head relax on the comfy pillow.

"And though I wasn't your clinician during the last couple years, the experience you've described in your intake form and our time during this session leads me to believe you suffered from PPD."

"How Roberta? I thought that was for mothers of infants. Like after three months the baby blues is over."

"For many mothers PPD ends within that time frame but not all. Post-partum fog can last for up to five years and in some cases turns into long-term depression."

"What?" I spoke as that realization set in.

"You mean that stuck feeling, that foggy feeling wasn't just me tripping."

"I mean, I can't say there weren't times you weren't 'tripping'," she said using air quotes. "But with PPD that looming feeling of overwhelm, spikes of anger, loss of control, helplessness. It read like a classic case in your intake. But if you were not in treatment, it's easily missed. I say all that to say, be easy with yourself and give yourself some grace."

"Hmmm," was all I could muster. She gave me so much to digest. I began to feel relief.

"Is God a loving God?"

"Yes." Thank God I could answer this question honestly.

"Then why would He want you to feel bad over and over again?"

"You're right!" I said.

Gratefulness washed over me.

"That's not God. He may highlight some things so you won't make the same mistakes again or so you're able to see your pitfalls. You have to let go of the anger and guilt toward yourself now that you've released your anger toward God."

"I want to let it go! I want to live!" I tapped my foot with built up energy. I wanted to go and become, so bad, I could feel the push pulsing through me. "We discussed me living my best life when I came after my mother died. I was making the steps to do that. But life keeps sitting me down."

"When we met, you had goals set. Have you worked on those?"

"I've tried." Sighing, I placed my head in my hands. "But no. I haven't been able to focus on my goals like I want to. Israel's hectic work schedule has taken so much of the time I need to get my goals accomplished. So, I start and have to stop. I'm always sacrificing me and my dreams. I have the kids from the moment I wake until the moment they close their eyes at night. What time do I have?"

"Exactly. And add depression and mourning and trauma."

"You keep bringing me back to the pain. I don't understand."

"You keep *glossing* over the pain and holding yourself to an impossible standard. I'm showing you the lie. I'm highlighting the impossibility of you doing all that you somehow have convinced yourself you were supposed to be doing. Healing. That is what you need to do after your mother dies. And that is what you need to do now. Everything else is a biproduct of that. And a beautiful manifestation of the healing."

"So, I'm supposed to not even try?"

"You can try but if you aren't also working on healing, you keep getting stuck. It affects your work instead of pours out through it. The projects you work on while allowing yourself to heal, end up healing *you.*"

"That actually sounds beautiful. I would love to work on what I love and have it assist me in healing."

"Here's the thing. You need to do the things that make you feel alive whether you have a husband or not. Whether you have the kids or not. This is the life you have *currently*. It's not perfect. You have handled tragedy with the grace many others haven't been able to. But are you truly living? No. You are surviving. That feeling of discontent that has caused you to complain and blame, a husband won't fill that, ever. He can't."

"Wait a minute. There *you* go. First my best friend and now my therapist. God is sending everybody with this message for me."

"You know I'm a Christian therapist Jasmine, so He's bound to show up somewhere in our sessions." She smiled kindly as I laughed at her quip. "And it's just proof for you how deeply loved by God you are."

Internally I felt butterflies. To be loved by God felt so good. "I'm blown away by His love for me. You're right in line with what my friend prayed. I know what God has been saying. I need to focus on me and let Him handle the rest."

"That sounds like a great plan. Let's set some goals that will shift you into living instead of survival mode. You can't help what has happened to you. You *can* enjoy each day exactly where you are as you learn to process and heal from trauma."

"I really want that," I said with a genuine smile feeling a glimmer of hope.

"I believe you can have it Jasmine. You just need to shift your focus. I believe you can benefit with working with me, but I have an additional resource for you as well. I know we joked earlier about all the life coaches and gurus but honestly, they're needed. We all have our purpose in the lives of those we serve. Have you ever heard of a purpose coach?"

"No. Sounds interesting."

"A purpose coach helps awaken your gifting. I truly believe stepping into your own venture, separate from your husband and kids, will restore some of your confidence and give you something positive to focus on besides what you feel you may lack."

"Okay. How do I connect with this purpose coaching?"

"The class is called The UnboxedMe. I will send you an email with all the details."

"Great. Thank you, Roberta."

"You're welcome. Open your heart Jasmine. Your life is still a gift."

I let her words sit on my heart and meditated on them the rest of that day.

Even though I could only feel pain right now, I knew she was right. *My life is still a gift.*

Chapter 22

Jasmine age 24

After six months with no luck, Jasmine was happy to find a job. Honestly, the job had found her and she was elated. A dear family member had offered her a part-time teaching position at a small private school. They knew she had been searching since graduating from college. The pay wasn't much but the children's silliness and the challenge of teaching in the inner city gave her a spark of joy, and adventure she needed to feel alive and like she had purpose.

"Miss Jasmine you should wear your hair like this," Deja, her seven-year-old student said as she twisted her hair every which way.

"Deja, can you do me a favor?"

"It depends Miss Jasmine. What you gonna give me?"

"It's not always what you can get. Sometimes you

do things just to be kind."

"Okay Miss Jasmine. You right. Well Deja is here. At your service."

Jasmine laughed at the little girl who kept her on her toes. Jasmine never imagined she'd be teaching. She got her degree in Journalism. She thought she'd be jet-setting, hotel hopping, writing articles for *Ebony* and *Essence* magazines…the life!

Five years. That's how long it had taken her to graduate. That first year had really set her back from meeting her four-year graduation goal. Overall, the experience was a pleasurable one that she'd cherish forever. She met awesome people, experienced ups and downs that helped her grow as a person, fell in love with herself, deepened her relationship with God and Jesus, and she accomplished her first major life goal: College graduate. The first in her family. And now almost a year later, she felt deflated.

All her hard work, the late nights and juggling a hectic social life with school; it all went veering off track that last year. She thought things would die down and she could finish her last semester strong after her mother recovered from her work incident, but no. Three months before graduation, the pain in her lungs began to bother her daily. It was relentless. Multiple hospital visits produced no answers. Her resolve dipped with each failed appointment. In between her part-time job, and all the sleep she needed from unexplained exhaustion, she was back and forth to the hospital. They were whispering autoimmune disease, just like her mother.

She thought she would be more scared hearing a possible diagnosis. Of course, she was *scared* but she wasn't terrified. She had watched her mother and grandmother live with autoimmune diseases. Taking care of her mother and helping take care of her grandmother who suffered many years with an autoimmune condition, had given her an odd sense of calm. She knew that if they could live through it, so could she. They survived and so would she. But man did she not want to have to go through a life devastated by a disease. Instead of walking into the sunset of her college experience and rising into a new career, the beginning of making a name for herself in the world and meeting an awesome guy to settle down with, she was walking into endless doctor's appointments, blood tests, CAT scans and prescription drugs that may or may not work to treat her emerging symptoms. Deflated, confused, and angry summed up Jasmine's mood. She had to endure so much without an ending in sight.

Jasmine felt engulfed by sadness and rather discouraged. The disappointment felt as heavy as a backpack filled with rocks. She carried it everywhere. And on top of everything, she couldn't find a job in her field that would pay what she felt was Bachelor's degree level money. She thought her degree would mean more. All her life she'd heard, "Go to college, get a good job." But she wasn't truly prepared for the real world with that half piece of instruction. She graduated college, in debt, with a degree in a saturated field and no related experience beside a 3-month internship at a TV station and the office work she'd done part-time for the school's president.

Jasmine believed the instructions given to the youth were flawed. She would tell her students and future children to graduate with minimal debt, if you have to get loans, get the minimum, never stop applying for scholarships, save money, don't declare a major until the end of year 2 after you have researched careers slated for growth and major in one of those, take financial courses as electives and lastly, *no* credit cards. All of that information would have been helpful. But in the end, when you graduate as the job market and stock market crash and a depression hits the economy, there's only so much a person can do. She could have done all the things mentioned above and still had trouble finding a great job in her field. With the way things were going, finding a mediocre job in any field was proving difficult. Her only consolation was that the job shortage was nationwide. She wasn't the only one finding herself settling for unlikely positions or not finding work at all. The epidemic was plastered over the morning news daily. In addition, her health crisis limited her search. She couldn't join the military or work on her feet for eight hours. The entire ordeal made her head spin.

So, when she landed the teaching position, she was elated. She had something to take her mind off the negatives and now she felt independent again. Deja was an added bonus. The sweet and salty little girl made her heart smile. Deja had given her the most push back in the beginning, but now they both treasured their interactions.

Jasmine was tough on her students. She wanted them to do their best and structure coupled with a strict schedule in the classroom was working for them. Her students were slow readers and not interested in the work when she first began. She suspected it wasn't lack of intelligence but they needed the right motivation. She gave them incentives such as winning a pizza party if they read a certain number of words before the month was up. They had fun reading and counting the number of words. When she saw the excitement build, she decided to start a reading program and writing club with a fellow teacher. That took their love of literature to the next level. Learning became exciting for all involved. And as amazing as watching her students excel made Jasmine feel, she knew teaching was not the right space for her long term. Writing as a career was too near her heart to let go forever.

Chapter 23

"Confused about your gift or purpose? Frustrated and stuck in regard to your vision and dreams? If the answer is yes, you are in the right place! Welcome to The UnboxedMe."

My skin prickled as I listened to the welcome video. My excitement was palpable. Roberta was right. "Hmm, Unboxed," I said under my breath. This course was exactly what I needed.

"These Units are designed to move you forward with purpose in your business and foster conversation about the collective movement to live in purpose, on purpose. Here you will uncover or gain tools to build businesses.

"Through virtual Live coaching, coursework, and community interaction, your mindset will shift and you will gain strategies to catapult you to your next successful endeavor or level in life. Remember, change will not happen until you do. This class is for those ready for the change. We will uproot patterns and lies that have stopped you in the past. Join me if you're ready to GO!"

Coach Myra's vision hit me like fresh air on a stuffy day. She was a natural motivator. But more than that, her words set a fire. I rubbed my arms. I sensed electricity all over. Not just my mind but my body responded to her call to action; awakened. By the end of the welcome video, I wanted to jump for joy. With credit card in hand ready to sign up, I steadied myself and inhaled a cleansing breath. Her class released the aroma of breakthrough.

Everything was online and it made me nervous but I had no time for apprehension. Virtual courses were definitely the norm in this era but I had no personal connection to Coach Myra. The classes weren't even through an accredited university or affiliate program. And the kicker, no refunds. Risky for sure. In the past, these facts would stop me. But the more I read through the material, the more I realized how perfect this course was for me. A tool I needed to make the shift Roberta mentioned. The best part was that Coach Myra took a biblical approach to purpose. Her course would not only direct me to purpose but feed my spirit as well? I needed in! I decided to take a gamble on myself. I had nothing else to lose.

Israel was still adamant about divorce. He had already started to separate us even though no papers were filed. He moved his things into the garage and removed my access to all company correspondence and accounts. He kept all the money in his accounts so I wasn't privy to those balances anyway, but he became very strict with my "allowance." I hadn't expected him to shut me out completely.

I felt like a fool that even though he was treating me harshly, I let my hopes rise up at the fact that he was still in our home. But lately he'd practically began to live out of his office. I knew I pushed him to that point.

Determined to change his mind, I ignored the instruction from Angel (*and* God). I hoped to change his mind by proposing unique date nights and quality time. I jumped right into a "What can I do for you; how can I please you?" mode.

Making myself crazy, I bent over backward trying to do and make everything perfect in our home. Extra chores, mine and his, buying his favorite snacks, and preparing his favorite meals in addition to the girl's picky favorites. I was pouring on compliments and sending him jokes and memes. I apologized to him, again and again, and told him I recognized my fault in our divide. Even though I knew it wasn't all my fault, I told him I would shoulder all the blame if that would make us right again. I just couldn't let it go. He was my first love. My only love. And the more I did, the more annoyed he got. The more I tried to change his mind in my own strength, the more distant he became.

I ended up even more heartbroken and in another health crisis from overexertion. My plate was already to capacity. And the wall Israel already had built seemingly grew taller. I was leaning on my own understanding and hurting myself in the process. Thank God He reminded me of what Angel prayed and thank God my first therapy session with Roberta was so impactful. It took *her* words to confirm Angel's words to truly spark a change in my behavior. I was supposed to be focusing on myself. And healing. Clearly there were no words to say or works to be performed by me to make Israel want to stay. My mind knew this but my broken heart had a difficult time catching up. I needed to focus on building myself up.

God is intentional. When Roberta mentioned The UnboxedMe, the idea stuck with me. It nagged at me until I logged on to explore. Maybe this was God's way to guide me back to me. If I were being honest, I lost myself right around the time I had our first daughter. And Roberta was right. Israel couldn't fix it. Working on fixing me was possibly the key to fixing us, but I chose no longer to focus on us at all. I alone needed saving.

The UnboxedMe course unlocked dreams and ideas I let lay dormant like my dream to publish one of my stories in a popular Black magazine. Or go back to school for education administration. I always wanted to be an author, so maybe this class could help me launch that career. It was definitely worth a try. The class was geared toward unlocking stifled potential and offered help to revamp or launch your business. I didn't have my own business, but what did I have to lose? Coach Myra encouraged you to use the resources you had available and your God-given gifts and talents, to awaken your purpose and create income. It was so perfect! I was ready to revisit my dreams. The UnboxedMe was a safe landing space to heal and gain the tools needed in order to launch. I hoped it would be the catalyst for the change I needed to feel alive again.

Chapter 24

Jasmine age 24

"Angel you know I'm not worried about a man right now."

"Girl you look good. You've been dressing so cute. Your makeup be poppin'! Y'all both love God, y'all both lost weight, y'all both silly. My cousin Izzy is a perfect fit for you. I'm going to set up a blind date."

Jasmine rubbed her temples before speaking. "Angel…how is it a blind date if I know who he is?! I saw him last month at your birthday party girl," she said and then let out a sigh. Angel could be so ditzy sometimes.

"Okay. It's a half-blind date. He will be down here visiting from Vegas next week for his family reunion."

"Vegas? What? When did this happen? How will we date if he lives there?"

"Girl if y'all like each other y'all will figure it out. *Any! Way!* I will set up the date with him. Then I will have him call you and that's when he will find out who he's going out with. I'm *such* a genius."

Jasmine sighed her exasperation. "Oh my gosh!" she huffed, smacking her forehead.

Angel usually tried to hook her up with the friend of the current man she was dating. This time it was different. This seemed like a worthy candidate. Jasmine met him and interacted with him several times before. She'd even met his mother at one of Angel's birthday parties. She had given up on dating after the health issues seemed to ramp up but she was on a good regimen and she was feeling great. She wanted to try for love. She still had her save-the-date in the back of her mind.

"Don't worry. It will be great. But let me go! I still have a million things to do for this cake tasting."

Jasmine hung up with Angel shaking her head and laughing. That girl was a nut. And her mother's vow renewal was sure to reflect that. Jasmine was looking forward to celebrating with Angel's family for her parent's thirty years of wedded bliss. Witnessing other's happily ever after caused the the flicker in her heart for her own happily ever after shine on.

As the week crawled by, Jasmine worked hard to get her nerves down. She didn't want to put too much thought into it or feel nervous and get her hopes up. Dating had been rough. What if he didn't like her? As she'd stated to Angel, he'd met her before and hadn't made a move and he lived out of state. What made her the most nervous was he wouldn't know it was her until she contacted him to make the announcement that *she* was his date *right* before said date was to take place. Angel had other friends. He could be disappointed it was Jasmine. All the factors threatened to make her a nervous wreck...that is, until three days before their date when Jasmine logged on to her social media account and found a friend request from Israel.

Her heart started beating fast. She nearly tossed her computer across the room when she saw the message indicator blinking as well. She knew Angel couldn't hold water. Half blind date her foot! Jasmine clicked the message so fast.

> **Israel 9:09 PM: Congrats on the weight loss. I see u and my cousin are doing your thang. U look good. I know it's hard work!**

Jasmine messaged him back as soon as she finished reading.

> **Jasmine 10:28 PM: Thank you so much Israel! It is hard work. It's choices ya know? I KNOW you know lol. You're looking good yourself! How is everything? Last time I talked to you, you were heading off to college…**

She typed her words carefully trying to sound confident and cool. She hoped he hadn't gone to sleep and would issue a quick response so she checked emails and graded papers to pass some time. She was bummed after an hour passed with no response. Jasmine padded to the kitchen to fix herself some tea when she heard the computer ding a notification. As she pivoted, she almost tripped over her foot. *Girl, calm down!* She internally chided herself. She couldn't make it to the computer fast enough.

> **Israel 12:52 AM: Aww thank u! I've**

just been doing a lot of growing up for the most part. And trying to live saved. I am working in real estate and getting ready to move back to Cali in a few months. What are u up to these days?

Jasmine could feel her heart thumping in her ears. Her nerves were frazzled.

Jasmine 1:02 AM: Man... Life! lol Living. Learning how to live for Christ with a what can I do for you attitude (nothing really which is why He's so amazing) because I've realized that my walk has been in a Lord show me state for a while. But God is faithful, we're the ones who need to work on it! Haha.

And I'm teaching (1st grade at a private school), Exploring careers. About to start applying to Grad schools. Working out, eating better (trying to! lol). Wow I think that's it! I'm long winded. How's real estate? I know the market is beginning to recover and that this is a "buyer's market" and when are you coming out here exactly? And will you be here for Angel's mom's renewal?

Jasmine pressed send and then read over her response. She smacked her forehead as she realized how many times she typed "lol." *Get it together Jasmine! Don't be so eager!*

Israel 1:16 AM: That's cool. I love kids. Yeah, the market is getting better for buyers now. I actually work for a property management company so I'm not actively selling homes at the moment. I will be in town tomorrow morning actually. I'm staying a few days. I will be back for good around October. I am in the process of becoming a snacks broker and I have to get back to help my dad with his church. I can't run from my calling anymore! And Yes I will be at Auntie Minnie's renewal as well.

Jasmine 1:24 AM: I love kids too! My kids are a handful but they are funny and sweet too. I'm blessed by them for they are teaching me patience! And I'm glad everything is going good for you but can I ask two questions? What in the world is a snack broker and why would you be running from your call? You know how the story ends. Moses, Jonah, Peter....hahaha must I go on?

Jasmine hoped he didn't take offense to her probing. When it took him a few minutes to respond, she thought she had. But before the wait time became awkward, his response pinged her notifications.

Israel 1:29 AM: Lol! I know but it's not easy knowing what's ahead of you sometimes. I don't take helping my

dad reach people for God lightly! Knowing that every step and move I make is being watched by people is tough. But it is what it is.
But a snack broker is one of the companies who supplies vending machines. They're still very popular at colleges and schools. It's become a niche market. I want to open up shop and expand to snack production.

And thank you for the well wishes and yes, kids teach so much patience!

Jasmine 1:32 AM: Wow! God gave you a call and I'm glad you aren't running anymore. People are waiting on you to be saved. That's what I keep hearing at bible study on campus. I truly believe it. So, Pastor Israel, glad you're answering your call lol. And that snack broker job sounds amazing! Sounds delicious. Hehe. And yes! Kids teach you patience like a big dawg. Never have I heard my name called so much! Miss Jasmine this, Miss Jasmine that!

Israel 1:45 AM: Haha! Watch that word pastor now! Lol. Ms. EVANGELIST Jasmine! And yes I'm very ready to do the will of GOD and I can handle the hard stuff. First Corinthians chapter ten, verse thirteen and fourteen reminds me of this!!!

Jasmine 1:50 AM: Evangelist? Oh my lol. I'm not currently running, I've just never heard that associated with my name. I'm very open to what He wants to use me for. God will reveal in time.

Israel 1:56 AM: Amen! Well, I gotta step away. I have a super early day. We will definitely keep this conversation going!

Jasmine ended the conversation on cloud nine. Israel hadn't said he'd see her soon or whether he was looking forward to their date though. Jasmine figured he'd just got caught up in the flow and excitement of their first real chat. She was now through the roof with excitement to go out with him one on one.

Chapter 25

Jasmine age 24

"What do you mean, 'he still doesn't know it's me?' We spoke for the whole night on Wednesday! He friend requested and inboxed me."

"Girl...I don't know what you're referencing. He was probably just being random. But anyway, when we get off the phone, I'm going to text message you his number. You text him, 'I'm ready.' Those are the keywords I told him to look out for. And BOOM! Half-blind date! I'm genius, I tell you!"

"I'm ready?' Angel," I smacked my forehead. "You are so dumb," Jasmine and Angel busted out laughing in unison.

"What?! I couldn't think of anything clever. But heck, you're the only one who will text message Israel that phrase today, most likely, so there shouldn't be any mix-ups."

"Oh Lawd, Angel. I was excited after I spoke to him online. Now I'm all the way nervous again," Jasmine said, stomping her foot in full tantrum mode.

"Well, what did y'all talk about?"

"I don't know. Nothing. Everything. Our careers, your mom's renewal, weight loss, ministry."

Angel rolled her eyes upward. "Ooh, y'all so saved and *boring*!"

"Shut up!"

Angel choked on her laughter before responding, "You'll be fine, girl. Just relax. Text him, 'I'm ready' when you get the number from me. He's waiting! Bye!"

Jasmine's fingers trembled slightly as she typed the keywords. She felt like an eternity passed before she heard the familiar chirp of her text message indicator. It had only been four minutes in real life. The longest four minutes she had ever experienced.

"Awesome! I will be leaving shortly. Please text me your address," Jasmine read aloud, her cheeks hurt from cheesing.

See, he knows it's me.

Relief washed over Jasmine. She sent Israel her address and put the finishing touches on her makeup. She heard the familiar chirp again and checked to make sure he didn't have any questions.

Her heart lurched as she read the message:

4:25 PM: By the way, who is this?

Jasmine almost threw the phone. Her nerves could just not take the suspense. Would he be happy with who Angel had chosen for him to go on a half-blind date with? This was just so weird. If it were a blind date for both of them, they'd meet, feel each other out, and take it from there, but she already knew who he was and already knew he was a great guy. He was finding out who she was moments before he was to pick her up.

Jasmine took a deep breath and quickly typed her name. She sat on the bed, unable to finish getting ready until she received a response from him. Again, those pesky minutes took an eternity to pass by. She jumped when her phone dinged.

4:29 PM: I'm glad it's you :-)

Relief washed over Jasmine. Her smile returned. She tried to play it cool, but she could not turn the smile off to stop her cheeks from hurting.

Israel arrived shortly after their text exchange. Jasmine walked out to his car with her nerves jittering. She tried her best to walk cute, switching her hips just enough to stay in the saved but still sensual category. Jasmine hoped he would like her outfit. She thought it was both trendy and showed enough of her curves, while it left something to the imagination. She gave herself one last once over, smoothing down the white form-fitting shirt with a buttoned-up black vest covering it. Both hugged her waist, giving it the corset look. Her boot cut jeans were slimming with their dark wash, and her black boots were dressy enough for date night but comfy enough to have fun still.

"Hello!"

"Hi!" Jasmine said with excitement. *Jasmine! Calm down girl.*

"Well...what would you like to do?"

She tried to play it cool so this time she casually answered, "Hmmm… I don't have any preferences. Did you have something planned?"

"I do. But I'm not sure of your interests, so I was

feeling you out a bit," Israel said nervously.

"Oh, okay!" Jasmine laughed.

"Do you like movies? I know *Wolverine* has been out for a while, but I haven't had a chance to see it yet."

"Yes. I love movies. And nope, I haven't seen it yet."

"Well, let's do it. Then we can get a bite to eat and talk afterward."

"Sounds like fun," Jasmine said, smiling ear to ear.

They enjoyed the action-packed movie with Jasmine's favorite Marvel character, delivering his signature bad boy/good guy performance. As they strode to the car, Jasmine and Israel's conversation flowed smoothly. They conversed like two old friends. Their ride to the movie theater had been way too short. Jasmine looked forward to more face-to-face time.

Just before making it to the vehicle, Jasmine's stomach rumbled audibly. She kicked herself for allowing her nerves to stop her from eating all day. She was mad at her stomach for the betrayal. She prayed Israel could not hear the disrespect going on in her body.

"So, I thought we should go to a low-key spot so we can talk. What do you have a taste for?"

If he heard her stomach, he didn't mention it. She was grateful either way.

"I'm honestly down for whatever. Let's go to the diner up the street and get like a table off to the side. The food is delicious. It's kind of late. The crowd may be low-key," Jasmine said.

Jasmine and Israel traded glances as they road to the diner. He cheesed. She blushed. They looked like two love-sick puppies. Those smiles turned into bewildered gazes as they exited the car and entered the restaurant.

Jasmine's prediction of a quiet space proved inaccurate as they entered the crowded restaurant known for its tasty breakfast platters and T-bone steak and eggs combo. They managed to get a table off to the side, but it was not quiet which caused them to have to lean in close in order to hear one another. They had an amazing time. The conversation flowed nonstop. Jasmine was so grateful. Sometimes when you speak to someone online and try to make the switch into real-life, face-to-face interaction, it became so awkward. Jasmine and Israel did not have that issue. They talked about anything and everything at the restaurant while they dined. They laughed and laughed.

As Israel drove her home, they laughed at Angel's hilarious invention of a half-blind date, and Jasmine revealed that she thought he knew who the friend Angel had chosen was based on their random social media exchange.

"I won't even lie to you Jasmine. Angel told me she was hooking me up with one of her friends, and I went and friend requested her friends I remembered meeting at her birthday party."

"What?! You're a *nut,*" Jasmine laughed as tears sprang from her eyes. "That is hil-*ar*-ious!"

"I was trying to figure it out," Israel said, wiping his own eyes as the laughter took over him as well. "Aw man," He said out of breath and still snickering. "I'm *so* glad it was you. Because the conversations I had with the others..." They both bubbled over with a fresh wave of laughter at his inference. Israel finally sobered enough to sincerely repeat, "I'm glad it was you, Jasmine," as he took her hand in his.

As he reiterated that sentiment Jasmine felt her heart flutter. And she felt a spark as their palms met.

Jasmine said, "Thank you," as they sat in his car, taking each other in. Blissful silence surrounded them.

"I had a great time with you."

"Me too. I think I could talk to you all night, but tonight, I have to call it a night."

"Oh yes, Miss Jasmine. My bad keeping you out late on a school night."

"It's okay. I enjoyed this. And I'm usually up late, but this week my students are releasing a journal to three local libraries. All the stories and articles are written by them and a fellow teacher. And me of course. So I need to get rest."

"Now that's dope. I'd love to hear more."

"Well, that just means we need to do this again."

With that, Jasmine tried to rush out the car. She didn't know where that surge of boldness came from, but embarrassment immediately followed her statement. *She* had a good time, and she hoped he had too, but she couldn't just assume a second date was in the plans.

"Oh wait. Hold on," Israel rushed to open her door. "Let me walk you up."

"Thank you, kind sir." She took the hand he offered.

They walked the winding pathway to Jasmine's porch. Jasmine was nervous with expectancy. *Defer to him Jasmine. Don't be weird.* She coaxed herself.

"Let's do this again *soon*," he said as he kissed her on the cheek.

It was the sweetest kiss she could imagine. Jasmine swooned internally. One thing was for sure, they had a deep connection. To Jasmine, Israel felt like home. The instant feelings for him both exhilarated and terrified her. Israel had made a lasting impression on her heart. She went to sleep with a smile.

Chapter 26

Jasmine age 24

The next day, Israel and Jasmine text messaged throughout the day. After she got off work, they spoke on the phone his whole drive to Vegas. Jasmine was grateful her mother wasn't home so she could continue without any interruptions or nosiness because there was no way she was hiding her smitteness with Israel from anyone. She couldn't keep the silly grin off her face, not that she was trying.

And they never stopped talking from that day. They spoke daily, any free moment either of them had. They learned so much about each other over the span of two months and decided they really wanted to give themselves a chance on love. But someone had to move. Jasmine did not do long distance. Touch was her top love language, so forehead kisses and bear hugs were a must.

"You're already planning on moving back to Cali. Just come now instead of the end of the year."

"I want to. Nothing I want more than to come be with you."

"Yay! Okay. Come on Izzy!"

"I have to put in a transfer for my job. They want me to stay out here until at least December. When I mentioned moving in October, they said they weren't sure if they could make it happen."

"Tell them you have extenuating circumstances."

"What? An impatient girlfriend?"

"Girlfriend?"

"Uh...yes silly. I don't just be on the phone and texting. I never text. You're pulling me out my shell."

"Texting is a shell?" They both laughed.

"And I *want* you to be my wife."

Jasmine's breath caught. "You…you do Izzy?"

"Yes. I told you. I've dated. I've had my fun. I've made mistakes. I'm almost thirty. I want to settle down and have kids while I'm on the younger side and travel with my family. My plan is simple."

Jasmine was caught off guard. *Nine. Nine. Nine.* The date popped in her head as he spoke. And she almost started crying. That was just a couple months away.

"That sounds like a solid plan for sure."

"I know when it's real and I would marry you tomorrow girl. Or I would marry you next year or we can wait two or three years. It's up to you."

"Wow Izzy. I'd marry you tomorrow too. But I'd love to plan a wedding."

She was nervous now. She felt herself about to trip on her words. She couldn't just act like she made up the date on the spot. But it was so soon. They couldn't plan a wedding that fast. And it sounded so silly. But if she lied, her nosy friends would surely mention it and he'd think he was set up. *But you don't even lie,* she thought to herself. That just never was a pitfall she had to deal with. She was a terrible liar so she never tried. *Just tell him,* she heard strongly and firmly within.

"Well…Funny thing… I...I-I -I made a half joke but was half *serious* too that I'd get married on September 9, 2009. Nine, nine, nine," she said and then braced herself.

She hadn't realized her eyes were shut. She peeped them open to look at the phone. The silence was getting to her so she immediately filled the moment with more words. "And then I prayed and said Lord I'd love to get married on that day if I meet an amazing guy. But it's so soon and it's on a Wednesday. Can you even get married on a weekday-"

"I love it. Let's do it."

She looked at the phone. "Huh?"

"Let's do it baby!"

"Just like that?"

"Just like that."

Jasmine smiled and giggled and they talked about their potential children and future plans and the grand life ahead. Things were looking so good.

Chapter 27

"I LOVE you little girl! Love you big!" I hugged Carleigh extra tight as she sat next to me on the couch.

I didn't want to let her go.

"And I love you little one" I gushed as I reached out to Mariah and allowed her to snuggle on the other side of my lap.

"Mommy. Are you okay?"

"Yes! I am. And I will be."

"Mommy what does that mean?" I laughed at the confusion on Carleigh's face.

All she needed to understand was that everything would be okay.

I knew my tears as I smiled were confusing her but I could not help it! The phone call I just received was life changing. With all that was going on, I was simply miffed at the idea of this opportunity reaching me at *this* moment in my life. Everything was falling apart. But it was also coming together. Who would have thought that simply saying yes to God would lead to an avalanche of blessings? I kept trying to make it make sense. I sat there hugging my children because it's all I could do so I wouldn't start screaming and jumping up and down again and scare them any further.

I had to tell an adult. Israel was out of the question. Telling him would just make me sad and take away some of the excitement with his lackluster response. He'd eventually need to know because soon, I wouldn't be as available for all of his and the kid's needs. On my quest to get Unboxed, I just got booked!

I longed to share my news with my mother. These moments made me miss her the most. I decided my sister was an awesome next best. Anise would be just as proud as my mother.

I waited anxiously as the phone rang.

"Yes?" Anise asked sounding hasty.

"Hi sister! You busy?"

"Kinda, but I can chat for a quick second. You know I make time for you. What's up?" she said in a rushed but pleasant tone.

"I had some news I wan-"

Before I could begin, she said, "Dang it! Jaxxie, let me call you back. I've been waiting on this call all morning," and abruptly hung up.

I really wanted to share my news with her. But nothing could take my joy away. God had answered my prayer. I was finally getting the chance to use my journalism degree!

Two weeks after beginning The UnBoxedMe, I received a call from an old friend. This was after Coach Myra warned us to be open to the new opportunities even if they were wrapped in an old package.

"Ladies, if you put in the work, the opportunities, your people, and your resources will come. Do not be surprised if He uses old connections and reunites you with seemingly dead dreams."

I buckled down and truly dived into The UnboxedMe coursework. It was so uncomfortable at first, answering questions about how my early familial interactions and experiences affected my ideas, behaviors, and patterns. The amount of self-reflection was sobering. God used Coach Myra to expose pitfalls, self-sabotage techniques we use repeatedly, poor business practices, disobedience to God's instruction, and more. She came for everything that would hinder one from elevating. The more I uncovered, the lighter I felt. And like clockwork, my phone rang with opportunity.

I worked as a teacher and part time assistant administrator for a few years before transitioning into the role of housewife and mother. I never thought I'd end up teaching more than a few months. I grew so much during that time, especially as a writer. I started a writing club called "We Write the World," with a fellow teacher, Ms. Jada, and together we put out a monthly publication featuring our writing and stories of children from each grade. That publication circulated to all the local stores and libraries. We were so proud.

In the years I stayed home to grow my family, Jada's career took off. I would smile as I saw her highlights on news outlets and on social media. Of course, the thoughts of where my career would have been had I stayed connected to her would resurface but I wouldn't trade my kids for the world so I tucked the what-ifs. Today, she called me with an opportunity and I said yes. My time to soar was here.

"Are you serious?"

"As a heart attack!"

"Jada!" I said as I shook my head so she could both see and hear my disdain. Perks of video conferencing.

"Sorry," she said as we both laughed.

"Can you repeat it please?"

"Girl I'm not saying all that again."

"Ja-daaaaa?" I dragged.

"Fine! It's paid. It's weekly. You'll have to drag ya-"

"JADA!"

"SO-RRY! I forgot you're all Christiany and stuff," before we both laughed.

"No, you didn't."

"I didn't," she admitted with a chuckle. "Give me a pass. You will have to drag your *gluteus maximus* out of the house. Is that better?"

"For sure! You're giving me a job. I will be happy to leave my cave. Now details please!"

"You come to the studio. There will be make-up, hair, cameras, lights, and you. It's that simple. I already have five approved stories I pulled from your work in We Write the World. I know you have a slew of stories kids will love to hear. You need to submit a few each week. Short ones like the ones we used to write because the segment is only ten minutes. The segment will air weekly and their advertising team is amazing. So basically, thousands of children, some of which never get bedtime stories, will get to hear one written and read by you! We are working with the social workers now to get these stories streamed in group homes."

"That's the best part! I just can't believe I get the honor to read to children who generally do not get read to. I had no idea there was an initiative to bring stories to them."

"Ma'am, I've been busy. You already know how serious I am about these babies."

"Wow. I just wanted you to repeat it so I could make sure I was hearing you correctly. I'm amazed!"

"Well, be excited and stay excited but you have work to do Jasmine. You need to get the proper documentation to protect your writing. You have two months before we start recording. You can get something published. You need social media accounts for your writing as well. And a landing page. So, you need to get all of *that*," she said waving a disapproving hand at my ensemble, "tahgetha. You're looking like a mom. You need a makeover and a photo shoot."

"Hey!" I said smoothing down my hair. I hated FaceTime.

"Girl! Now is not the time to be in yo' feelings. Get polished and get visible. Where can people find you? Where can people purchase the book? Books! Please. Get. Ready! Book clubs, book tours. You never know."

I gulped at all she was throwing my way. "Slow down Jada."

"No. You speed up. I told you to publish years ago. I know life and yada, yada but you're not getting any younger Granny."

I laughed at the familiar nickname only Jada could get away with calling me.

"Jada this is a lot to take in. But I'm excited! Who are the other storytellers? We can't fit two in the one ten-minute segment. And you said it is weekly. So, will me and the other storytellers alternate?"

"Jasmine pay attention dear. You are the only storyteller. And stop saying storyteller. That sounds dumb as hell. You're an author. It's just you! Come on sis... Get with this program! You are it. It is you!"

"I can't stand you Jada!"

"Girl you love me. And you about to love these checks!"

"Just me? But how? Why? You don't want to share your work? You *are* published."

"I just want to be behind the scenes. I've released books, done book tours, and sold thousands of copies. I've made best-seller lists and all that. My royalty checks flow consistently. I like being in the background most."

"Shoot, me too!"

"But you were made for this Jasmine. Why *not* you? But hey, I don't have any more time to convince you. The confidence is your responsibility. I will talk to you soon though. Get busy!"

I pondered her words and they sent a shiver down my spine. *The confidence is my responsibility. What kinda cryptic statement is that?* Though I had much to ponder and complete in a very short amount of time, I couldn't help but feel grateful and excited.

This was a dream come true! Bigger than my initial plans. I just wanted to get a piece of my work out there. This was what I asked for and so much more. An answered prayer of a dream completely buried coupled with a mind-blowing opportunity. I needed this evidence and reminder of how good God is and how following His path leads to breakthrough.

Chapter 28

Jasmine age 24

Lord, I don't know what the end will be of this health issue. But I know it's something. I feel it in my lungs and I feel the changes in my stamina and energy. I don't want to go through this but if I just have to, send me someone to walk it through with me. It doesn't have to be a boyfriend or a husband. That would be amazing but even a best friend. Someone who won't put me on the back burner when I need their help or to accompany me to a doctor's appointment or just sit with me if I get too overwhelmed. I know it's a tall ask, but if I have to go through this, help me in this way. In Jesus' name, Amen.

Jasmine remembered her prayer request from college. She hadn't known exactly what to expect with her health. Hoping it would go away on its own was not working. But Jasmine's main issue was feeling alone. She did not want to go through this, whatever it ended up being, all by herself. And for a time, Jasmine's childhood best friend was there. Any time she could be, Ebony was there. Friends since the tender age of eight, they had a tight bond that had held steady through the years and Jasmine was so grateful for any time she was able to give. Having someone there made the difference. But then Israel came along. She was so grateful because his quiet strength comforted her in a way she had never felt comforted before, even by her mother, who also was a great support even though she had her own health challenges.

After a year of prodding and subpar healthcare, Jasmine was able to have access to some decent health insurance and a higher level of care, and she was finally getting the answers she needed. Jasmine knew Israel was the real deal when she went to her first diagnostic appointment. She finally got a definitive answer of what she was dealing with. The mystery had been solved. Jasmine went numb as the doctor in a monotone voice, read off possible prognosis of Jasmine's rare lung condition - fibrosis of the lungs: prognosis possible lung failure and transplant patient. They didn't have all the answers and treating her would be in part experimental. The doctor tried to inform her of what symptoms may develop, life expectancy, prescription medications she'd need to add to her regimen, and he advised her not to google. Her eyes were as big as saucers as he finished and invited the two medical students to press and probe as he pointed out indicators and symptoms of the disease that usually go unnoticed. Jasmine began to feel overwhelmed and like a science experiment. Israel could see her discomfort immediately and began asking questions of his own.

Once he had the doctor's full attention, Israel asked the medical students to leave the room so they could speak to the doctor alone. Everything Jasmine couldn't think to say or ask, Israel did. He didn't freak out. He looked unfazed. He seemingly felt none of the confusion and angst Jasmine was feeling. At that moment she became even more smitten with Israel. How he stood up for her was such a turn on and she immediately felt heartbroken because she knew what she had to do. She could not let this man live this life with her. He didn't deserve a sick woman to spend his life with. The doctors said this would be a lifelong battle. The tears wouldn't come because the numbness wouldn't subside. This was her life. Good with the bad. And she knew it wasn't fair for Israel to be stuck carrying this burden with her. It was too heavy.

Jasmine hung her head with the weight of her declaration. As soon as the doctor left, she blurted out what was on her heart.

"You don't have to marry me Israel. This is a lot. You don't want to be with the 'sick girl.' And I just-"

"Jasmine. Stop," he said without a pause as he casually picked lint off of his pants. "This is not the end of the world."

"But-"

"Stop." He said it with finality causing her to lift her head and find Israel's eyes. Israel's commanding tone brought her eyes to his. He hadn't yelled and he wasn't angry. She could see his eyes glazed over with compassion and love. That much love in such a short amount of courtship. She could barely believe it. But then she remembered, she had prayed for exactly this. His tone, his compassion, and the look in his eyes warmed her heart and calmed her spirit.

"Thank you for stepping in."

"It's okay. It will be okay. This is something we will deal with. We hear what the doctors say and we will deal, but you don't accept this as the final word. God can do anything."

And with that she felt her mustard seeds grow.

Chapter 29

Just as I suspected, Israel wasn't overly excited by my news of landing an entire segment on television. He was cordial and congratulated me but was still standoffish. My feelings were hurt. I had shared SnackJoys with him, even helped it grow. I felt like I was winning but didn't have *my* person to share it with and that stung, but I couldn't live there. I could hear Coach Myra in my ear saying, "Focus on yourself." That was her famous tagline.

The UnboxedMe course and community quickly became a support system in my life. I almost had no chance to miss him. Almost…

I enjoyed my one-on-one sessions with Coach Myra. And I always left empowered after a class. When I found out I would be able to make income sharing my stories, I immediately went on social media and posted in our group. The congratulations I received warmed my heart. But I couldn't help but feel sad I wasn't receiving that same reception in my own home. I wanted to share this with Israel...

Things between us were quiet. That's the best way I could describe it. He announced last week he would be moving out in the next few months. After I was convicted for trying to make him change his mind, I went through an internal battle. If I wasn't going to be syrupy sweet and try to win him over, did I need to stop all wifely duties? It came up in my counseling session with Roberta.

"So how am I supposed to treat him? He basically wants a roommate because when I try to be a wife, he rejects it."

"Look at it this way. You have a choice. Excuse my terminology but I want to paint the picture clearly. There are two paths you can take: wife or baby mama," She paused to see if I was following.

My eyebrow reached for the ceiling. "Please explain."

"Okay. So, as a wife, you would treat Israel as your husband with honor and stay committed to your vows by continuing to do the tasks you figure are becoming of a wife. You do this with no expectation. You do this regardless of how he acts. You do this effortlessly as if things were perfect but you keep the emotion away. You do this with a pure heart, not expecting anything from Israel. You weren't wrong before when you tried to ramp up your wifely duties. Your posture and reasoning were. They were manipulative and Israel wasn't receptive. Is this connecting with you?"

"I wasn't manipulative. I was trying to make him see…" I stopped mid-sentence. The realization set in. "Dang…I was manipulative. Whether purposeful or not."

"I know it wasn't malicious."

"Okay. I see my mistake. I'm following. More on wife versus baby mama." Trying to bend Israel's will had backfired miserably. I was not eager to repeat it.

"Now I know it's hard to carry out your wifely duties and be met with a stone wall. That's why you do it as unto God. You can never go wrong when you're submitted to God."

"Okay. But I must admit, I'm still confused. Why did you mention baby mamas?"

"It's all about perspective. If you take the baby mama route, you would start distancing yourself – and your services – in anticipation of the two of you separating anyway. You know, let him feel what he will be missing. Pull back and only do for yourself and the kids."

"Is that so bad?"

"Well, you tell me. What is the end result you desire?"

"I desire reconciliation. But I can't make him turn back to me. That's painfully clear."

"But if you never stop being a wife, when and if he comes back, you won't have to get back into that mode."

"And if he…never turns back," I could barely get the words out.

"You can't worry about it. Right now, you are a wife. You take your vows seriously and you honor God by honoring your husband. And you posture yourself for the future you *expect*."

"So, I continue with my wifely duties but with no expectation and even if he's mean and seems annoyed? That's tough. And honestly, *that* seems manipulative."

"Treat him like a guest in your home. Treat him as if you were entertaining an angel. Listen to him. If something you're doing makes him uncomfortable, stop. But cooking, cleaning, washing clothes, that's normal household routine. You'd actually be going out of your way to *not* do those things for him."

I pondered her suggestions for a moment and began to feel at peace. That feeling was one of the signs I had grown familiar with over the last few weeks as an indicator of solidarity with God. “I can do that,” I said with conviction.

“Good. Next session I want you to have several examples of how you chose to be his wife when you didn’t feel like it. I know it seems tedious to write down, but having proof of small victories along the way helps to keep us motivated and track the change we want to see.”

“Will do,” I said gathering my belongings to exit.

Although I was excited to feel as connected as I did to God, I had to admit that some of the instruction was hard to follow. Not literally, but I simply didn’t want to do it. But I had to admit, praying and journaling and actually hearing the heart of God for my life kept me in a space of joy I thought was unattainable with the way things that had gone on and were currently happening. Landing the show had instantly changed my life and I knew staying connected to God and listening for his direction was key for my success. But that hadn’t made it easy. *God, it sure is hard to wait.* It was hard to be obedient with a husband who was acting like a total jerk. All of me wanted to just say forget it but I knew that fueling the fire was not the path God had for me. The future I prayed for was reconciliation so why would I act like it was the end? And as if God heard my thoughts, upon arriving home, I quickly had a chance to put Roberta’s wife versus baby mama theory to use.

“Israel, I am making tacos tonight. How many would you like?” Tacos were his favorite dish. He never turned them down.

“Nah. I’m good,” he said without looking up from his phone.

Until today. His answer caught me off guard for a moment. I took a deep breath and let the disappointment go.

"Okay," I said in a cheery tone that was not fake.

I had no energy to let his callousness change my mood. *Wife or ratchet,* I thought. The ratchet would simply not make his tacos, put the food up, serve myself and the children and call it a night. The wife made extra taco shells and set the meat and toppings out like a taco bar for a self-serve option. I then made plates for the kids and I. Me, Carleigh, and Mariah ate and laughed as we sat at the dinner table. I was grateful for the joy my kids brought.

"Daddy," our daughter Mariah called. "Come. Eat."

"Not tonight baby. Daddy's not very hungry."

He's hurting. Extend grace. Focus on you. I heard the gentle reminder and immediately said a silent prayer. I wanted to be angry that he refused to sit down and eat with us. I wanted to be angry that he wouldn't even try to work it out with me but expected only me to change and like magic our marriage would be fixed. But I chose to extend grace and let him process his own emotions. I would never be able to change his mind. I wouldn't be able to keep the house clean enough or make enough tacos to make him want to stay if he was hellbent on leaving. Only Israel could do that. And only God could change his heart.

All I could do was focus on me. At the same time that one piece of my life was falling apart, opportunities for me to live, expand, and grow kept popping up.

After being a stay-at-home mom and homeschooling for several years, my kids were transitioned into private school. Carleigh and Mariah loved their new normal and I all of a sudden had more kid-free time than I had in years and it immediately filled up with purpose! I went from changing diapers, potty training, homeschooling, and playdates to writing deadlines, dress fittings, makeup and hair consultations, and planning a small watch party for my debut episode. The watch party was Angel's idea. I could not hide my excitement even if I tried. That was the odd part about the pattern in my life.

Whenever something devastating was happening, there was usually something amazing on the horizon. I had to admit that the latest journey was a pleasant surprise.

"Mommy. I'm sleepy. Can I go take a nap?" Mariah's little voice snapped me out of my thoughts.

"Okay little one. Let's go night-night. Carleigh, mommy is going to put your sister to bed. Say good night to Daddy, Mariah."

"Night, night Daddy."

I left Carleigh and Israel to get Mariah in the bed. Bedtime was cherished in my home. I would read stories, sing songs, and say prayers with the girls nightly. I longed for Israel to join in on this time of pouring spiritually into our kids but he was always working on something or too tired. Still, we tried to never miss a night. Especially with them starting school, and my schedule ramping up, bedtime bonding was that much more important. But tonight, Mariah was drifting before she hit her bed. I decided to lay down with her to insure she went to sleep and drifted off myself. I jolted awake after what felt like five minutes. I looked at the clock and it had been two hours. I made my way to the kitchen to put up the food. I knew I'd have to toss the sour cream but figured some of the other fixings would be okay.

To my surprise, all the food was put away and I noted Israel's favorite plate in the sink with taco residue on it. I guess he was hungry after all. My heart twinkled. And then took a dip. I didn't know what to feel. I hated this emotional rollercoaster.

Chapter 30

Jasmine age 24

On the evening of Wednesday, September 9, 2009, Israel and Jasmine prepared to join in holy matrimony. They were set to be wed in a small ceremony with just their parents, siblings, and a few friends. Jasmine suspected that less than fifteen people would be present and she was perfectly fine with the arrangement. Israel's father was set to officiate. The couple was quite eager to say, "I do."

Jasmine dreamed of having a beautiful wedding decorated with all white flowers and accents of gold and lavender. Her vision included bridesmaids in simple A-line gowns that flowed to the ground. She wanted them to look flowy and regal. Her guests would be invited to wear shades of purple and gray. Intricate lighting detail and high-low center pieces would highlight the reception and her guests would sit down to family style dining. She'd put all her favorite ideas from the wedding shows she grew up watching together to have her dream day. But with the added conflict of managing her health and how tired she'd get from time to time with her "struggle lungs" as Angel jokingly called them (her humor helped Jasmine stay positive), Jasmine's heart was just not into executing such a major production. Her energy was all over the place as she learned her triggers, figured out a medicine regimen, and tried to find more stable employment with better benefits. Wedding planning was just too stressful. She did have fun at bridal shows and a special outing with her mother and besties to try on wedding dresses, but the elaborate wedding planning pretty much ended there. And Israel could not care less. He just wanted her happy. He was ready to begin their lives as Mr. and Mrs. Israel Ford. So was Jasmine. And she would always have that special memory of their humble beginnings and God's favor to answer her prayer. They could always plan a vow renewal for an anniversary in the coming years, God willing.

Jasmine fangirled inside her own mind. *You're really doing this Jasmine,* she thought as she laid on the floor of her soon to be father-in-law's study. *This is a beautiful day and your marriage is what matters. Get it together.*

Though she was excited, she was still nervous. She tried to speak these words strongly to herself but she still felt all the nerves churning at the bottom of her stomach. She knew she was tripping because being a known germaphobe, having her head and body on the nasty unknown floor was an absolute disgrace. She hopped up quickly as she tried to sober her thoughts and calm her nerves.

Jasmine left the study to go get some water, pizza, a drink or anything to calm her nerves. She needed *something*! She ran into Israel's cousin Stacy as she turned the corner. She wished she'd gone the other direction.

"Oh my gosh girl! Welcome to the family! I'm so excited for you girrrrllll. Marriage is such an amazing experience," she said speaking a mile a minute and smothering Jasmine in a bear hug.

"Thank you," Jasmine said as she tried to rush past Stacy with no luck. Stacy positioned herself in a way that prevented Jasmine from clearing the hall. She needed to go outside for fresh air. Beside her nerves, the impromptu but fun karaoke bachelorette girl's night Anise surprised Jasmine with also had her a little groggy. She needed air, quick! But Stacy clearly had other plans.

Jasmine only met Stacy once before but she'd heard countless stories about her from Angel. Israel had stories too. Not as many as Angel, but more than enough to let Jasmine know she probably should stay away on her wedding day if she wanted to clear her mind.

The history between Angel and Stacey was very thick due to the fact that Stacey was married to Angel's favorite cousin Lemar who happened to be one of Israel's best friends and Angel felt like Stacy was terrible to Lemar. It was all so confusing for Jasmine when they first laid out this family tree until she realized Angel and Israel were Black cousins (not blood related but related by their parent's friendship). "Play cousins," Anita and Israel had grown up more like siblings along with Angel's cousin Lemar. Lemar and Israel were best friends and more like brothers from birth and Stacey was Israel's *actual* blood related first cousin. The funniest part of the story is that Jasmine had the biggest crush on Lemar when she met him in high school, and now she was marrying his best friend, that is if she could get past his wife…

"Yes girl. I'm excited."

"Thank you so much Stacey," Jasmine said as she once again tried to pass by.

"Girl, wait! I have these videos of the kids. You

know we have 5 girls now! And I'm pregnant again. Hope we get our boy. You haven't seen how big they have gotten. Hold on, let me find this one song Lemiah made up," she said as she placed her hand on Jasmine's forearm to stop her escape and then went back to scrolling and chatting.

Jasmine couldn't even hear what she was saying. She was trying to blink and lift herself from this chick's presence by osmosis but it wasn't working.

"Jasmine! Girl. You need to get dressed! Come on," Anise said as she came from seemingly nowhere dressed beautifully in a crisp purple pixy cut dress.

Her best friend Joissa trailed behind her with Jasmine's dress and make up bag. Her glam squad had arrived. And not a moment too soon. Jasmine knew God loved her in that very moment if she had ever doubted before. Anise snatched her by the arm and breezed past Stacey. She wasn't being rude but she was on a mission. Anita had sent her to find Jasmine so they could get the show on the road.

"But wait, my video is loading," Jasmine heard Stacey say as her words trailed behind them.

For this special day, Jasmine decided to honor her husband and accent the limited decor with his favorite color. She wanted the day to reflect both of them. There weren't many decorations involved but she had a small beautiful bouquet of blue hydrangeas, tweedia, and white roses, her sister wore a lovely shade of indigo, and Israel, the officiant and Lemar were all given blue hydrangea boutonnières. They kept it simple only choosing one attendant each. Israel chose his best friend Lemar of course and Jasmine chose her sister Anise.

"Alright Nonnie. You look so pretty," Anise said as she smoothed the bodice of Jasmine's off the shoulder cream colored chiffon A-line swing dress.

Jasmine loved her dress! It was floor length but flowed with each turn. And best of all, it had pockets.

"You ready?"

"No…"

"Jasmine!"

"Anise!"

Jasmine swiveled from Anise's mama bear gaze and took a moment to admire her dress, loving how it flowed as she swayed slightly. She patted the sleek chignon Joissa styled her straightened hair into, happy and surprised at the quick but beautiful job she'd done. Jasmine smiled when she saw the natural glow make-up was applied beautifully by Anise. She went back to her dress and stared at her reflection. It wasn't the beautiful ball gown she'd always envisioned, but she felt pretty. *Nine. Nine. Nine.* She shook her head. An answered prayer from God.

"Girl come on."

"Okay."

Jasmine and Anise made it to the door. She hadn't wanted to, but her parents made her walk down the aisle. Jasmine literally wanted to meet Israel at the altar and get married. This wasn't a traditional wedding. But she gave in to their small request.

She steadied herself as the doors opened. She was ready to see the small group. The more she thought about it, the intimate guest count made her smile. But to Jasmine's surprise, the church was packed with people. Every pew was filled with faces. Some Jasmine recognized, but many she did not.

"Anise," she whispered.

Anise shrugged and began walking down smiling and waving. Jasmine couldn't believe what she was witnessing. Somehow, the whole church found out about their ceremony. Jasmine had a gnawing suspicion that someone announced it at midweek bible study. However they received the memo, many church members decided to stay and watch the nuptials. Jasmine was already nervous because you know, marriage...but now she had to do it in front of a bunch of people she didn't know? That was not the plan. None of this had been the plan. Getting sick, then meeting an amazing man, and falling in love so quickly, and getting married this way because of the stupid sickness making her too tired to plan her own wedding. The best and worst things were happening to her at the exact same time and her mind just could not fathom how she was supposed to feel. Jasmine was worried and stressed about the future but she was also ecstatic about uniting with an amazing and handsome man. How was she supposed to embrace it all?

Walking down the aisle was a blur for Jasmine. She felt like she was out of her body watching it happen from above. She remembered her dad William coming alongside her after Anise left to walk down the aisle first. She was so grateful that after years of separation, they were reunited and William got to be there for her special day. His presence was comforting as she walked down the aisle with him. She remembered seeing Anita cheesing which was great, because she was no longer stressed about Jasmine marrying a man she dated for less than a year. Previously, Anita was dead set on it not happening until Jasmine's aunt pulled her to the side and helped her understand Anita couldn't make Jasmine's choices for her. After releasing her blessing, Anita was thrilled with the idea of being mother of the bride as she sat there beaming in her blue dress. Jasmine remembered seeing some familiar faces in the crowd as she made her way down the aisle and she wanted to make eye contact and wave but she also wanted to concentrate so she wouldn't trip and fall. When she locked eyes on Israel, all her nerves melted away. His smile made her heart skip a beat.

The ceremony was quick. Way quicker than she

expected. It took less than fifteen minutes to get through the vows and for Israel to kiss his bride. And just like that, they were married.

Jasmine thought, *I'm married on nine, nine, nine,* and it made her smile.

As she began hugging family and friends, Jasmine saw Stacy elbowing people to make it to the happy couple.

Oh Lord.

Israel and Jasmine greeted their guests, collected gifts, and headed to a small restaurant for dinner with a few of their close family members. The laughs were endless and the mood festive as the two families exchanged pleasantries and tried to learn names. No huge fanfare. No huge wedding. But definitely a sweet beginning of the Ford love story…And a night of sweet love Jasmine and Israel had saved for that special night. They planned to enjoy communing and bonding in covenant all week in their honeymoon suite. Jasmine was so glad she waited for her Izzy.

Chapter 31

Israel and I got dressed in separate rooms for our non-date night outing. I knew what to expect. No holding hands. Or even walking together. No contact at all as Israel would be sure to walk several paces in front of me. I hated these murky waters.

Two days ago, I received tickets to see a local jazz artist, Nikki Byard. They were a gift from my show's producer. Matt was a dream to work with and he always had a perk or gift to share. The sixty-two-year-old plump, white guy definitely had a crush on this Black girl excellence. He knew I was married but that did not stop him from flirting and teasing. I knew it was harmless but did not engage. I took the jazz tickets though. Mama ain't raised no fool! But seriously, our interactions were definitely professional. And he let it be known he respected and admired my mission and knew I was created to bring joy through my words. Having Matt and the rest of the staff constantly affirm and stand in awe and fan-ship of my work was a bit overwhelming at first but it ended up being exactly what I needed to break out of my self-depreciating box. My dealings with Israel left me feeling insecure, broken, and less than. I needed to be built up.

I asked Israel if he knew of the artist. He had, so I offered the tickets to Israel thinking he'd take a friend. He loved jazz. I wanted him to enjoy it and I knew that probably wouldn't happen for him with me. I was surprised at his response.

"Who's babysitting?"

I was caught off guard. I almost told him we wouldn't need a babysitter because he could go with a friend but I thought quickly and said, "Possibly your sister or I can call Mindy."

Mindy was our part-time nanny. In preparing for my debut, we had to get more help with the kids and Mindy was an excellent addition to our family. She cooked, cleaned, folded laundry, and handled my rambunctious youngest daughter like a pro. She was a true dream; Carleigh and Mariah adored her!

"Okay," he said sounding annoyed. As usual. Annoyed that I was in his space. Annoyed I had to talk to him. I wondered each day when he'd just serve me the papers and go.

"Okay..." I said and walked away to secure our childcare.

The night of the concert, we met at the car at the designated time like two strangers. The car ride to the venue was silent beside the R&B music playing softly. Each time a ballad came on, Israel would skip the song. I wanted to slap him and just take control of the radio and put on ratchet gangsta rap. All of our time together was spent navigating this weird energy. He was short, blunt, or cross with me through every interaction using the shortest amount of words to answer me or inform me of something.

He had cut off all pleasantries, idol conversation, laughter, fun – with me – for some time now. We'd be with a group of people or even the kids. He'd laugh and joke with everyone around but as soon as I joined in or tried to engage him, he'd shut down and turn monotone. It was like he wanted me to stay aware that he was not feeling me. He didn't have to. I knew. All the energy he was using to make sure I felt that he was not connected and there was no glimmer of hope, it was exhausting me so I just stayed quiet around him and when my feelings were too hurt by our lack of connection, I would pray for peace and restraint to not just ask him to leave. What an existence.

We pulled up to the concert venue and the place was packed. The line stretched outside the door and half way down the street. I hadn't expected such a turn out. This piqued my interest. What type of Jazz artist had people lined up like they were waiting for admission into the hottest night club?

From the first melodic note, I was hooked. Nikki Byard's smooth tone serenaded and livened my mood. Her voice mesmerized me with its rich tone and depth. And the lyrics to her latest album resonated with me deeply. She sang about finding yourself after getting lost in life. Self-love, preparing for romantic love, and healing were the main themes.

The concert was simply amazing! I had never even been to a live jazz show. I honestly thought it would be a little boring to sit through an *entire* jazz concert. After two or three jazz songs during a car ride I was usually fighting a nap. Not at Nikki Byard's show! She was so engaging. All around us I saw people in love, dancing, cuddling, handholding. In my determination to live each moment to its fullest, I danced and grooved where I stood, by myself. I let the music pulse through me and swayed my body to the smooth rhythms. I danced as if no one was around and even sang along to the songs I was able to pick up easily. I was in my own world so deeply, I almost forgot Israel was there. When I glanced at him, I couldn't read his expression. It was a bit of confusion, mixed with dare I say, wonder? For a moment, I held his gaze. Then I smiled. The corners of his mouth began to turn. For an instant I saw a smile flicker. Like a millisecond. And then his scowl returned. I returned to my grooving. And it felt good. My lungs felt good. Tonight, my breathing wasn't labored and I refused to need permission from anyone to have a good time.

The concert ended too quickly for me. Nikki Byard had earned loyal fan-ship from me.

Just as we turned to leave, I heard Matt's familiar voice.

"Jaaaazzz! Hi honey!" he said, gathering me in a bear hug. "You look *good,"* he said as he grabbed my hand and turned me in a circle.

I had taken Jada's advice. My long, drab curls now framed my face and shined with deep brown chunky highlights, covering the blonde highlights I rocked for years. I enjoyed the stress-free styling of shorter hair. Matt hadn't seen me since the makeover. Jada treated me to a mini shopping spree and overall wardrobe facelift. Basically, she tried to throw away all my clothes that didn't make me look like a "hot babe," in her words. I fought her. Like I literally chased her around the house. I was no match for her athletic lungs and height as she held the coveted items over our heads when she ran out of space to run. I was able to hide some of my comfort/mommy essentials. Thinking of that day made me chuckle.

Israel cleared his throat.

I turned to face Israel as I touched Matt's shoulder to redirect his attention. "This is my," I swallowed hard, "husband, Israel."

"Buddy!" He proclaimed as he vigorously shook

Israel's hand. "Your wife is *spec-tac-u-lar!* But I know you know that. Can't believe you were hoarding her all to yourself from the world. This lady has *it!* Don't be surprised when her show becomes nationally syndicated."

Matt's words were giving me so much life. He believed in me so much. I heard Jada's words. *The confidence is your responsibility.* I'd been working on believing and affirming me. the makeover helped but daily I had begun the work to love myself exactly where I was. I knew the responsibility lied on me but Matt's validation sure did help. Debuting on television was a huge leap for me. I quit in my head daily but moments like this gave me the extra push to go after this once in a lifetime opportunity.

"Oh, Matt stop," I said giving an obligatory downplay to his hype.

"Jasmine, I mean it. We truly lucked up landing you. It's like you were handpicked. Divine intervention because our first choice was great but she was missing something. I couldn't place my finger on just what until we met you. YOU are *made* for this!"

Fighting back tears I said, "Thank you."

"Oh Jazzy, Jazzy, Jazzy," he said calling me the nickname I usually hated. "My pleasure." But that was just how Matt rolled. He was smooth and so quick. He made you feel like a million bucks. I had to make sure I kept my eye on him.

"Thank you so much for the tickets Matt. Israel is a huge jazz head."

"You're welcome gorgeous," he said in his New York accent. Being affirmed by him filled me with joy. With the drought at home, it was much needed.

In the beginning, it made me a little uncomfortable, all the pet names he used but he used them with everyone so I knew it wasn't special for just me. That was just Matt.

I glanced at Israel. I wasn't surprised to see his face

angry. I immediately became alarmed. Though I knew this wouldn't be a date, I can't even lie and say my hopes weren't up that we'd find a moment of connection, a moment to laugh and get back to us so he could remember our love. I knew it was silly. And judging by the look on his face, our night out had just come to an end.

As I prepared to say my goodbye to Matt, we heard the room erupt with chatter as Nikki came out with her entourage. Half of the crowd had dispersed but the club was still pretty full. Everyone's attention turned toward Nikki. Claps and cheers went up. She looked so peaceful taking in her accolades. She smiled and waved and made her way right toward us.

"Nikki. Baby!" Matt held his arms open and she melted into his embrace.

It was like she was a long, lost daughter coming home the way the two connected. It wasn't romantic but something so sweet, tender even, about the way they held each other. I was immediately intrigued. Matt was always so flirty. Not with Nikki.

Matt held her shoulders and looked at her with a proud gaze. The two shared a private moment of knowing. I almost felt like an intruder. I wanted to turn away and almost did until Matt reached out and grabbed my arm and pulled me toward them.

"Nikki baby, please meet Jasmine. She's the host of my new children's show. The one I told you about."

"Oh, how nice it is to meet you Jasmine. My uncle told me so many great things about you. But honestly even if he hadn't, I would have wanted to meet you. You're the type of guest an artist loves to see at a concert. Your energy was love! The way you vibed to my music made my heart sing."

"Thank you, Nikki! I must admit I'm a new fan. And Matt you didn't tell me she was your niece! Wow! Such talent in your family. Matt is amazing to work with."

I hope I kept the surprise off my face at the mention of their kinship. Nikki was clearly Black. Either she was biracial, Matt was her uncle through marriage, or he was very light skinned.

"He is. I owe him my career. My dad wasn't much into music so he let his brother mentor me. Uncle Matt saw in me what I didn't know was there. He pushed me to pursue this thing full out and I'm grateful. Because of him, I'm able to sing music I love, and keep my identity in Christ. He helped me understand my gift didn't have to be presented any other way than how me and God felt comfortable and that God would bring my people. I've sold out shows ever since!"

She was a believer! My insides got all happy. Her songs weren't gospel or "Christian" in subject matter but there was definitely a purity to her music.

"What a testimony. I too am grateful for the opportunity to work with Matt. He will have you feeling yourself. We call him Dr. Cheer at our production meetings. I'm so excited to film our first segment."

"Music! Do you have an intro song? I'd love to help you create one."

"Nikki!" Matt exclaimed. Both Nikki and I jumped. We had been in our own world as we conversed. "That's perfect! This is why I love ya!" he said and grabbed her cheek to kiss it.

"Oh Nikki, I'm sorry. I'm being rude. This is my husband, Israel. I must admit, he's the jazz connoisseur."

"Hello Israel. Nice to meet you. Your wife is a gift!"

"Thank you," he said with an uncomfortable smile that surprised me. Then angered me. He was too good at being fake for others. But it went with his line of work. He always had to be "on" to push those snacks in his competitive market. He never missed a beat. His whole business was making people feel good as he sold snacks with the offer of joy. But I knew how he truly felt about me. He did not consider me a gift.

"Dinner? Sleep? What are you doing next my love? Where's Kendu?"

"I am starving. Kendu, was just-" she said as she searched the room. "Oh, there he goes. He was tying up loose ends. Honey!"

She waved a deeply chocolate man over to where we stood. He was easily six feet, three or four. He was muscular with a manicured beard, low fade with waves dipping, and just classically fine. Like Denzel Washington, Morris Chestnut fine. I had to act like I was checking my purse for lip gloss so I wouldn't stare too long.

Now when *they* embraced, I wanted to blush. It was so sensual, tender, and loving. Their love was palpable. My eyes stung a little as they watered. I forced the tears to hush. I prayed my eyes didn't betray me.

"Kendu! Maaaaannnn. *Yo'* wife was up there killin'!"

I was grateful for Matt supplying a moment for laughter. I needed the mood to shift, quick!

"She did. She always does," Kendu said reaching down to kiss her cheek. He settled on the side of her with his arm resting around her shoulder. They looked freshly, deeply, in love.

"Kendu, this is Jasmine and her husband umm… ummmm. I'm so sorry."

"Israel," I said softly.

"Yes. Israel!"

"Hello Israel and Jasmine," Kendu said with a nod.

"Jasmine is doing an amazing project with Matt. She will be reading bedtime stories that she wrote for kids across the state. I mean the station is local but with the internet and social media, word will travel fast. I'm sure this project will go national. Global if God says so. We never know."

"Wow, Nikki. Thank you for the encouragement."

"You're welcome. I'm so eager to partner with you," she said warmly toward me and then turned to face Matt. "Unc, I am tired but you know I could always eat."

"Well originally, I was hoping you wanted to do dinner. I had a reservation for us three but I have to cut out. Duty calls. But I was gonna send you love birds. Double date!"

I gasped internally. I had to come up with an excuse before Israel declined. I didn't want to feel embarrassed in front of these people I just met.

"What duty Uncle? Who is she?" Nikki asked with a teasing glare.

"Mind ya business! But hey. The night is young. Y'all have to get back to New York tomorrow but you can do dinner with Jazzy and Iz tonight," he said totally making up a nickname for Israel. I shook my head.

"Can we?" Nikki asked Kendu. "I'd love to pick Jasmine's brain. I want to collab with her for the theme song for her show."

My heart beat fast. *Trust me* I heard God say. One thing was for certain. This trial had brought me into such a new and profound relationship with God and the Holy Spirit. I was now able to experience Them, hear Them, and trust Them in a new way. Having comfort, guidance, and newness in such a turbulent time restored my faith and helped me realize I could actually pray, relax, and watch God take care of it all. I let my guard down and decided I'd go alone and catch a cab or car service home. If Israel didn't want to come, I wouldn't block my blessing.

Kendu spoke, jolting me from my thoughts. "I'm down," he shrugged.

"The dinner is paid for already. They know me there. I will phone them and let them know of the changes. Jazzy can you and Iz extend your babysitter?"

Before I could tell them there was no need to

extend the babysitter, let them know my plan, and excuse Israel, he spoke up.

"I'm sure the babysitter can be extended."

"Okay! Y'all are set. It was really good seeing you all." Matt gave us all parting hugs and made his exit.

"We will see you two lovebirds there," Nikki said as she and Kendu turned to leave hand in hand.

My mouth was left slightly open. The confusion left me in a stupor as I tried to figure out what just happened.

"Well come on," Israel said.

His tone was a little softer but that familiar, I don't fool with you, vibe was still there under the surface. I decided to roll with it. I had a theme song to create. God told me to live, and despite current circumstances, I would take every opportunity to do just that!

Chapter 32

Jasmine age 27

"Mrs. Ford, we have to take in account your future quality of life. You have serious choices to make. It is not in your best interest to become pregnant right now. It could literally kill you. Your body is already under attack. That's the nature of living with an autoimmune disease. And with pregnancy, all your organs get compressed. That could become critical in a patient with lung fibrosis who is already dealing with issues of expansion of the chest cavity.

"I just want you to hear it straight, even though it's tough news, but we can discuss the process of harvesting your eggs. I can give you more information on the new meds we'd like to start within the next two weeks. Remember it is an infusion so you'll need an IV each time but I will have my nurse go over all the information alriiiiight," Dr. Ambrose said as her business tone turned into a cheery cheerleader tone at the end of her diagnostic evaluation.

The icing on the cake was the back rub. Jasmine hated the non-comforting back rub and she hated these appointments. Jasmine shut down so her mind could process all this new information. *Infusion? Freezing eggs?* Jasmine's head was reeling.

Israel spoke first. "By infusion you mean through the veins?"

"Yes Mr. Ford. That's the best way to get the medicine through at high doses in the shortest amount of time. The lung disease is active right now. We want to calm it down as quickly as possible and other methods haven't worked as quickly as we'd liked."

"But have they worked at all? We can't just stay on that regimen and give it more time? We *have* to switch to these infusions?" Israel spoke up.

"Well sir, Mrs. Ford has been seen on and off at our office. We get baselines and manage as we are able to see her but there have been gaps in her care with us..."

With over 3 years of marriage under their belt these doctor visits and conversations weren't new. They'd been pushing these same drugs from the beginning. Experimental. Known to possibly (definitely) cause more symptoms unrelated to what you were being treated for or fail to rectify the current issue. Painful side effects. The list went on. But Jasmine had been able to calm her body and her symptoms with less invasive drugs, dietary changes and a deep faith that God would heal her and that though she was going through a painful trial, she would make it through victoriously. But this felt different. Things were getting out of hand. She was walking around feeling as if she could not breathe, barely able to make it from the car to her front door without needing to sit down. Depleted. Barely able to handle her students the whole day. She loved teaching. The position had grown on her. She did not want to give it up. But standing up for extended periods of time was becoming increasingly difficult.

Lord is this the trend of my life? Is this how it's about to be? Always something? Always?!

Things were not easy for Israel and Jasmine from that first year and hadn't yet balanced out completely. Jasmine let her mind drift back to their wedding night…

Jasmine and Israel had in fact made sweet love the night they got married, but Jasmine was unsure it would actually happen *that* night. They were so tired from the wedding; they fell asleep in the car before making it inside their suite. They woke up after about an hour due to a couple walking by their car arguing.

Jasmine gulped as she crossed the threshold. Her eyes became shifty as she watched Israel's actions. He was undressing while undressing her with his eyes. Why was she acting like she hadn't known this part was coming? *Sex. Sex, sex, sex!* She said to herself in her head. *Stop acting weird Jasmine. Sex is normal. It's beautiful. It won't hurt forever. Just probably this first time.* She winced at the thought of the pain.

Israel watched Jasmine with a smirk. It's like he could read her mind. And clearly, he could see the trepidation on her face. Before he could say anything, a deep belly laugh erupted from his diaphragm. It started as a slow rumble and quickly turned into hysterics. At first Jasmine shook her head in disdain. Her agony was not funny. But then Israel closed the gap she had maintained between them since arrival, and tickled her. That set off giggles of her own and opened her up. The two laughed to tears!

After the laughter ceased, the two embraced. They let their bodies touch as closely as they could as they slow danced in the silence, their in-sink heartbeats the only music they needed. Israel whispered, "We have the rest of our lives baby. We can just hold each other tonight."

Jasmine swooned and tears filled her eyes. She felt so seen in that moment. And instantly she felt her heart open more to her husband. *My husband*! She smiled at the thought. *Nine. Nine. Nine.* Her prayer had been answered. Her heart then swelled with great fullness and her body spiked with heat. She felt a sensual tingle take over her. She stopped their dance, let her shoulders relax, grabbed the sides of Israel's face, and kissed him sweetly at first. It felt good.

Israel placed his hands over hers and deepened the kiss. They got lost in one another as they attempted to simultaneously devour and show one another their burgeoning passion. Jasmine broke the kiss. When she opened her eyes and looked in his, she saw a fire in Israel.

"I'm ready husband," she said. And with that, the two began the slow dance of learning one another's bodies and anointing their union with tender love making. Israel was careful to take his time with Jasmine and led them through their first love making session leaving Jasmine sprung. They were both smitten and drifting in love fumes after their time together on the best little honeymoon they could afford. But reality met up with them as soon as they made it back home.

Jasmine and Israel shared a car initially. Both working part-time, they struggled financially. Israel was developing his company SnackJoys during his off time as well, so he basically worked two jobs for the price of one. Their apartment was in the 'hood and they were making every dollar stretch. Far.

And beside all that, the two becoming one was rough. You can take driver's education for six months and pass your written test but until you get behind the wheel of a car and actually get a feel for the road, you are no driver.

Israel had seen his parents married all his life but there's was not perfect, no marriage is. And Israel definitely wanted to learn from their mistakes so he didn't repeat them in his own marriage. Jasmine had witnessed her parent's divorce. Anita remained unmarried so Jasmine being raised by a single mother and taught to be independent, did not transfer well into wife life. Jasmine prayed all the prayers and thought she read enough books but respecting your husband as the Bible commands was tough for her because she'd never seen it in action. Israel was loving and gentle as he tried to guide her on his expectations and how he needed to be treated as a man and though she wasn't used to this new sense of responsibility she felt to please him, it was growing on her. He was her family now. She wanted to make him happy but the independent woman mentality was hard to break and many times what he saw as disrespectful was innocent on Jasmine's part. She saw what needed to be done and did it. No questions asked. But that doesn't produce partnership.

And of course, the health issues. Even if they said nothing and chose not to have open discussions about it, it was like an elephant that traveled into each room, the car, and with them into every discussion of the future. All of these elements made for a rocky start. But both Jasmine and Israel were determined to make it work. They chose to choose one another and build a legacy together by both digging their heels into their careers and working hard to secure their future.

As year one flew into year two and year two flowed into year three, they began to see their hard work pay off. Israel eventually acquired contracts for two school districts and had SnackJoys honey buns in stores across four Southern California counties. Israel worked early mornings, and late into the night developing the business and Jasmine helped whenever she could. She was his cheerleader. He ran every idea by her in the beginning. She did get overwhelmed with the ups and downs of budding entrepreneurship, but she always rebounded when she realized he was her partner so she could feel safe to give him her all and trust his decisions for their family.

When Israel, started school to learn the business side of his operation, he became overwhelmed fast with still working as a property manager and handling SnackJoys' rapid growth. One night, Jasmine heard him grunt loudly in frustration. Shortly after that, she heard the thud of his fist hit the table.

"Hey babe," she said as she came behind him and rubbed his head. He let his head drop so she could rub his shoulders too.

"Ooohh…that feels so good honey," he said as he grabbed her wrist and pulled her around to sit on his lap.

"What's wrong Izzy?"

"I know I will be fine but tonight, it's a lot."

"Let me help."

"I got it honey. Just having a moment."

"Hey! We're a team, right? Team Ford! I can take *something* off your plate."

He thought for a moment and seeing the sincerity in Jasmine's eyes, he relented.

Jasmine began helping Israel get on a schedule. She completed papers and class assignments for him, took over all the household duties, and made sure to help him stay on track of his calendar. She did this while working full time as well. They had a rhythm going. They spent a lot of time coming and going but made sure to connect over dinners and movies. They were balling on a budget so the dinners were home cooked or cheap take out and the movies were red boxes but they made it work. Things were looking up. Their hard work was paying off.

And currently, Jasmine made decent money as a now full-time teacher and assistant dean. She also helped with writing club, so her schedule was quite busy. And they were able to move to a beautiful suburb, no longer having to come home to trap music, drug deals, and gang activity. So naturally, they were ready to expand their family.

But as Jasmine sat listening to the doctor, she felt hopeless. She knew what she had to do and it didn't feel good and she hoped Israel would agree. Jasmine needed to quit her job and focus 100% on her health so that her body could become strong enough and heal enough to carry a baby.

Jasmine worked from the time she got up checking emails and conversing with parents, and organizing her day so she could get to work and be present for the kids, to the time her eye lids closed as she completed paperwork for SnackJoys and graded her student's assignments. Many days she barely got dinner on the table. Though she was grateful for how their life was shaping up financially, and the consistent health insurance, the time to dedicate to her care was not available. She wasn't eating well, picking up fast food more time than not. Jasmine didn't even have time to make regular appointments and she was not consistent with her medicine. Something had to give. The opportunities were amazing but they weren't more important than her life.

During prayer and bible study one night, Jasmine felt led to research herbs, natural remedies, and natural healing. She found so much information and she wanted to dive in to create her own remedies but she needed her time freed up. But she knew Israel was working so hard and his company wasn't able to sustain the life they were getting accustomed to. She was scared to ask Israel about quitting but she knew together, they would make the right decision.

Chapter 33

Jasmine age 27

It sounded great for Jasmine to quit her job and focus on her health, but bills. And health insurance. And money. Those are all real things that never stop. Israel said he could handle it and Jasmine expected he would. But Jasmine quitting her job created a domino effect for which neither of them was ready.

At first, Israel made it look easy. He slowly began removing tasks from Jasmine. She had been over the budget and paying utilities and car insurance but Israel was on board with getting her stress down and her body being able to heal. He wanted a baby just as much as she did. He promised Jasmine they would be okay. Having signed a contract to acquire distribution in two more counties, he had every reason to believe they would be. In just two years from the time SnackJoys officially launched, the company was bringing in enough revenue for Israel to quit his part-time job and focus on pushing business even further. He now had five full-time employees. Things were going so well. Israel believed they would continue to soar and Jasmine did too. And her research was paying off. She found a supplement that helped sooth the inflammation in her body and she was always researching and adding natural elements to her regimen. She was starting to get relief from some of the symptoms. Things were looking up all around.

Three months after Jasmine quit her job, there was a snag in the system. A new company offering cheaper products came for Israel's distribution in a few of his districts and some of the schools decided to go with the cheaper company. There was no way Israel was willing to lower his prices and take a pay cut across the board. It would set a trend and show his clients and other competitors that he could be bullied. He knew his pricing was fair, he trusted the relationships he was building with his clients, and when the consumers began complaining about stale and low-quality snacks, the clients who left, would be back. But in the meantime, business suffered.

Israel told Jasmine they'd have to cut back. She knew the drill. No expensive date nights during the week and no fast-food for a few months. But this was something different. Jasmine wished there had only been a small dip but it was more like an avalanche. Money dried up fast. Israel had to pay his employees to keep the company going as he worked to get his actual products in more grocery stores so he would not have to rely so heavily on school vending machine sales. Quickly, they went from tight finances to the threat of eviction, and termination of healthcare was on the horizon as well. Jasmine's emotions took over. She tried to be supportive but she was shaken to her core.

"Baby. I know this looks bad. It feels bad."

"I don't like this. We are supposed to be on our way to stability. Starting a family. And I need health insurance." Jasmine was scared and she could not hide it.

"This is all a part of entrepreneurship. There will be ups and downs. Most companies don't even turn a profit in the first five years. We have surpassed that. This is a hiccup. Roll with me."

"But what are we going to do? I no longer have a job to help make ends meet."

"Don't worry. I will get a second job again if need be. And you know me. I will get three and four jobs if I have to."

"Oh yes," Jasmine laughed.

Remembering the time he got hired at Taco Bell and worked there one full day before landing his new property management job. It was right before they got married. As suspected, his job did not transfer from Las Vegas with his hasty move, but he chose to move back to California anyway so they could begin their life. He was not willing to enter their marriage jobless. She smiled at the memory as she cuddled up next to him.

"We will be fine," he said as he hugged her tight. "We will be just fine."

Jasmine tried to stay positive and not nag. Although she had quit teaching, she decided to go back to school to pursue a second bachelor's in creative writing. She loved the work she did with We Write the World and their student newsletter project immensely. She hadn't realized how deeply connected she was with writing, storytelling, and literature. It felt natural and like the perfect addition to her healing journey to further her knowledge and perfect her craft through higher education. And all the writing kept her busy. That along with researching health remedies and trying new healing recipes. Doctors said she would be on prescription drugs forever to keep the inflammation down in her lungs but she still wanted to use natural healing as well. Nonetheless, no matter how busy Jasmine found herself, worrying about her and Israel's finances still took up a huge chunk of her time.

As their finances continued to take a downturn, Israel kept his promise. He picked up a job working nights as an after-hours apartment manager. With their schedules flipped, never seeing Israel and feeling alone became a new issue. They barely had two hours of awake time together each day. And Israel's second income was still not enough and finances continued to dwindle. They had to cut back even more. Anything extra had to go, including Jasmine's natural supplements that were not covered by insurance and her organic diet. And again, Jasmine found herself feeling sluggish and faint. Her lungs were inflamed. She found herself in the doctor's office *again* getting faced with the decision to get intravenous injections. Last time they declined the drugs but this time she considered it. She was done fighting. The natural route was hard and slow. She wanted to feel better, not just for a few months. She thought, maybe the doctors were right. Do the IV drugs for a year to see if they stop the disease quickly and then pick up the natural supplements when her body was more stable and they had more money. The insurance would help with the cost, and she wouldn't have to burden Israel asking for yet another thing they could not afford.

Israel came home from a long day and greeted his wife with a tired kiss. He hated the long hours. Having to be "on" all the time was mentally draining. Jasmine knew he was tired and barely wanted to bring up the conversation of the infusions to him but she had no choice.

"Babe?"

"Yes?" He said, one eye open.

"My numbers have been way off. My lungs...They want to put me on the chemo injections."

He straightened his body and opened both eyes. "The same injections that could cause blood or bone cancer?"

"Yes," Jasmine said.

They knew the risks. They also knew the possible benefits. Treating autoimmune disease with chemotherapy was a common medical practice. The idea was that killing the body's immune system would allow it to stop attacking vital organs and hopefully cause the body to reset itself, putting the body into remission. Sounded pretty straight forward but for many, the treatment did not even work. And it took away the chance to have children by over seventy-five percent, hence the egg harvesting, another expensive procedure, not covered by insurance. They did not want to risk their chance to birth a biological child.

"Babe. We have had this discussion before. But I am here to support you. I want you to live."

Jasmine wasn't sure how to take his answer. He hadn't wanted her to take the chemo in the past and neither had she, but she was tired of the health rollercoaster. She needed a solution. Some peace.

Jasmine decided she would go on a three day fast to clear her mind and really hear from God. She'd done seven days with just water and even a fourteen-day fruit and juice fast. What was three days?

Day one, Jasmine woke up, prayed, and headed to school with her gallon of water which would be her only sustenance for the day. Prayer and the word of God would be her daily bread. Jasmine prayed as the hunger pangs churned and read her bible when she heard the rumbling of her stomach. By 10 am, she was so hungry that she literally felt like she would die if she did not eat. She had never been so hungry in all her life. This hunger was different. It caused Jasmine to feel faint, like she would pass out if she did not eat immediately. Jasmine prayed and asked God for forgiveness and promised to continue with the fast the next day. She said a prayer of thanks as she finished the last bite of her breakfast burrito, grateful there was a cafe next to her class.

Day two started off just as successful as day one with the intention to fast but unfortunately ended the same way. This time Jasmine made it to noon before the relentless hunger returned. Jasmine was so thrown off while sitting in her class feeling as if she were going to pass out.

Come on God. I'm fasting to hear from You. I need clarity right now. For my health. For my future. Why isn't my fast working?

Jasmine couldn't even make it through class. She rushed to the student center to get food. She scarfed down the chicken nuggets and fries and cried as she broke her fast day two. *I'm so sorry God,* she silently prayed. She knew she probably looked silly crying and stuffing her face at an alarming speed but she couldn't even help the tears. Too much was going on. Her emotions were high. Life was intense. As the thoughts of life, Israel, her decisions, and his company, all swirled in her head, Jasmine felt her stomach lurch and barely made it to the bathroom before losing the contents of her stomach.

Relentless hunger and now vomiting? Jasmine decided she was going to call her doctor and make an appointment because these could not be good signs. She knew ulcers could rise up when on one of the meds she was taking, so she wanted to check on it before it turned into something else chronic.

She woke up on the third day wondering if she should even fast. She decided she wouldn't call the hospital but just go as a walk in. She got a pregnancy test out because although her doctor had *sworn* her to use protection and not get pregnant as she waited for her health to stabilize, Jasmine knew, "Are you pregnant?" Would be the first question they asked her as protocol and she wanted to have a confident "no!"

They kept a box of pregnancy tests under the sink like most newly married couples, just in case, so it was not unusual to have them on hand even though they were not actively trying for a baby. Jasmine took the test with ease because after three years of marriage she was definitely a pro. She went on brushing her teeth and as she was humming her favorite worship song "As the Deer Pants for the Water," a plus sign caught the corner of her eye. She gasped and almost flung her toothbrush in the toilet. Jasmine had figured out her mystery. The soul crushing hunger that had almost brought her to her knees was her baby letting her know to keep the meals regular and tasty.

She flew in the room and tried to hand the positive pregnancy test to Israel while shaking him awake.

"Wake up Israel!"

"Huh?" He huffed trying to wake himself enough to understand what was going on.

She stuck the pregnancy test in his hand and held her breath.

"You're pregnant," he said rubbing his eyes.

"Yes…pregnant."

"You're pregnant!" he yelled as he hopped out the bed. He grabbed her up, hugged her, and they jumped up and down.

Israel was bursting with joy and surprisingly so was Jasmine. The joy that rushed over her surprised Jasmine. They had just recommitted to no more slip ups during sex. They admittedly hadn't done their best to avoid pregnancy upon their first warning, but when the financial issues hit, they became sticklers. To get pregnant when they were really trying to do the right thing, was truly an unexpected occurrence. So many thoughts rushed through Jasmine. She had two paths she could let her mind take. Think about all that could go wrong or pray, trust God, and expect everything to go right. Israel's utter euphoric state made it an easy decision. The Fords were getting ready to welcome baby Ford!

Chapter 34

The conversation flowed effortlessly between Nikki and I. Her ideas for the theme song sounded amazing. Gratefulness overwhelmed me as I sat listening to her and I couldn't help but smile even though it began to hurt my cheeks.

I felt my fears about Israel tagging along dissipate. He seemed to be enjoying himself. He discussed SnackJoys' latest distribution acquisition with Kendu. I knew I shouldn't care, but I was also grateful he was able to share his love while I shared mine.

"Well, we are set then!" Nikki exclaimed. "I will have a track laid for you before this week is up. You tell me what you think. Honestly. Hold nothing back. Please! I want this to be perfect for you. I'm too excited!"

"Me too," I agreed. I was over the moon.

"Honestly, I'm being a little selfish," Nikki said as she cozied up to Kendu.

There they were again with their sensual embraces that would make anyone blush. These two had a blazing chemistry. You could feel it in the air. The tenderness in Kendu's gaze made my heart ache. Israel used to look at me with such admiration. I missed my husband.

I asked "How so," intrigued by her confession.

"Okay so enough business chat. Let's talk looooove and marriage!" Nikki livened up.

Both Israel and I looked at one another briefly and then looked back at them.

"I'm so excited and honored to be a part of this project becaauuuse," she said drawing out the word as she made a drum roll noise with her utensils. "We will have a little one next year that will be sure to tune in. So sorry if my ambition is a little selfish."

"Wow! That makes it even more special. Congratulations," I said genuinely happy for them.

"Yes, congratulations man," Israel shook Kendu's hand.

"We are still new in this thing! So, we know adding a baby will shake things up. We've only been married for eight months," Nikki revealed crinkling her nose.

I guess she was waiting on judgment from us. I had none. And I really had no answers for them. Everything I thought I was doing well clearly wasn't working. But I wasn't going to admit it sitting at the dinner table with strangers. I liked Nikki but I didn't know them like that. Israel glanced at me. I thought I saw a look of solidarity. I hoped he was on board.

Grasping for something relevant to say, I decided to stay neutral. "Almost a year. Time sure does fly. I can tell you that," I said with a nervous laugh.

"Help us out. How long have you two been married?" Kendu inquired.

"Eleven years," both Israel and I said in unison reminding me that our connection was undeniable.

Kendu nodded his head and continued speaking, "Okay so how about you give us five things you've learned in eleven years. A cheat sheet of sorts. Tag team style! I know marriage is about teamwork. I'm sure you two have it down."

*If only you knew...*And just like that, my stomach was back in knots. My hands moved to rub my temples but I stopped myself and put on a smile instead.

"Um...I-I-I can give you the five. Israel isn't much of a talker," I stuttered trying to save face.

"Aw come on Israel," Nikki prodded.

"Okay," Israel replied blandly.

"Hmmm," I had to ponder where to start. I prayed silently for the right words. "I guess one of the most important aspects of marriage is perception. The way your spouse experiences you needs to be discussed. You can truly think you're giving your all but if that's not how your spouse sees it...or can receive it, conflict and resentment can arise," I said somberly.

"Perception..." Nikki pondered.

"That's good," Kendo chimed in.

"And expectations. The two go hand in hand." My words became stronger as I continued. "Your spouse cannot read your mind. Communicating what you need is important," I added.

I was ready to go on when I heard Israel clear his throat. "Resilience. You have to be resilient in your marriage. Things, some unfathomable, may come. You can't crumble when the winds of life blow."

"Oooh Israel and Jasmine. These are so good! You don't have to go on but if you have more, we'll take it," she said as she softly kissed Kendu's cheek.

"You both may change," Israel said looking straight at Nikki and Kendu. "Physically, health wise... there's *no* guarantees. Of anything! Accept that things. Will. Change. Don't even bank on them staying the same."

Israel's words were true. And real. Too real. Both Nikki and Kendu looked worried as he finished speaking.

"But even though things change and dynamics can change, the vows you took never change. The expectation of commitment does not either," I somberly finished, completing the requested five. "Love is a choice. Actively choose one another daily."

I was startled at first as Nikki and Kendu both began clapping.

"Bravo you two! Now that was solid," Kendu said.

"Yes guys. Thank you," Nikki spoke humbly.

"We appreciate you pouring into us. We truly believe marriage mentorship is so important to the health of a marriage."

Marriage mentorship. The irony, I thought but said, "No problem." Israel remained silent.

"Uh, oh! That's my jam baby," Nikki said to Kendu as an unfamiliar but groovy R&B song began to thump through the sound system.

Nikki nibbled on Kendu's ear lobe between words. This chic was insatiable. I felt the heat rise on the back of my neck. I couldn't tell if it was embarrassment of feeling like I was spying on their intimate moment because I couldn't look away if I tried, or the passion I'd been holding back from involuntary abstinence threatening to burst through my pores.

"My lady," he said as he held her hand, lifted her to her feet and grabbed her by the waist in one smooth motion. I wanted to shout out, "You go boy!" He was so smooth with it.

"Come on Israel, take your lady for a spin."

I almost yelled, "Oh no, it's o-"

I paused mid-sentence. My heart almost stopped when Israel stood, extended his hand, and looked me directly in the eyes. For just a moment, I saw a glimpse of the love we shared when we said, "I do."

I grabbed his hand. He held me gingerly and I felt secure. He felt so good. Too good. What was I doing?

What was *he* doing? This couldn't be good for both of us. But this felt *so* good. *Dang it!* I knew I was in trouble. I sank into his embrace and let myself enjoy the moment. Eleven years with this man. He was my first love, my best friend. I was trying my best to get over him so he could move on and be happy if it wasn't with me but in just an instant of his touch, I felt all the feelings return. I laid my head softly on his shoulder as I let him guide me in a slow two-step. I couldn't help the warm tears as they spilled from my eyes. He lifted my head and looked me in the eyes once more. I saw his pain. And I know he saw mine. He closed his eyes as one tear escaped. I wiped it away with my thumb. He kissed my head. And we continued our slow dance. No words exchanged. The best communication we'd had in months.

The ride home was quiet at first. We clumsily parted after the song. We excused ourselves, citing early morning and work schedules. I had done a good job of keeping conversation with Israel centered around the kids lately. He was uninterested in anything else from me. But tonight, after the dinner, and the dance, I felt moved to engage.

"Can I ask you something?"

He was silent for a few moments before responding, "Yes."

"Have I not followed your lead? You said I made the transitions hard. I can own that. But once I got my bearings, each time we had a major shift, I was right there with you."

"Yes, you followed but it was the road to you following me. It was always bumpy. I messed up along the way, but once we landed there was always an elevation. But it happened in spite of the pressure I felt from you. I felt pressure from the world. I felt pressure from myself because the weight of family is heavy and then I felt pressure from you too. Sometimes, I felt like you didn't ride with me during our lowest moments. You walked in fear and it just didn't help."

"I did my best Israel. I felt like I was drowning. SnackJoys took off so quickly. It felt like you left me. You started making all these decisions without me. I felt blocked out so the transitions were hard to handle. But before everything blew up, I had my hand in everything right along with you. Heck, when you were in school, I even wrote papers for you."

"You did not write papers for me," he scoffed.

"Oh yes I did. I aced your macro-economics midterm and wrote your cheat sheet for your business marketing tier-one course. Don't play."

"You did?"

"Yes," I said laughing. "You had fallen asleep. I finished it and went to my mom's to print it for you at 3:33 am. You almost cried when you saw it the next morning."

"There you go. Exaggerating…"

"Okay, okay. Maybe not teary but grateful."

I thought I saw the beginning of a smile as his memory kicked in. "Wow…I do remember that." Yep. I saw a smile creep up.

"And before the kids, I did all the house work, cooking, errands. And worked full time. I tried to take on as much as I could so your focus could remain on SnackJoys. Even with my health going up and down. That counts for nothing?"

"Jasmine. I never said that counted for nothing. But it doesn't erase the fact that you were hard on me during some of those downs."

"Israel did you hear me? It felt like you left me. You shut me out. You started hiding what you were doing with the money from me. Then next thing I know, boom a new building. Or bam, tax lien! Many of the times I lashed out or was hard on you, I was just trying to get into your mind. Or get you to see me. I felt shut out. So, I felt like I had to nag to get you to talk to me. And tell me *something*. *Anything.* I went from handling everything to having to rely solely on you and you weren't always honest. You know how important trust is to me."

"I wasn't dishonest with you. I kept certain things from you to protect you."

"Izzy. That's the *definition* of dishonest," I said with a chuckle trying to make sure our discussion didn't shift into argument territory.

"Okay. I see what you're saying. I was dishonest but you seemed so fragile and like things would break you if they weren't perfect.

"That's so unfair. I was in my early twenties when we got married. Yes, I needed time to mature. And the health issues took my breath away, literally. I never expected it to be something so devastating and present in our lives. I can't get grace from you?"

"I tried to forgive you. I didn't know what I was signing up for or the magnitude either. And yet you still managed to make me, the person who chose you despite your sickness, feel like anything I did for you was never enough. So, excuse me if now that you've realized it, I'm not overjoyed about your realization overnight. I'm not willing to just jump in line with *your* timeline. I have prayed. And tried to move on. This didn't happen overnight. The hurt feelings don't just go away."

"It was enough. I was grateful. I apologize that I didn't convey that enough. You were not the issue. I just wanted and needed wholeness. And validation. I tried my best to convey I felt like I was alone and drowning. And you supported me financially but do you realize you weren't *there* for me? Emotionally. You said we wouldn't get lost in the diagnosis but you acted like it was invisible. I couldn't even talk about the pain, emotional or physical, and you acted as if I should just do all my wifely and motherly duties and be quiet. I needed to talk and express and process and I wanted to do that with you. I felt silenced. For years."

"Yeah…I hear you Jasmine. That was never my intention. I didn't know you felt that way…But it doesn't take away the fact that I'm tired. And I just don't know how to move past it."

We sat in silence with the weight of his words. He was right. I had to let him go through his process. I so wanted this process to end with a resolution for us *tonight* but he said he prayed. He was still distant and for the most part detached. At times mean and very grumpy. God had a tall order. I had to accept the fact that maybe this was the end for us. I wanted to rest on my prayers but it was getting harder by the day.

I silently prayed, *God, heal his heart.*

"Thank you for writing my papers," he said looking straight ahead as he drove.

I smiled and shook my head but kept my hopes down and the surprise of his acknowledgment out of my voice. I stayed looking straight ahead too.

"You're welcome," I said softly, the memory of our dance floating in my head and heart.

Chapter 35

Jasmine age 27

Israel and Jasmine were too excited to share their news with their parents. They began making calls immediately without even knowing how far along they were. One by one they heard the screams of joy from ecstatic family members. It felt amazing to have family just as excited as the couple.

Jasmine headed to Dr. Melbourne's office as soon as the doors opened. Jasmine expected a reprimand. She remembered the warnings to refrain from getting pregnant. To Jasmine's surprise, her doctor was excited for the couple. She expressed her nervousness but sent Jasmine to the gynecology department after a sincere hug.

Jasmine's nerves hit an all-time high as she entered the office. She wasn't sure what to expect. Her doctor told her she would need to see a high-risk obstetrician. Jasmine did exactly that and through the grace of God was blessed with an amazing doctor.

Jasmine and Israel felt like they hit a stride. SnackJoys was doing great, expanding, and adding employees again. Jasmine was acing her coursework and nesting. They each had an extra pep in their step due to the excitement of the pregnancy.

And the best part, beside normal pregnancy related activity like hormones and round ligament pain, Jasmine's health felt amazing. It felt miraculous. There was a shift in her body as if pregnancy was helping her heal from the inside out. Her mind was completely blown. Symptoms were dropping off left and right. She wouldn't have believed it unless she lived it so she was grateful for the opportunity to experience such a phenomenon.

One day Israel came home with a brochure for a beautiful space. Jasmine was impressed. She loved the layout and how the fixtures and amenities flashed "new money." Everything was beautiful.

"Wow! These are dope babe! Are these homes? Condos?" She asked rhetorically. "One day. One day," she said not waiting on an answer.

She continued fumbling with her latest crochet project. She hadn't crocheted since she was a little girl. She tried to pick it up again when she quit her job but the lung disease had affected her in such a way that even the usually soothing movement of crocheting or knitting could cause her to become exhausted. Since being pregnant, that was not the case.

Though she was physically able to crotchet, her skills had not progressed. Anita would have been shaking her head if she were in the room. Saying Jasmine was out of practice was too kind. She would definitely need Anita's help to make the blanket believable. Because after all these years of watching her mother crotchet beautiful full-length blankets, aprons, sweaters and scarves, Jasmine hadn't progressed further than a chunky, one chain link scarf. She wished she could instantly snap and create a blanket for the baby.

"Today. Well...in the next two weeks."

"Huh? What do you mean?"

"I got us one of these luxury town homes!" Israel was beaming with joy.

Jasmine didn't want to crush his spirit but she didn't want a luxury town home. She wanted a luxury house. She liked those fixtures and that new money look but she wanted it for their home that their baby would grow up in. She wanted a backyard. And a driveway. She was ready to dig in to a town and grow roots.

"Israel...I thought we were saving for a house."

Jasmine knew it would take a while with one income but Israel was making great money and SnackJoys was growing by leaps and bounds after their setback. She was willing to wait for a home. She thought that was the path they were on. They were finally stable again. She didn't want to rent a more expensive place. She wanted to save more until they could buy a home.

"That will come in due time. Just trust me," Israel responded. Some of his excitement was deflated. "This is a better move for us financially. We need to prove we can handle reoccurring payments in this price bracket and have a record of it on paper. As an entrepreneur, that paper trail will be important for us. We have the income. Now this move will make us look better on paper since you're not working. And it's so close to my job."

"But I love it here. And I'm close to all my friends. And our church. And you work so many hours. I will need a support system when the baby comes," she said.

She'd really come to love her little town. She had created her own schedule and daily routine and she was sad and scared to have that shift right at the time she felt she needed it the most with a new baby coming. The remainder of Israel's excitement faded from his eyes. He sat on the couch, defeated. Here he'd done something he thought she'd love and she voiced concerns and asked a million questions before simply saying thank you. Jasmine finally took notice of his changed mood.

"Babe, it's beautiful to me. I love it and I love you!"

"It's five minutes from the office Jasmine. I will be adding two to three hours to my day if I remove the commute."

"Wow. Five minutes?"

Israel commuted daily to and from the warehouse he leased to house SnackJoys. He acquired the lease for a steal through a family friend but the cost of the commute was not cheap, though it wasn't a monetary cost. Each work day he drove forty minutes to work which wasn't so bad but in rush hour traffic that forty minutes could double but usually tripled which forced Israel to stay later and caused Jasmine to spend way too much time alone. He needed the warehouse. SnackJoys would not be as fruitful as it was had it not been for the expansion, but leasing a property that far from their residence was tough on both of them. Moving closer was the best option.

"Yes! You know that commute is the bane of my work day. It's really killing me. This way, I will have more time to spend with you and our baby," he said scooting close and rubbing Jasmine's protruding belly.

Jasmine took a moment to think about it. Jasmine did not want to move. Especially pregnant. But what choice did she have? Here she was crying over friends and a church that she could commute to once a week. Israel had to commute five times a week. Sometimes more. As the boss, he really had limited down time. She knew the choice was obvious. She just wished she actually had a choice. The lease had been signed already. He did it without her even knowing. A surprise. It felt more like an ambush. Hopefully their next move would be a forever home that they chose together.

Chapter 36

I pulled up to my garage and felt a jolt of excitement to see Israel's car there. I hadn't expected to see him. He rarely worked from home and I was supposed to be picking up the children anyway, but my sister offered to pick them up and let them spend the night. I was so grateful for the break. I'm sure Israel would be too. Things had been peaceful since our night out. There were no hints at reconciliation but he wasn't so angry. This made me happy and dare I say, lifted my hopes.

I walked in to hear Israel on the phone so I quieted as not to disrupt his call. He needed it quiet when he worked from home. I sat at the foyer and slipped off my shoes. Before I made my way to the couch, I sat there just relaxing and hoping he'd wrap the call up quickly so I could watch my show. And then I heard it. Relationship voice. You know that low, sensual, voice people use when they're talking to that special someone. The relationship is fresh, you want to sound sexy and intriguing. It had been years since I heard it but I knew.

"Israel!" it was evident by the look of shock that he hadn't heard me come in.

"Hey. I'll call you back," He quickly disconnected his call.

My furrowed brow said all I needed to say but you know that didn't stop my words. "How freaking *dare* you? In our home?"

"Jasmine. You already know what it is. I told you I was filing for divorce."

"Yeah, and you haven't filed anything! And you're living here. At least respect that before you're talking to other women in my face!"

"See. I've tried to be cool with you and just stay here until I could get my place together but I already see I've gone about this wrong. Here you are cooking, washing my clothes, praying for us to reconcile. I see and hear all of that. You're not getting it. I'm gone!"

"Yes! Clearly. Because you are crossing lines I never thought you'd cross."

"Jasmine. It's over. I'm moving out the end of next week and I've already had the paperwork drawn up. You will be served a few days after I move. I was going to talk to you about it this weekend. I didn't want to tell you like this."

"Israel, save it! I just cannot believe you!"

The rage hit me like a Mack truck. My heartbeat fast. I refused to faint again. And I refused to cry again, especially in front of him. There was so much I wanted to say, but what was there left to say in this moment that would do a bit of good? In all this, I hadn't blamed him or brought up what he did. But now as I grappled with the fact that he held me at an impossible standard, the decision of divorce on his part felt so cruel. In the past, whenever he would bring up grievances, I admittedly would bring up my own. But when he told me he wanted a divorce, I ate it and I worked on myself. He just pointed at my wrong, not even acknowledging how he mishandled my emotions, repeatedly faltered in providing, and left me alone to handle the home and kids on a regular basis, further aggravating my fragile health. And now he'd already moved on? Pissed was an understatement.

I walked to our bedroom and closed the door. I let myself cry bitter tears. I didn't pick up the phone to call anyone. He told me this was coming. His actions told me this was coming. I sat with my pain and cried. And then, I got up and sat at my desk. I let myself coast on autopilot. I had a deadline to meet and I was letting nothing stop me. Not even the shattering of any hope I had left that he'd change his mind on ending our marriage. Coach Myra warned us just last night that everything, anything, would come to derail us. We had to focus if we wanted to make it to the other side.

I desperately needed to be on the other side. This pain, realizing that I had to let him go fully, threatened to suffocate me but I chose in this moment to let my work heal me. Oh, how I needed my work to heal me!

I tried writing the finishing touches on a few new stories I wanted to submit to Jada and Matt for consideration. We had a pretty solid lineup so far, but I wanted to stay ahead. I felt a deep sense of gratitude to have something just for me again. But who was I kidding? This is what I always did. I didn't allow myself to sit in the grief long enough. This level of pain can't be scoffed over.

The sting of Israel's latest announcement lingered as I tried to stay focused. And my tears would not stop falling. Visions of him with the other woman ran rampant through my mind. And our conversation with Nikki and Kendu kept popping up in my mind. Just a few nights ago, we sat giving marriage advice to newlyweds while our marriage was ending. Tears spilled from my eyes onto, my keyboard. I wasn't getting any work done in this condition. Before I knew it, the kids would be out of school. I had to get myself together.

I opened the app on my phone to begin reading my homework assignment for The UnboxedMe course. Our task was to jot down the ways our emotions were holding us captive. I took my journal from my desk drawer and began to write. My feelings almost poured out quicker than I could capture them.

As I turned the page to continue, I heard, *allow your heart to break,* before I could write another word. I took a deep breath and closed my eyes. I let the tears fall and relaxed my shoulders. Trying to keep it together the last few months had been weighing heavy on me. I was holding on and walking around feeling tense while still trying to embrace the newness of opportunity and restoration God was bringing to me personally. Today, it wasn't working. *You keep looking back,* I heard the Holy Spirit utter. It was that simple. I kept looking at Israel. I knew I could not make that man do anything. My mind understood that, and as my heart began to get the memo, my resolve began to crumble. Right at the brink of a breakthrough in my career, while my personal life was crumbling. Good. And bad. Always together for me. Wrapped up in the same gift box. It was such an ugly reminder to be careful, no matter what. It was also annoying.

"God! Help me to trust You?!" I sobbed.

Give me all of you.

God wanted my full trust and my submission. He wanted me to surrender everything. I thought I had. But as much as I'd like to say He had it, it would have been a lie. There were places in my heart closed off to God and I didn't know how to let Him in.

And you didn't let Israel in, I heard the Holy Spirit nudge.

I never let Israel in completely. How could I trust Israel if I couldn't trust God? I was aimlessly searching for something to fill a space that only God could and Israel became a casualty of that pursuit. And as a result, I was not living but waiting to live. Waiting to enjoy. Wondering why I had to suffer. God could literally say "no more" at any time but yet, I suffered year after year with sickness and pain. And the deficit eventually destroyed myself image and how I was able to see myself as worthy and even beautiful so I stayed in a marriage that was no longer serving me.

I never imagined this would be my life. I felt robbed. My best years had been taken away. I got sick in my prime right when I was getting ready to enjoy life. I studied the word. I believed God would heal me. I had faith and I was faithful to pray and proclaim what I wanted to see take place. I trusted God would heal me supernaturally like Pastor Bill taught. I had seen so many others healed. But for me, nothing. The anger I harbored seemed righteous. And it prevented me from fully enjoying my life with all the obstacles and pain.

I will restore the years. I heard that loud and clear.

"Restore the years God. Help me believe in your healing power again."

Do your part and trust me to do the rest.

I knew what God meant. It was time for me to clean up my diet, bust out my remedies, clean my vessel with the best nutrition I could afford, and then stand. Israel had made his final decision and I wasn't going to lay down and die because he chose to leave.

"I choose to live," I firmly stated as I opened my computer to begin working on my stories again.

Chapter 37

Jasmine age 27

"Ladies, thank you for helping me pack all this stuff up."

Angel's side eye reached Jasmine's gaze before they both laughed.

"Please! As if you thought you'd be left to pack with your delicate pregnant self."

"Shut up," Jasmine said laughing. But within seconds her laughter turned into sobs."

Ebony, Angel, and her sister Anise surrounded her on the couch as Jasmine wiped her tears with the tissue Angel handed her. Anise rubbed her back.

"It's okay Jax. What's wrong?"

"I'm just going to miss this area. Stupid hormones! I'm a thug! I don't cry this easily."

"Child…these hormones and this pregnancy has turned you into a whole pregzilla."

"Angel!" Ebony and Anise said in unison as

Jasmine smacked Angel's knee.

"Ya'll know she's been tripping." They all laughed.

"Jaxxie, don't worry. You're only an hour away from us. That isn't so bad. We will be there when you need us. It will just take us a little longer. This is a new beginning for your family."

"You're right sister. Thank y'all for packing this place up. So many memories."

"We will make new memories in your new place," Ebony reassured her.

Jasmine knew they were right, but she still cried leaving her little community and safety net. She would miss her church. She'd been there since college. But she had to admit, having a beautiful, brand new never before lived-in state-of-the-art home sure made the landing soft. Israel should have led with that when he introduced the move. He would have been met with less protest.

Angel and Ebony continued to pack while Anise loaded the car with smaller items. She planned to drop Jasmine off so Jasmine could pray over the home before any of her baby's items got there.

"Why Jasmine. It's a NEW home. Ain't no spirits," Angel teased to a retreating Jasmine.

Jasmine was so grateful that in a turn of events Israel was able to secure a new build instead of the condo. They were moving into a new two story, colonial style home. She got to choose some of the finishing touches like shutters, paint colors, carpet, and the backsplash design. Th best part, they had a spacious backyard for their baby to play in. Jasmine was elated.

"It's necessary to *me*."

"You are *so* saved Jax," Angel quipped as Jasmine made her exit.

"One day you will be too," Jasmine tossed behind her shoulder before shutting the door.

Anise decided to drop Jasmine off and head back to

finish packing. Jasmine was grateful for her sister's willingness to make the hour-long trip both ways. Jasmine could get used to how people went above and beyond when you were pregnant.

Jasmine entered the beautiful arched double doors of the house and was met by new couches, end tables, and the rocking chair she wanted.

"Surprise!" Israel said as he greeted her with flowers.

"Oh baby," Jasmine said as she grabbed Israel's neck and kissed his lips. "Baaaaabe! You did gooooood."

"Thanks babe. I'm glad you like it."

"I don't like it, I loooove it." Jasmine said as she kissed him again. He deepened the kiss and whisked her away to their new king-sized bed.

Israel was so perky in the coming weeks leading up to Jasmine's due date. Now that he ditched his commute, his stress level was down. Jasmine could see the benefits immediately. He was crushing his goals at work and he came home in time for dinner. Sometimes he made it in early enough for them, to catch a movie or go out to a restaurant. They were both on cloud nine.

Jasmine went fully mommy mode. She threw herself into planning a gender reveal, maternity photo shoot, and baby shower. She wanted to celebrate the arrival of her baby girl with a bang. She was so excited to be a mother! Pregzilla was in full glory.

Carleigh René Ford entered the world bright eyed and ready for all the hugs and love Israel and Jasmine could give her. As the doctor lifted her cute little almost chocolate body for Jasmine and Israel to see, Jasmine squealed with delight. Carleigh was the spitting image of Jasmine and had Israel's rich skin tone. She had won the family bet of who Baby Ford would favor.

Jasmine and Israel were so in love with their little girl. She was a welcomed surprise. Her arrival highlighted their love in such a deep way. The fact that they came together to create life made Jasmine fall more in love with her husband and feel connected to him on a deeper level. And you could see the love between the three of them. Israel was in awe of his baby girl because she was an extension of him and he was in awe of and had a profound respect for Jasmine as he watched her go through the miracle of childbirth.

Each of them knew their life would never be the same. Jasmine was determined to fight to stay alive for her perfect little angel. She and Israel had definitely been blessed.

The first year of Carleigh's life was a blur. It flew by but was filled with so much. Milestones, so many firsts, family outings, baby's first trip on a plane and so much cuteness. But the year also had a dark side. Just three months after Carleigh's birth, that health elephant was bobbing so loudly it couldn't be ignored.

Jasmine began to feel all the progress her body made during pregnancy fade away as if someone was siphoning her life force with a gigantic straw. It was surreal. She had been naive to believe the healing that occurred during pregnancy would last. She realized this is what the doctors had been referring to. During pregnancy as your body harbors the fetus, the autoimmune attack can go into remission. That is what happened for Jasmine. She hoped it would stay at bay. And for a while it did. She felt empowered and like a true gangster the moments and weeks after birthing her daughter but the triumphant feeling did not remain. Within three months' time, her energy was beginning to tank, her hair began to shed and thin at an alarming rate and she was losing weight, which she thought was normal at first. But it did not taper off after a few months as her research suggested it should. When she began to feel the familiar aches, pains and the heavy feeling in her lungs, Jasmine knew exactly what she was dealing with.

These health developments made the year tough. It made her relationship with God difficult. It made enjoying her baby a challenge. And it tested her marriage in such a layered way that it was hard for Jasmine to explain. She knew none of the health issues were Israel's fault and that he worked hard to provide but dealing with her health issues overwhelmed her and when he got home from work, he'd often have to cater to her and the baby, leaving no actual downtime for himself. Jasmine knew it felt unbalanced but was unsure how to handle it when she literally had no energy to do anything after a certain point in the day. Each day wasn't terrible. And if she were honest, her sweet daughter brought her so much joy that many times her smile was enough to ease the pain, but she had to admit she felt cheated. Year after year there was something major for her to deal with. Something chronic. Life and death. Her doctors were sure to always be firm with her that she could easily and quickly slip into the "you may not make it sis" category at any time with the nature of her condition. The weight of that was crippling at times. But she had so much to be grateful for too. And that's what she fought for. On her good days she tried to make them her best, and on her bad days she resigned to be grateful to be alive, even if the circumstances weren't ideal.

One thing was for certain, Israel was doing his thing with SnackJoys and having the money to buy everything she needed to start back on her health and wellness journey gave Jasmine much needed security.

While searching for an after-pregnancy detox,

Jasmine came across a video about supernatural healing. The words of the preacher jumped out at her and caused her heart to beat fast.

"God wants you healed! And he heals, supernaturally. Today!" Pastor Bill proclaimed in his country drawl.

Jasmine had heard of instant healings before but would God do it for her? She began praying and asking God to heal her supernaturally and instantly. She inhaled teachings on supernatural deliverance and decided she'd expect God to heal her supernaturally while taking her natural measures in her own strength. She was starting over but she knew what to do and this time she felt like she had an extra boost. The new level of faith and teaching and understanding she entered allowed her to begin to see God as a loving father instead of a dictator. A father wants you to have every good and perfect thing. You don't have to beg for what's rightfully yours from a good parent. So Jasmine amped up her prayer life, restocked her health arsenal of organic foods and natural supplements and continued the fight for her life in prayer.

Chapter 38

Jasmine age 29

"Be healed in Jesus name! By HIS stripes you are healed," Jasmine heard Pastor Bill pray and she felt her heart racing.

She had watched so many sermons online and now she stood steps away from him ready for him to pray over her. Jasmine heard about him raising the dead. She heard about him praying for arthritis, AIDS, lupus, cancer, dead babies in utero; the testimonies were endless and many were healed instantly! The more she watched him; the more Jasmine believed it could happen for her too!

For the past year and a half, since randomly finding his first message on supernatural healing, Jasmine had become a student. Some would say fanatic. She downloaded podcasts and listened to them in the car and around the house and fell asleep watching his YouTube videos. She pulled away from her diet and supplements and focused only on praying, proclaiming, and believing God for her healing. She knew God had originally told her to focus on the health aspect too, but Pastor Bill constantly reiterated how God didn't need any help. He said you could diet and take medicine if you needed it to stay alive but he had seen God heal and he trusted God alone. Jasmine wanted to be healed instantly and she removed all perceived hindrances to her faith which included diet, supplements, and prescription drugs. She felt like she could only choose one thing to focus on without her heart being divided. She decided God would heal her supernaturally, instantly, and it would be through the laying on of hands from Pastor Bill.

Jasmine got Israel to listen to the videos too. He wasn't into it like her but he thought the theology was pretty solid. Pastor Bill taught straight from the word of God and that's all that mattered to Israel.

When Jasmine broached the subject of taking the family down to Georgia to visit Pastor Bill's church, Israel was on board. He wanted her healed too. Jasmine felt relieved. She just knew Israel would complain about spending his vacation at a healing conference.

With the hotel and plane tickets booked, Jasmine felt giddy. Pastor Bill was about to pray for her and she could not contain her excitement.

The night before their trip, Jasmine listened to Pastor Bill's latest Sunday sermon. She was preoccupied as she half listened and half packed the last suitcase but then he said one thing that made her stand at attention.

"I've failed you all if you think you *need* to hop on a plane for *me* specifically to lay hands on you. God is the healer and He does the work. I am just the vessel. You can be healed from anywhere. Just believe."

Jasmine had heard him say that countless times. She knew he believed that but she knew that for her it was different. The way she found him was so divine. It had to be God. It was so random, but right on time. He was her answered prayer. So, though her heart beat with apprehension, she kept packing. She wasn't the only one in her family in need of healing. Israel had a work injury that required surgery and Carleigh had reoccurring thrush that just wouldn't go away. The way Jasmine saw it, she was going to get healing for her entire family.

As they sat in service, Jasmine felt all types of emotions. What she did not feel was peace. She felt anxious and ready for it to be her family's turn. As they stood in line to wait for Pastor Bill, he walked away from the line and grabbed the mic.

"Okay so I've been teaching you all day at this conference. How many of you know you don't need me to pray for you for you to receive healing?" Most of the hands went up. Jasmine slid hers in the air but her heart was set on him praying for her anyway. "Well, now it's your turn to get activated and practice what you've learned. If you'd like to pray for people, come to the front of the church and stand across this way," Pastor Bill said as he motioned for people to stand across the stage in a line from left to right. "And if you're in need of healing, you walk past the healers and each person will pray and lay hands. We will do it assembly line style. You'll get the virtue flowing from each person as you walk by!"

Jasmine's heart sank. And Israel had to slip out of line to go change Carleigh's diaper. This was not how it was supposed to work. Jasmine felt herself internally panic. She had not flown her family across the country for this. Pastor Bill was *right there.* He *had* to lay hands and pray for her. He had to heal her.

I am your healer. The Holy Spirit spoke softly to Jasmine. She heard His words but she had to let Pastor Bill pray for her. In her mind Jasmine knew he was right, but she had been praying, proclaiming, believing and *not* seeing. What else was there left to do? She was still sick! And faith without works was dead she reasoned. Having Pastor Bill pray was her works. She was so tired of not receiving what she knew was available to her from what she read in The Word.

Jasmine followed protocol and walked down the assembly line but she felt her heart breaking. As each person prayed for Jasmine, she felt no different and it broke her resolve. Jasmine replayed all Pastor Bill's teachings as she received prayer in the ministry line. He had said faith is not seeing or feeling but simply believing even if you still have symptoms. You stand on God's word. He said God is the healer and not man and reiterated that the healing did not come from him and not to put stock in his prayers. Jasmine was in denial that she had willfully ignored all that. She ignored the pull of the Holy Spirt to stick to her supplements and diet because that is what God told *her* to do. She ignored the fact that God never told her the only way she could get healed was if Pastor Bill prayed for and laid hands on her. But as she walked down that line, the realization set in. The tears streamed down her face and soaked her shirt.

As Jasmine made it back to her family deflated, she saw Pastor Bill speaking to Israel. He had his hand on Israel's injured shoulder. Jasmine briskly walked up to them.

"This is my wife Pastor Bill."

"Well, hello there."

"Hello Pastor Bill! I'm so encouraged by your ministry."

"Thank you. Your husband told me you're from California. Y'all came such a long way! How can I pray for you?"

Jasmine almost sank to his feet with relief.

"Please pray for my healing. Full body healing."

Pastor Bill nodded and grabbed Jasmine's hands.

As he prayed, Jasmine felt warmness release from his hands and flowed up her body. She could not believe it.

"Healing virtue flow from me *now* in the name of Jesus! Be healed in Jesus name! Amen."

"Amen," Jasmine said.

As they boarded the plane right after service, Jasmine still felt a sense of wonder. Israel's pain in his shoulder had gone away instantly and Dr. Bill hadn't even prayed for him, only touched him.

"The pain is gone?"

"Yes. It feels a little stiff but it's so much better. No more pain."

"Wow," Jasmine said in awe.

Over that next week, Israel's shoulder gave him no more trouble. He had been healed supernaturally. Instantly. Carleigh too. That same night Jasmine went to apply the medicine to the thrush in her mouth and nothing. All the white spots were gone. Pastor Bill had played with her hands and cuddled her cheeks. And healed! Jasmine felt excited. If God did it for her husband and daughter, he could do it for her. She left that building with hope.

But as one week slipped in to two, nothing. She still felt all her pain and every symptom. Jasmine's discontentment grew. How? And why would God heal her family but leave her stranded? Jasmine could not comprehend it.

"Israel, how did it not work for me but worked for you and Carleigh."

"I don't know Jasmine," he said with sadness in his voice.

"I'm so confused."

"I believe God will heal you. Don't give up."

"I won't," Jasmine said non-convincingly.

She was dispirited. But she couldn't say she was confused. She knew she'd exalted Pastor Bill and his ability over God and in the end, she had only hurt herself and bruised her faith.

Chapter 39

Jasmine age 30

The sun peeking through the window caused Jasmine to stir. She listened for the sound of tiny feet or infant murmurs. Satisfied with the silence, she basked in the fact that she had a moment to herself. Today was a milestone, her thirtieth birthday. Jasmine tried to muster up some joy. She knew life was a gift. Even if it currently sucked.

She lifted her arms and said, "Thank you for my life." Her tone was low, almost a whisper. She tried to mean it. The sentiment had a hard time reaching her heart.

Three months prior this day, Jasmine had lost her mother Anita to a heart attack. Two hours after they pronounced Anita dead, Jasmine went into labor with her second child. She experienced an intense, agonizing but thankfully rather quick birth. The aching from having lost her mother just two floors down, moments before she was made to push, caused each contraction to feel like daggers ripping through her body. Four hours after her mother was pronounced dead, Jasmine and Israel's second daughter Mariah was born. One of the best and the absolute worst things that could ever happen, happened to Jasmine on the same day she brought forth life. Good. Bad. Together again.

Jasmine had been ecstatic to find out she was pregnant. After the Pastor Bill fiasco, she needed a win. And just like with Carleigh, her disease responded well to pregnancy. The pain stopped and her body's brutal autoimmune attack of itself ceased. Everything was normal until half-way through her pregnancy. The lung fibrosis stayed at bay, but her cervix threatened to give out at week 26. The cerclage was too risky so they administered several drugs intravenously to stop contractions. But for the rest of her pregnancy Jasmine was on strict bedrest. When at week 29, the whole thing happened again with dilation to six centimeters, Jasmine was admitted to the hospital.

"For how long Nonnie?"

"Mommy, until I deliver. I'm on strict bed rest too. They only let me walk a few times a day."

"Look at my grandbaby already causing a scene," Anita chuckled.

She sounded so weak. Lupus had attacked her heart. She was on her own version of bedrest and couldn't make it out much. They both were grateful for FaceTime as that had become their main mode of communication in the last few weeks but today, Anita made it to the hospital to see about her baby.

"This baby needs to chill!"

"Yeah, just like her mama chills so well," Anita side eyed.

"Whose side are you on mommy?"

"The truth. And history. They never lie. And I birthed drama queens so that baby's behavior is fitting,"

Anita chuckled softly.

"You sure did Mommy."

"Jasmine," the sudden seriousness in Anita's tone caused Jasmine to stiffen.

"Yes Mommy?"

"I love you. And I'm so proud of you. I want you to make sure you live your *best* life. No regrets! I know you have the challenges with your lungs," she said as her voice broke. "But go on the trips. Even if you have to walk slow. Even if you have to rent one of them scooter thangs to get around. Go!"

"Okay Mommy," Jasmine whispered in tears herself. "Mommy why are you saying this?"

"No regrets. You *Live*. And you stop faking and hurry up and have that baby. We all know you in here so you don't have to clean up all that pretty house."

"There you go mommy!" They laughed and hugged. They let the hug linger.

Anita gave the best hugs. Jasmine had no idea that would be the last time she physically touched her mom.

Three days later, Israel came in for his daily visit with Carleigh, but she was not with him.

"Hey baby, where's my baby?" Jasmine spoke in a cheerful tone.

"Jasmine. I need you to stay calm. Mommy is here."

"She is? Yay!" Jasmine lit up with surprise.

Israel spoke firmly. He needed her to understand. "Babe. Listen." Jasmine's confusion caused him to soften his tone. "She was brought in by ambulance. Anise found her nonresponsive. We don't know all what's going on. They are working on her now."

"What?!" Jasmine ripped the covers off and moved remarkably fast for a woman 35 weeks pregnant, weak from bedrest.

Israel stopped her before she ripped the IV out and

stormed out to see about Anita.

"No Jasmine."

"LET ME GO ISRAEL!" She screamed.

Fighting against him was useless, but still she tried. After realizing he wouldn't let go, she allowed herself to melt into his arms sobbing. Her water broke as he held her.

"Doctor!" Israel held her close, not caring about any bodily fluids that spilled on him.

The untimely death of her mother and best friend rocked Jasmine to the core. The stress of having two children under three years old. The tumultuous years of marriage that tried to flourish under all the weight of these issues but seemed to be drowning. The recent expansion of SnackJoys' operation which took more of Israel's time from the family. The ups and downs of the finances because entrepreneurship is unpredictable. And her wavering health. She prayed and believed for healing but yet, here she was, still struggling. Jasmine was finding it hard to feel truly grateful because she felt like her world had collapsed.

Jasmine let out a sigh.

She took in as deep a breath as she could, lifted her arms again and repeated, "Lord...thank you for my life," this time a little louder, as she allowed tears to stream down her face.

She couldn't believe she had to enter her thirties without her mother.

There's no back to reality when you lose your mother. Some things you think can be restored or revived if given enough time. When you lose your mother, there's a hard stop. A page break. There's nothing you can do beside move forward and establish your new sense of normalcy because life will never be the same. With two kids and a husband, she had no other choice but to forge ahead.

Jasmine thought of her two beautiful children. Carleigh was her spitting image in looks and attitude. She was the sweetest little chocolate girl with gorgeous dimples. She dawned the same bouncy curls as Jasmine and her personality was just as lively – her laughter infectious. Just thinking about it made Jasmine smile. And even though the sadness of losing her mother wanted to engulf Jasmine, the special gift of Mariah's arrival would not let her succumb to the whispers in her mind to give up. She had no choice but to fight.

And Israel. He needed her. He couldn't raise the girls alone. And he deserved a present partner.

Thirty years old. Not old. No longer a kid. Adult in every sense of the word. But she felt so vulnerable. So new.

And so much life ahead, Jasmine heard the Holy Spirit distinctly.

She lifted her hands again, willing the love of God to comfort her and bring her joy back. "God, THANK YOU for my LIFE!"

Jasmine felt something flicker in her heart as she thanked God. Right then and there she decided life was going to have to square up and fight if it wanted her to stay down. She had taken some devastating blows but she kept swinging and she was determined to see the light again. Of course, losing her mother hurt deeply. It always would. But she chose to latch on to their last conversation. She chose to live and to make herself and Anita proud with her life. Jasmine had her own beautiful family to live with and for in the memory of Anita.

So, she cried her tears while lifting her hands and said at the top of her voice now, "I AM GRATEFUL FOR MY LIFE. THANK YOU, GOD!

Chapter 40

Jasmine age 30

"Hello," Jasmine greeted Angel.

"Hi Jax," Angel said in her cheery tone.

"Hey girl!"

"Heeeeeyy," Angel sang. "So…how's it going?"

"Angel… what?! Because we don't even do small talk."

"Girl…."

"Girl!"

"Sis…"

"Angel?!"

"I just wanted to check on you. I see you've been posting a lot on social media lately and I just... wanted to make sure you are good."

Jasmine withdrew from social media while pregnant with Mariah. With the complications, she wanted to keep a low profile. But after Anita died, social media became like a diary. Her release. She wasn't able to grieve like she wanted. She *wanted* to lay down somewhere to eat chips and watch endless episodes of "Martin," or "Moesha," drinking root beer with no other responsibilities but she had two kids who needed her and a husband. She had to find a way to grieve and still be present so she began to share on her social media again. Writing was her therapy.

The posts weren't long but they were contemplative, raw, and deeply personal. Some of them were funny memories but most just relayed her experience of grieving the loss of a life pillar and welcoming new life simultaneously. That best and worst trend continued to show up in her life.

"I'm good. It's hard, but I'm making it. The posts are just therapeutic."

"Hmm… well about that."

"About what?"

"Have you thought of going to therapy?"

"Yes...I actually just mentioned it to Israel. But my posts aren't an indicator I need to go."

"I'm not saying that."

"Okay…"

"I found a really good therapist after losing a few of my coworkers back-to-back and it really helped me."

Jasmine rolled her eyes so hard before saying plainly, "Angel you are bullying me. I am in bereavement."

"I am not!"

"Are!" Jasmine said, in full brat mode. *I can write statuses on Facebook and still be grieving well,* Jasmine thought. *Wait...*"I can write statuses on Facebook and still be okay *Angel*. I'm fine. I'm grieving in my own way. It's a normal release."

"Jax. Hear me. I'm not saying it's not normal. I'm just saying it would help to get some additional support. Just think about it. I don't think there's anything wrong with how you're processing. I just wanted to add to your healing process. You've been through a *lot.*"

Jasmine had, and she appreciated Angel for acknowledging it. And Jasmine knew therapy could help but she was offended at the idea that writing on social media meant she wasn't dealing with all this muck in her life. She thought she was handling it like a boss actually. The amount of strife she'd faced made her shudder if she thought too long on it. The fact that she could formulate cohesive sentences surprised her daily.

"I've been considering therapy and will consider it. Thank you," Jasmine said curtly.

"Yes friend. Just think about it. And if you need someone, I have a friend who just started her private practice. She's a licensed therapist. You two have so much in common. You're both moms of two young kids, same gender and around the same age. You're both married, Black, and Christian. Having the Christianity aspect combined with the mental health component will be amazing for you."

It actually did sound pretty amazing to Jasmine. She had just mentioned to Israel she wanted to try grief therapy. She wasn't opposed to therapy. She had gone to therapists before. She was literally offended at the suggestion that she wasn't dealing well and probably a little prideful that someone had the audacity to suggest it. But Angel was right, therapy was in order to help Jasmine cope with her mother dying and having a baby the same day. Jasmine just didn't want to give Angel the satisfaction of admitting she was right.

"Thank you," Jasmine said still tight lipped.

"I will send you her info. I love you Jasmine. I'm here for you. Don't go into your shell. Don't become a hermit."

Aghhhhhh, Jasmine growled in her head. She was annoyed and wondered why Angel was stepping on her toes.

"Bye Angel."

"Jasmine!" Jasmine stayed quiet. "Jasmine I know *darn well* you didn't hang up this phone!"

They both laughed.

"I'm not going to be a hermit Angel."

"Jasmine don't try to play me. That's what you do. When life gets tough for you, you go in and you close those who care for you out. You try to deal alone and we don't hear about it until it's over. You don't have to do that this time."

The tears came instantly for Jasmine. Angel was right. Jasmine knew she couldn't afford to go this one alone. She needed to get all these feelings out in whichever ways she could whether it be therapy, writing, girl chats, beach trips, or shopping. Because she did not want to look up in ten years and still be in the same amount of heartache living the precious moments of her life as a memorial billboard of sadness at the death of Anita. That is no life worth living. That doesn't bring honor. It just feels like two lives are lost instead of the one. She already had enough obstacles hindering living her best life. She decided to take a state of perpetual grief off the list.

"Thank you, friend. I love you."

"I love you too Jax. Kiss my babies for me. I will talk to you soon."

"Talk to you soon."

As soon as they hung up, she received the text with the therapist's information. Jasmine called and made her appointment immediately then she stuck her tongue out and rolled her eyes at the phone. She still wasn't telling Angel she had been right!

Jasmine knew therapy would be amazing for her right now. She could start getting some normalcy back to her life, creating a schedule, getting time away from the kids to think her thoughts. Therapy could be her day! She could go to lunch after therapy, do whatever. There was so much she wanted to work on in therapy such as her marriage and communicating more effectively with Israel. They were just not as connected as they used to be and she wanted to help them get back to how things used to be. Their anniversary was coming up. Maybe they could reconnect then? Maybe this therapist could help her devise a plan.

Chapter 41

I sat waiting for the doctor's recommendation on which medicine I should take. I was happy to be off of all but one. I felt great! I hoped they weren't trying to add anything but the doctor seemed stuck on something. *God you are with me.* I prayed silently. She was giving off nervous energy but I refused to let that dampen my mood.

"Mrs. Ford…how are…you feeling?"

"I'm feeling fine Dr. Benson. Why? What does the blood work say?"

Dr. Benson scratched her head.

"Hold on Mrs. Ford. Let me get my attending because… I'm stumped. The head of rheumatology is here today. I'd like him to consult as well. I need them to look at this bloodwork with me"

For a moment I got nervous but then I remembered what God told me. *You will live. So live!* I was holding on to that word. I had no room to worry. I trusted God to restore me so I refused to become alarmed as I sat waiting.

Instead, I began humming the words to "Victory is Mine."

Both doctors came in and washed their hands.

"Hello Mrs. Ford. How are you feeling?"

"I feel great!"

"Sorry, I'm Doctor Nguyen and this is Doctor Kent. Can I listen to your chest?"

"Sure."

I took deep breaths in as Doctor Nguyen listened to my chest. Lately my breaths felt so normal. The heaviness and weight were just not there. As I walked in purpose my breathing continued to improve.

"Call pulmonary please Doctor Benson. Have Doctor Yasick come on over?"

"Doctor, what's going on?" I said with my nose scrunched.,

He looked bewildered as he re-hooked the stethoscope around his neck and placed his hands behind his head like he was surrendering to a cop. He let his hands fall to his sides and then brought the left one back up to scratch his head.

"Mrs. Ford, I want to wait until Doctor Yasick comes in. I don't want to say the wrong thing but your lungs sound abnormally clear and the blood work we got back this morning… This just isn't making sense."

Three more doctors and thirty minutes later and I was finally released. The doctors were baffled by how clear my lungs sounded and the results of my most recent blood work which told them I had no markers for inflammation or active autoimmunity. It was as if I had new lungs and new blood. They asked what I had done. I gladly told them about my natural supplement regimen that I had been strictly following and my daily affirmations and prayer. They were in a stupor.

"Mrs. Ford, supplements and diets don't cure disease."

"I know. God does," I said laughing. I had so much

joy.

"Wait Mrs. Ford. You don't understand. This is a miracle."

"I understand," I said, my eyes filling with grateful tears. "Thank you, God!" I began worshipping and thanking God right there.

I had been feeling so great lately. But I had no idea I would get medical proof of what I was feeling deep down on the inside. God had truly healed me? Me?! Just how He said He would! Just Him and I and my faith.

Just then, Dr. Melbourne walked in. She wasn't a specialist so they didn't have to call her but I'm glad they had. She had been the medical professional who walked this journey with me the longest. They ushered her in to look at the labs before I could greet her. She scrolled back and forth three times. When she turned to face me, her face was struck with tears.

"Jasmine," she whispered. She hugged me. "Thank you, God!" she cried.

"I knew you were saved!" I said laughing as I grabbed on tightly to her.

"Oh Jasmine. I have had one toe in and one toe out for a long time. But this is the evidence I need to know God is listening. He's real!" She let go and looked at me. She shook her head in wonder. Both of us were unaware what the other doctors were doing as we shared our moment.

"He *so* is Dr. Melbourne. He *so* is real," I said wiping away my own tears.

I almost ran out of that building. As the fresh air hit my face I yelled, "Thank you GOD for my life!" Not caring who looked at me strange.

The physical manifestation of the healing God had promised; every symptom gone; every deficit restored. I took in a deep breath that felt like it reached the depths of my soul. “THANK YOU, GOD!”

I stood amazed at all that could happen when you trusted God and followed His instruction. For years, I prayed for this and like a blink, things began happening.

In two weeks, I would go live for the first time on my show reading my books to thousands of people. In two weeks, I would get all dressed up with my children, and family for my launch party.

I needed this win. It felt so good to win!

Chapter 42

Jasmine age 30

"The look on your FACE when we pulled up to the 'drop off,'" Jasmine said using air quotes as they both doubled over with laughter.

They were at one of their favorite restaurants, Sparkie's Delight Brewery. It was an upgraded bar that served creative takes on classic American favorites. They stuffed their faces with Bavarian pretzels, blue crab and artichoke dip, Caribbean coconut shrimp, and grass-fed beef sliders, as they recounted Israel's reaction to Jasmine's big anniversary finale surprise.

Jasmine was elated that their trip was ending on such a positive note because the beginning was rough! Israel was present and pleasant but he seemed reserved. He wasn't letting loose like pre-fatherhood Israel. He wasn't bubbly. It didn't feel like a celebration. She'd worked so hard and she really wanted him to enjoy it and to spark some passion back into their friendship marriage.

Jasmine had several activities planned over the span of 4 days. The plan she devised with her therapist Roberta was to not sit idly by and wait for Israel to plan something and then be sad or upset if it was whack. Roberta told Jasmine to switch the rolls and figure out what Israel could enjoy. Jasmine had fun choosing the activities.

First, they attended a Los Angeles King's game. They *loved* hockey. Those fights were epic. They were able to sit just a few rows from the ice. That's the closest they'd ever been. Next, they checked into their beachfront hotel and had drinks under the night sky. The beach was so peaceful. It was Jasmine's happy place and she felt like beaches were romantic.

On night two they had a dinner cruise. That was a total bust. The food was awful, Jasmine forgot to bring her coat so she was freezing on the boat which caused her lungs to react and resulted in a nagging cough the whole dinner, and to top it off, a woman tripped and spilled her wine all over the front of Israel's pants. They were stuck on the boat for two hours, freezing, wet, and hungry.

"Agh!" Jasmine yelled as Israel opened his door and got in. He had gotten her in to the driver's seat so she could quickly heat her hands with the heated stirring wheel, and then came around and got in the passenger side. The burst of cold air shocked her.

"What?"

"That cold air."

"Jasmine, you're so dramatic."

"I am," she said laughing and grateful the heat was now on full blast. "What a night."

"That was terrible and I'm hungry. no more dinner cruises please?"

"No more. Promise!"

Jasmine started the car on the way to their suite.

"Ooh honey. Popeyes. Let's get some of those

biscuits! Can you forget your diet for tonight? I just want to be."

"You know what babe," Jasmine said thoughtfully, "Let's just be! I like the sound of that my love."

"Me too," he said holding out his hand. Jasmine grabbed it and drove carefully with the other.

That night when they got in their room, they peeled their clothing off, showered together, and spent the night watching movies and eating the crunchy chicken, biscuits, fries and sweet tea just like old times. And they laughed. They hadn't just hung out, in so long. It felt great.

They spent the next day hanging out again. They went to the movies, ate lunch at a local sandwich shop and did some shopping at the mall. Jasmine kept waiting for them to click. She couldn't put her finger on it. They were talking, they were laughing, and Jasmine felt the wall that had been between them falling down.

They ended the night before the finale activity with a candlelit dinner. It had been three days of just the two of them. It had been months since they had alone time which was understandable with where they were in life, but she knew for their marriage to survive they needed alone time. She was hoping this was the beginning of a new trend; a sort of rekindling of their snuffed love flame.

"So, what's the big finale you have planned that you're keeping so hush?"

"You want me to tell you? You said I could keep it a secret," Jasmine said grinning.

She wanted to tell him *so* bad. She loved surprising people but was terrible about keeping surprises.

"Is it bungee jumping?"

Jasmine's heart started beating fast.

"No. It's not bungee jumping." And it wasn't.

"Alright. Because I'm *not* doing that. Anything else should be fine."

Jasmine almost choked as she sipped her water. She

hoped those words were true when they pulled up to her surprise.

The look on Israel's face when they pulled up to the meeting spot and he saw the truck with the basket for the hot air balloon in it, was priceless. Jasmine had never felt threatened or unsafe with Israel but on this day, she was a little nervous. He looked like he wanted to hurt someone. She looked down at her hands avoiding his gaze.

"How much?"

"Five hundred."

"But you know I don't like heights."

"I mean I know you wouldn't want to do a free-falling activity. Like bungee jumping…" His stony glare caused me to stop talking.

"This is crazy. *We,* don't do this," he said pointing to their skin. Jasmine stifled her laughter. She knew when to hold it.

"But babe, this is different."

"You already paid?"

He was looking for an escape. He was clearly cheaper than he was scared though because after Jasmine's nod of confirmation, he went radio silent. He refused to waste that much money but he was not happy. He couldn't even look at Jasmine. Jasmine felt so bad. She knew she had messed up now. He had *just* started feeling loose and like old times after three nights together and now he was actually angry with her. This was not in the plan. She thought he'd be surprised and a little nervous and that they'd laugh it off and continue the fun they'd been having. She was scared too of the new experience, but she hadn't expected him to completely shut down.

Jasmine tried to make small talk but Israel didn't have much for her. He sat quiet on his phone as they rode in the van to take the take-off zone with two other couples who'd be their companions on the trip.

They watched as the crew worked to get the

balloon inflated. It was a pretty cool process. One Jasmine enjoyed watching on her own because Israel was sitting down stewing and she wanted no parts. She wished she could make herself invisible but decided to chat with the other couples instead.

Israel was looking more jittery by the moment. She kept sneaking glances at him. He was sweating and pacing by then. He looked angry at first but as the crew got the balloon in the air and their basket was almost ready for loading, he looked more nervous than anything else. He came and stood by her but still wouldn't say a word.

"Okay ladies and gentlemen. I am excited to say we will be airborne in less than ten minutes! We have to go over some rules and procedures."

The pilot went over what they could expect on their trip and possible dangers and the rules. Jasmine wished they could skip that part. He was making it worse. She thought she would faint when he said on his last trip the basket landed sideways and started giving instructions on how to brace for impact. Israel just looked at her and shook his head.

They finally entered the basket and Israel got in the middle! Jasmine couldn't believe it. He left her on the outside nearest the edge. She couldn't help her laughter. He looked straight ahead at the pilot and stood as still as a statue in the center of the basket. The basket began to ascend and it was amazing. The flight was so smooth. The sites were beautiful. Within five minutes, Israel was laughing and cracking jokes and laughing at himself for tripping so hard. Jasmine felt so relieved.

"Yeah babe. I was tripping," he said before polishing off his half-pound Colby and mushroom stuffed burger.

"I was over there on my phone googling fatality and accident rates of hot air balloons. I was contemplating how many hours I had to work to make that five hundred."

They both laughed.

"I'm so glad you ended up liking it babe. You looked like you wanted to kill me!"

"Jasmine that was so amazing! I just feel good! That was so dope. I feel inspired. Did you see those houses?"

"Yes! The neighborhood we passed over at the end was beautiful. You saw those kids waving? Ha ha!"

"Yes. How cool for hot air balloons to be a fixture in your neighborhood."

"Right! So cool."

They chatted and laughed and it truly felt like old times. Jasmine was pleased with the end result of their anniversary trip and looked forward to more times like these with her Izzy.

Chapter 43

My weekly one on one with Coach Myra ended up taking on a more personal tone. I hadn't known Myra before taking her course, but after knowing her for a few months, she had grown to be a person I deeply admired and looked up to. So, when she asked me what was holding me back from reaching my full potential when I had opportunities knocking at my door, I did not hold back.

I learned early on that you don't just share your private marital business, but I had grown to trust Myra. I truly felt she would speak life into the situation and pray.

"I reached out to Roberta because my husband wanted a divorce and I felt lost. She directed me to your course because she felt like I was too wrapped in my husband's identity. I got into your course and amazing things have been happening ever since. But honestly, it's hard to enjoy without my husband."

I felt a relief as I revealed what I had been holding. God truly met us in the UnboxedMe course. He revealed, pruned, encouraged and left us with tangible work that would take us to the next level and heal the places that were hindering us from making forward progress. Each of us was blown away by how God met us regularly. But as I stood on the brink of my success, something felt like it was blocking me and Myra had picked up on it.

"I knew you were having marital issues. You briefly mentioned it. But I didn't know you were facing divorce. Have papers been filed?"

"Yes," I breathed deeply. "Last month he had me served. I dropped the papers off to the lawyer yesterday. He has also moved out."

"Wow. That is a lot to take in."

"It is. And I am trying to focus on myself. It is so hard to not long for him but I'm staying focused."

"What's the motto I live by Jasmine?"

"Focus on yourself?"

"Yes. I know it may sound harsh after you shared what you shared with me, but this is it. This is where you dig your heels in and you trust God. Didn't God just miraculously heal you?"

"Yes!" I said, tearing up instantly. I would be crying tears of joy over this for the rest of my life!

"God has you. You posture yourself as if it is done. Whatever you have asked Him for. And you keep going after the assignment He called you to do. Don't ignore your emotions but never let them stop you or lead you. How were the men healed?" she said referring to the lepers in Luke chapter seventeen.

"As they went."

"That was your hang up. That is what used to hinder you in your parenting, in business, in your marriage, and in your relationship with God. You miss your go, for trying to figure everything out to the very last step. Right now, you're going to feel pain. You don't know the last step nor how God can move in the last minute. But you have to keep going."

"I know. You're right. And I have been…"

"Jasmine. For over *twelve* years you suffered and in the span of *less than A FEW MONTHS* God healed you. Miraculously! You. Don't. Know. What. God. Can. Do. So, don't let your actions, or lack thereof, tie up the hand of God. When do we see God move?"

"When we are obedient and surrendered."

"You're right there. Your book show launches in days. Don't let the enemy steal this moment."

When I initially reached out, I wasn't sure about UnboxedMe but Myra's handling of me was exactly what I needed. She was like Angel, my mom, and a Gospel gangster all rolled into one. Myra ministered to me with enough firmness that didn't push me away. I was so grateful I said yes to taking her course.

That night, after my one-on-one, during class, something magical happened. When Myra asked us if we wanted to go off the book and share our hearts, each woman agreed. I asked them if I could read a journal entry and they encouraged me to share.

"Please bear with me ladies. I may cry. These words are from week one. So much has changed since then. Here goes." I cleared my throat before I began. "I have decided I am done living an unfulfilled life and I am ready and willing to do the work to change it. With a pending divorce, something in me has broken. I felt things brewing years ago, after my mother died. I felt the need for change but was stuck. I was more than stuck. I felt lodged down deep in a vat of quicksand. And I frantically tried to fix it in my humanity. The more frantically I moved and tried to work, trying to fix things on my own, the more stuck I became. I lied to myself, convincing myself I was leaning and trusting on God. I was praying and worshiping and reading my bible, sometimes. But I wasn't doing what it said and I was half doing what God said. I would hear the Holy Spirit and not treat the instructions as if they were from my father in heaven because I thought they were just my thoughts and would dismiss them or talk myself out of them. People spend their whole lives being mystified and begging to hear from God. And there I was with access and I treated the utterances and direction as mere suggestions to possibly follow. Of course, my life was a wreck. I needed God to complete a supernatural, miracle working power type of move in my life but I thought I could lead the ship. My enrollment in this course is my first step of surrender." I let out a sigh of relief as I finished reading. "And now I stand here seeing what true surrender looks like. I'm healed! I said yes and God met me. I'm so grateful. Thank you, ladies for journeying with me and imparting into me."

"My God," Darla said. We heard the sniffles.

Sarah followed up with sniffles of her own, "Jasmine has us all crying!"

And one by one, each of the ladies began sharing their testimonies and their struggles they'd overcome over the duration of the course. I was so grateful to hear their testimonies. We ended that night praying and worshipping. And I felt set to keep going and keep seeing the amazing things God wanted to accomplish.

Chapter 44

"You ready?"

What a loaded question Angel let slip from her lips. Petrified was more like it. Why did I agree to record the first show live? I worked for weeks with sound engineers and production, wardrobe stylist, hair stylists and makeup artists to develop the perfect looks for filming my segments. We already had four recorded, edited, and ready for release. But somehow Matt convinced the network the *first* segment needed to be live. I could just kick Matt right now as my stomach churned.

"Angel help. I can't do this," I said as I got up.

"SHE'S GOING TO RUN! BLOCK THE DOOR!" Angel yelled. Everyone within ear shot burst into laughter.

"You know what?! Can't even escape in peace messing with you," I playfully pushed her hand away from fixing my hair.

"I just wanted to make you laugh. I'm so very proud of you friend," she said as she embraced me. The hug lingered as we took a moment to bask in joy.

"Let go Angel. I will not cry and mess up this makeup. I cannot be puffy on camera. Anita will be giving me major side eye from heaven."

"Okay, okay," she said as she released.

"I'm ready," I sighed contentedly.

"You are beautiful. Today marks the start of something special."

Before I could respond, I heard my name and whispering behind Angel. Everyone was trying to be as quiet as possible on the set. They didn't have to be, but I appreciated the respect. I turned to see Nikki and Kendu and got up to give them a big hug.

"Are you ready?"

"Yes!" Nikki exclaimed.

"Awwww. Hi belly. You were not showing like this last week," I squealed.

"I know! You told me I would just pop one day. Well, here I is. Or should I say here *they* are."

My face lit up. "They?"

"Boy, girl *twins*!"

"Oh Nikki! That is just amazing," I said as we both jumped up and down.

"I'm so excited but right now, I'm excited for this venture! I've seen you work so hard. I'm so proud you get to shine today."

"Thank you. I'm honored you get to usher me in with those smooth vocals."

"It's gonna be a party! Let me go sound check. I will see you soon," she said as Kendu ushered her to the stage.

"Okay Jasmine," Matt said walking up to me.

"We have five minutes. Don't be nervous. You got this. Let's get 'er done!" He walked away before I could get a word in.

"He is something else," Angel said shaking her

head.

"Yoowho," I heard a familiar voice call.

"Myra. Oh my gosh. I'm so glad you made it backstage."

"I would not have missed this. Look at what God has done."

"Yes," I said tearing up instantly.

"No!" Angel tried to catch my tear with a tissue but she was too late.

She beckoned the make-up artist for a touch-up.

"These are tears of joy, for what God has done. Tears of restoration. Tears of healing," Myra spoke as my tears flowed.

"Oh enough Mrs. Myra," Angel said exasperated, wiping tears of her own.

The three of us shared an embrace.

I sighed contentedly as I sat for the second time getting my make-up done. Healing, restoration, and joy reverberated in my heart. Nothing could dampen this moment. I wondered how I would feel in my big moment without Israel and in this moment, I honestly felt too happy to consider any lack. God did too much for me to feel anything else but grateful.

Show time. I made sure my posture was perfect and I was looking in the correct camera lens just like we had rehearsed all week. I wanted to make sure I was ready before Nikki finished her last note. I tried not to dance too hard in my seat but her song was definitely a bop!

She sang about rainbows and roses, fairytales and creating anything with your imagination. I did not want her singing to end. But of course, it did and the cue cards began my countdown. I read along in my mind: *five, four, three, two, one.*

"Good evening ladies and gentlemen. Boys and girls come, gather in. Prepare for a literary treat tonight. Surly your imaginary world will shine bright. Relax, take a deep breath, and come in real close. Let this story entertain you from I, Jasmine Ford, your host. Welcome, to Story Time!"

I could see the cue cards scrolling but I didn't need them. I chose to memorize the welcome and my story. I would use them for backup if need be, but I decided to rely and bet on God. He hadn't let me down.

I began my fairytale, a modern-day twist on Cinderella. I wanted to make my introduction with a story that was recognizable by many before introducing my completely original pieces.

"Cinderella's heart was overcome with joy. Her stepsisters had finally done the right thing. They stood up to their wicked mother and let her stew in the shame of her actions.

"She hugged her stepsisters Laquisha and Dawn. She refused to let the ugliness she experienced turn her heart black. Cinderella gave them an open invitation to the palace and with that she turned on her heels never to return to her father's home.

"Cinderella was welcomed to the palace with the wedding/kingdom block party of the century. Her prince had spared no expense. He hired chefs from all over the world to cook an array of culinary delicacies including an entire room for desserts featuring vanilla and banana swirl, buttercream cupcakes – Cinderella's favorite treat, and endless flavors of cheesecake. There were dancers, singers, a band, DJs, jumpers, slides, face painting, a petting zoo, and endless activities for all the kingdom's citizens and children no matter their social status. The royal's children played along with the bread maker's children. The Prince knew Cinderella would be filled with delight! After the most beautiful ceremony, Cocoa village had ever seen, Cinderella and the Prince lived happily ever after. The End."

I read the last sentence and breathed a sigh of relief.

I blazed through my ten-minute segment with ease. It felt like I blinked when I was ushered from my seat at the production desk into the embraces, cheers, and congratulations from the whole production team. All the blood, sweat, and tears that went into the project and we were done. And it was perfect.

I found myself being whisked away to another room to put on some comfy shoes. Angel told me we were having a small dinner to celebrate the launch of Story Time. I should have known. Angel was known for her grandeur. This woman turned the back-parking lot of the studio into a party for me! There was a step and repeat, with my picture and sponsors for the show. The vendors had everything from vegan ice cream, fried Twinkie's, gyros, and turkey legs to fresh juice and a chopped salad truck. It looked like the county fair! And the best surprise, my book which compiled a set of my stories had arrived. I thought it was delayed and wouldn't make the Story Time segment launch! That's what Jada told me. Clearly, she and Angel were in cahoots. There was a whole table set up for me to sign and giveaway copies to the guests. My heart overflowed with joy. I would never forget this night.

"Angel! You did all this?" I said as the tears streaked down my face.

I was now safe to let them fall freely after taking countless pictures on the step and repeat.

We embraced as she let me cry in the comfort of her arms. Tears of utter joy and relief.

"I cannot take all the credit. Each of these vendors came together for free. And I didn't ask them. Israel put that all together."

"Israel? What? Why?" Confusion covered my face.

"Yes girl. And why not? He got it! He said he would take care of the food and he did that!"

"Hmmm." I found it interesting that he paid for *any*thing for my event when he'd significantly cut my allowance and stopped my access to all our joint funds. The divorce proceedings were underway, no need to be extra friendly and giving now. *Girl. Let it go. Enjoy your moment.*

I looked up and saw the SnackJoys table in the distance. I heard the little voices of my children asking for snacks. Israel hung in the background watching over the whole operation, thankfully not catching my gaze. I was not ready to have any real conversation with him. I would have my assistant send a thank you note and a tax form for his contribution just like all the other vendors (yes, I had an assistant now). I just wanted to just heal and move on.

Carleigh and Mariah got their snacks and then ran to me with their arms out. I embraced my blessings with all the strength I had. I embraced what mattered and what was mine today. Everything else, could wait.

"I will take three copies," a videographer came to my table with cash in hand.

"Oh no, books on me today! Especially for all those working hard."

"Nope, God told me to bless you. It is an honor for us to sow into the work you are doing. Please accept my gift."

I was taken aback by his words and gladly accepted the money. God was truly showing out. As my babies sat beside me eating their snacks, I happily signed all three copies. This felt *so* good.

Chapter 45

I loved the soft damp feel of the sand as I walked along the shoreline. I walked close enough to feel the warm water wash over my feet every now and then. That was my favorite part of the beach, the shoreline. And I could stay there for hours but I had to get back to the airport. Carleigh would have a conniption fit if I missed my flight and wasn't able to attend her very first dance recital. My phone was on silent so no one could disturb the moment I'd chosen to take for myself, but my alarm was set to alert me when it was time to leave.

"Whoo-hooo," I heard and it jarred me from my thoughts.

"Hey!" I waved at the ladies.

I began walking toward them, my dress flowing in the wind.

"Uh oh! Look at them thick thighs," Myra yelled.

We all laughed.

"I know you said you were going on your solo walk but Sarah has to leave early and we wanted to pray and dismiss from the first The UnboxedMe Retreat!"

We all cheered.

"This has been such an amazing journey to walk with you ladies. The work God has been able to do with this core group will change so many lives. It's already begun. We have a children's modern-day fairytales book published, a nationally syndicated Story Time, and a series of teen chapter novels coming soon," she said as she nodded my way. "We have national speaking engagements for moms and families and a worship album," she said as she squeezed my classmate Sarah's hand. "We have a book, workbook, and bible study course in its second cycle, with requests from several well-known pastors," she said as she beamed at my classmate Darla. "And my podcast is successful y'all. I just got my third advertiser and the course for fall and next spring are both sold out with a waiting list, my master class is filling up quickly so I may close registration early, and my membership group just reached ten *thousand* members. God did that!" Myra said as she lifted her hands. We all let thankful praises rise up.

"Yes!"

"Hallelujah."

"Thank you, God!"

"The UnboxedMe was more than we bargained for, in a good way. You ladies have made me so proud to do life with you. None of us will ever be the same. Wherever we go from here, I pray we stay connected. But remember this. Your obedience got you here. You already had the knowledge. You already had the faith. But you put the action behind what God told you to do and He made it pop! Don't go back. Stay wrapped in Him and stay open to Him. Stay vulnerable so you can go unbox and unveil those you're assigned to."

Chapter 46

I sighed as I opened my app to request an Uber. I still became a little sad when I did some things on my own that I used to do with Israel. Though I didn't feel like I was ready for a new relationship, I still longed for companionship. I loved togetherness. But day by day, it was getting easier. Though he'd moved on, I still didn't feel ready. And I wouldn't rush my healing either. I was excited about the prospect of a new love though, in the future.

"Jasmine!"

I looked up in time to see Israel rushing out of his car from the passenger loading zone.

My heart instantly began beating fast. My babies? Why had he come here? He hadn't even known my flight information or terminal. I hated how quickly my mind tried to flash into my old ways of thinking negatively first. *My babies are fine. Lord protect my babies wherever they are,* I prayed as I gathered my things to meet Israel halfway.

"Israel is everything alright?"

"No," he said but quickly changed his answer when he saw the concern begin to turn to panic on my face. "I mean yes. And no... the kids are fine."

"Whew. Okay. You scared me!" He just looked at me. I looked back at him, confused. Waiting. "Excuse me," I said as I cleared my throat. "I canceled my Uber because I thought it was an emergency. I'm tired and ready to go home so…"

"Oh yes. Yes. I'd like to take you. If that's all right."

"Take me where?"

"Home."

"Um…that's okay. I'm good. Just let me know what's up if it's not an emergency with the kids." I said as I grabbed my bags and headed back toward the airport.

"Jasmine. Please. I really need to talk to you. Let me take you home and we can talk on the way."

I sighed and turned apprehensively. He had me messed up. "Okay," I said solemnly. I would listen but I didn't have much to say.

Israel clumsily walked in front of me to retrieve my bags. *What in the world is going on?* This was becoming awkward. Fast! I felt myself catching an attitude. He had been so indifferent to me over the last year. Now he wanted to carry my bags and give rides without being asked? I wanted to give him major side eye. Thank God for growth.

We made it to the car and he fumbled to open my door while balancing the bags in one hand. When he finally got the door open, I saw a picture of us on his dashboard. *Oh, now he wants to feel nostalgic?*

"Israel...what are we doing? What is this?" I was immediately on the defense.

"Just give me a few words with you."

Stop, I heard God say. I took a deep breath and got

in the car. I couldn't stop the tears if I tried; those angry tears you cried when your parent jacked you up on the low and then said, "Stop crying before I give you something to cry about." I tried to quickly wipe them away before Israel finished putting the bags in the trunk and got in the car so he couldn't see. I was annoyed at myself too for almost letting an attitude surface. It was the reminder I needed that my humanity would always be available to play.

"Jasmine," he said and then paused. "Jasmine I'm sorry."

Something in me broke as I heard those words from him. The tears were now seemingly endless. He reached over for me and I flinched.

"Hold on Israel. I need a second."

What in the world? This man had done everything he needed to do to make sure I "got it" and understood we were over. He was full on dating while still living in our home!

"I can't do this!"

"Jasmine. I had no business trying to date anyone before we were officially over. I told them I felt confused and I needed to end things."

"*Them?!* Israel you cannot just do this! You're bombarding me. No," I said grabbing the handle to the door. I had to get out of there. I couldn't let him take all the peace that had settled over me at that retreat.

"Jasmine I was never intimate with any woman. I cared nothing for them. We did not have sex. At all."

"Israel, please. That doesn't absolve you," I said opening the door now. He could mail my luggage to me.

"Jax wait."

He tried to hold on to me but I gave him the look of death and he released me. I briskly walked away from his car. I had to get out of there immediately.

Israel got out too. He began yelling at the top of his voice.

"Jasmine, baby I was wrong!"

I shook my head and kept walking. "You sure were," I said in a low voice I knew he couldn't hear. "And I'm over it." *But are you? Is this not what you prayed for?* The Holy Spirit literally had bad timing. *Hey! Not right now. I need to process this. He doesn't just get to show up.*

And then I heard it. It stopped me in my tracks. I turned, stunned, as I saw Israel standing on top of his car belting the lyrics to Ruben Studdard's "Sorry 2004." My mouth hung open.

"Girl this is my sorry for, 2004. And I ain't gonna mess up no more, this year. I'mma take this one chance. And make it real clear."

"Israel, stop."

He continued. "I'm sorry for May."

"Israel, you are embarrassing yourself," I said taking rapid steps toward him."

"And I'm sorry, for June." He sang even louder and even more off key.

"You're embarrassing *me!*" I said closing the gap.

"And I'm sorry for July. In case I don't tell you."

"Israel," I said making it back to the car and looking back up at him with my hands on my hips.

"August, September, October, November tell you December I'm sorry 2004." He finally stopped singing but kept yelling even though I was standing right there. "And I'm sorry for today. And yesterday Jasmine. And all I put you through, all the years but especially this year."

"Hey guy! You have to clear out of here. No extended parking," an LAWA officer (the airport version of police) came now to warn him? After all that? I rolled my eyes. Couldn't even help it.

I got in the car without another word. The car rumbled and felt like it was involved in a crash as Israel struggled to get off the top. Those thirty-nine-year-old knees knew better.

"Jasmine. Say something."

"You don't get to do this Israel. When you're ready, you leave. When you're ready, you come back? You did a work on meeeee! And now you wanna sing a song and like a Hallmark movie we all buttoned up? What exactly are you sorry for?"

"God showed me."

"Showed you what? Because that apology, though sang movingly," I stated sarcastically, "Was pretty vague. Especially for someone who told me that our divorce, that will be final in two weeks, was all my fault," I said as the tears started again.

He tried to grab me again. "Jax I –"

"Israel please do not touch me. You no longer have those privileges."

"Hey man, I mean it. You have to move your car," the officer warned again.

Israel put his hands up in surrender and pleaded for me to get in that car with his eyes.

"Fine," I relented.

We road in silence several miles before he began speaking again.

"I was selfish Jasmine. And I know the breakdown of our marriage was not all your fault. I was so hurt and angry at God, and you, that I felt like your wrong outweighed mine. I felt like I busted my butt and you should be grateful with my leftovers, all I could give after those long days working. All the ups and downs of SnackJoys were tough on me. I *had* to make it work."

"Israel. I was right. There. With. You! And you shut me out! we started SnackJoys together!"

"I know! I didn't want you to have to worry about it anymore. I wanted you to stay stress free."

"It didn't work. That led to more stress."

"I see that… now. I didn't communicate well enough. I didn't let you know that I worked so hard because I was afraid to run out of money again and have you without treatments and your medicine again. Do you know the hit my pride took when after building for YEARS I had to use the money your mom left when she died to bail out my company after yet another hit? So, I just worked harder. And internalized my pain. I had to keep making money. So, I could provide for you."

"Israel we could make that money back. It wasn't your fault the company tanked. Miguel was foul and mismanaging the funds when you trusted him. I don't care about that money. I just wanted you."

"I see that. I just put my head down and kept working so I could make sure nothing like that ever happened again and that there were no more lapses in your coverage because...because," he was tripping over his words. "I didn't want you to die," his voice caught. "I didn't want you to get really sick again because I didn't have the right healthcare for you. That responsibility felt like it would crush me sometimes," he said, his voice breaking.

"Wow..." was all I could manage as the tears flowed. He hadn't been this honest with me, ever.

"Then when you would complain about a bill or something, it would make me so angry. I see you were just fighting for stability I lacked to provide. But I felt like you couldn't see me. I shut you out to protect you at first. But I kept you out even when you tried to help and that was wrong. And worst of all, I did not love you like Christ loved the church. I sacrificed but it had limits. Now I see what you mean when you said you couldn't trust me completely. I knew I wasn't giving my best in our marriage. I put everything into SnackJoys. I just wanted enough money to keep you healthy."

"You were afraid I'd die?"

"Yes Jasmine! You're my whole heart," He said unable to hold his tears back. He began sobbing. I was totally undone.

"Pull over Izzy."

He did. We sat there. Both crying. He held out his hand. I stared at it. Then at him. His eyes were pleading. I grabbed his hand. I closed my eyes and let the rest of my anger flow out through my tears. He let go of my hand and looked into my eyes. We embraced. It felt so good. We sat there holding one another and we both let tears flow.

"I'm so sorry. I've been awful to you this past year. I held the money from you. I acted like I didn't see you working on Story Time. God been kicking my butt over it too! He let me see how I hindered you from creating a solid family and community for us and the girls by isolating you.

"Spending time with the girls alone showed me how much I really didn't know them with being at work all the time. And I just got caught up in pride. I just couldn't bring myself to say anything once He began showing me ME. I went out and started talking to those women to ease my own guilt. I was so wrong," he said shaking his head. "But I surrendered and now God has been building me up. I knew I needed to come back to my wife. Together we have to fix it."

"I have a question," I stated as we let one another go.

"Why didn't you tell me you felt this way? About me dying. You've been so indifferent these last few years about my health and the burden everything was on me. it felt like you didn't really care."

"Pride. And part of me wanted to keep acting like it would just go away. I didn't want to keep giving in to my thoughts that you could die. I just wanted to work and make sure I could provide either way."

"Wow…that answers so many questions for me. And guess what? I suffered Postpartum depression after Mariah was born. So, I was intense but I really couldn't help it."

"I didn't know that," he said looking shocked.

"Me neither Izzy. But moving forward, we need to communicate and learn to be a safe space for one another. Let's invest in us. Let's go to counseling and have date nights. Let's go slow and see where this can go."

"Wait, you don't want to be with me? You want to date? This standoff between us should have ended months ago."

"Yeah, it should have!" I said as I playfully swatted at him.

"When Angel told me God healed you, I wept. I was completely broken. I hadn't realized how disconnected I was from Him. But when He did that for you?!" He couldn't finish his sentence as the tears overtook him.

"He did it for *us* Babe," I said, easily recalling my favorite pet name for him.

"Please forgive me," he whispered through tears.

Without hesitation I said, "I forgive you."

"I love you so much baby," He reached in for another hug.

I held up a hand to stop him.

"Aht, aht! I forgive you but yes, I want to date. And get to know who we are now. After the pain, after the trauma. And counseling. Those are my demands," I said with a sly smile, crossing my arms.

With a suggestive grin he asked, "Your demands?"

He quickly kissed me before I could back up enough. He kissed me again and let it linger when he didn't feel me pull away. Ooh that man was definitely on some new, new. He hadn't kissed me like that in…Wait. He hadn't kissed me like that ever!

"Hey! I don't kiss on first dates."

"Jasmine," he said laughing as he grabbed me up. "I love you girl. I missed you."

We held each other in silence and let our hearts begin to reconnect. We broke our embrace reluctantly when Israel's phone rang. It was SnackJoys. I moved nervously in my seat.

"Hold on babe. Let me quickly take care of this."

My heart beat fast and my confidence in our newness dipped a little. I wanted to believe Israel could change and prioritize us over work.

"Hey Jake, what's up?" he said as he grabbed my hand with his free one. I sat there twiddling my thumbs. "Call Joseph. He's the manager on duty and can handle any urgent matter. I am not on call today. Please follow the protocol's we have in place." I could hear Jake's exasperated tone, though I couldn't make out exactly what he was saying. "Calm down man. You won't get fired. And I know Jonathan can be tough but it's been a couple months now. When I'm off duty, I'm completely off unless it's level 5 emergency. Look in that manual we had drawn up. It will show when you need to call me. This is level 3 and Jonathan is completely capable. Please respect the boundary."

Israel finished up with Jake and wasn't even on the phone for two minutes. I was pleasantly surprised. He had systems in place to carve out family time. Whoa.

"Now that's sexy!"

"What?" He said looking confused.

"You ending a work call and letting them handle the urgent matter."

"I hired people I can trust and have systems in place to watch them like I can't trust them. I am here for you and my family. No more SnackJoys over everything."

"You go boy!" I said in my Gina from Martin voice. We both laughed. It felt so good to laugh with my man.

"Whew! I feel light! Let's go eat."

"Israel Ford," I said as I shook my head in awe of

God.

"Jasmine Ford?" He asked as he lifted his eyebrows with a hopeful glint.

"Always and forever," I said in a shaky voice.

"Always and forever," he said confidently.

We sealed our renewed commitment with a kiss.

Epilogue

"Get back here Mariah!" Carleigh yelled after her little sister.

"Nooooooooo," she said as she grabbed the last cheeseburger slider on the small table and ran away.

There were stations of finger sized portions of veggies, burgers, chicken strips, fruit, hummus, pita chips, cheeses, crackers, and chocolate sprinkled throughout the ceremony and they were constantly being refreshed by the wait staff. A perfect alternative for those who needed a lighter option instead of the family style dining stations placed in the center of each guest table. The southern feast, complete with fried chicken, fried catfish, baked mac and cheese, greens, yam-mallow (yams with caramelized marshmallows on top), black eyed peas, cornbread and yeast rolls, had their guests with "the i-tis."

"I'm glad they're the only kids here," Israel said.

"Izzy," Jasmine said laughing as she reclined against his chest.

They lounged comfortably on the white chaise.

Nikki Byard's beautiful voice could be heard crooning the sweetest love song over the speakers. Jasmine took a moment to let the not-so-distant memory of Nikki singing that exact song as she walked down the aisle to Israel tickle her heart. The vow renewal was heartfelt and beautiful and Jasmine could not have been more pleased.

Jasmine and Israel were so cozy in their piece of paradise. A small section of the venue had been roped off just for them. It was decorated so beautifully. Flowers that cascaded down the accent wall to create a weeping willow effect and a beautiful crystal chandelier were the main attraction for the space. They had food, comfortable seating, and a perfect view of the entire room.

"Oh, get a room," Angel said as she plopped onto one of the lounge chairs. "You need anything?"

"No. We're good best friend. You did such an amazing job. Everything is so beautiful. I'm so grateful."

"You deserve it. I love you two. Enjoy this moment. I'm going to check on the staff."

Jasmine could not believe she'd gotten her dream wedding. And best of all it hadn't been stressful. Their family and friends planned an elaborate surprise for Israel and Jasmine. All they had to do was show up and get dressed.

Jasmine gazed across the room. She saw her loved one's dancing and rocking to old R&B tunes. The picture booth was packed and Angel was chasing Carleigh and Mariah away from the peach cobbler bites.

Jasmine told herself she wouldn't cry any more today! As she reflected on the last two years, she was truly blown away. Her "yes" had done all this? *Yes!*

She remembered where her and Israel started, how they had to fight, and when she thought they wouldn't make it. She remembered how low they had gone. And she thanked God for his faithfulness, restoration, and healing.

Her "yes" moved things and started an avalanche of

greatness throughout her life. She said yes to writing again and her books were selling out of stores everywhere as Story Time gained popularity and viewership. She said yes to obedience in prayer and God healed her body of an eleven-year infirmity. She said yes to submitting to God and her husband and watched God restore her marriage after years of drought. All the years she thought God did not want to move, like He had forgotten about her. He needed her yes, her discipline, and her consistency. Her mind stayed blown over how He moved once she fully trusted Him.

She said yes to the type of wife God wanted her to be and she and Israel had never been happier. Each day with him was like a dream. Their love was growing sweeter and stronger. It was nothing like before. And that was a blessing. They were living an abundant life. They were living a life that would create a strong and beautiful legacy for years to come.

"Izzy?" Jasmine interrupted him as he hummed "Ribbon in the Sky," while stroking her right thigh.

"Hmmmm?" He breathed into her curly ringlets.

"Baby, Carleigh and Mariah aren't the only children here." Israel stopped stroking her scalp. Jasmine placed her hand on top of his and moved it to her stomach.

They made eye contact and she bobbed her head up and down.

Israel kissed her passionately. He got up, pulled her up and twirled her around!

"Mrs. Ford. You were a virgin at your first wedding and now you're pregnant at your second. You're getting fast in your old age."

"Oh, Izzy hush!" She said as she pulled him closer and laid a kiss on him that knocked his socks off.

"Alright y'all, wedding over," he yelled.

"Hush!"

"Baby! You having my baby again?"

"Yes honey. Yes!"

"We can really shut this thing down. I just want to go lay with you and love you."

"First, we dance. Then we play," Jasmine said with a mischievous grin.

"I can dig it. Let's go!" he said as he playfully slapped her on the butt after helping her stand.

With that, they cued the DJ for the turn up music and danced the night away with their children, family, and friends.

Acknowledgments

I want to first say thank you to God for guiding this story. I began writing this story in May 2019 and finished it in 30 days! Yes. You heard that right. This story has been written from beginning to end since May 2019. It started off as a prompt from the Holy Spirit, given to me by my dear big sister in Christ. The prompt was short, but the story flowed from there. It resulted in a 32k-word eBook lol. Not the full-length novel I attempted. My goal was 60k words, but the story was great so I went with it. But God clearly had other plans because I felt so unsettled. Like I felt like it was okay, but not great. So, I left the story alone for a while and then the Holy Spirit prompted my big sister again to tell me to finish! This time I had two weeks. I was like wait? Why are you rushing me God? Because the story had been sitting there looking at me, feeling like a weight in my pocket for two plus months. So, I did it. Two weeks, 55k words! I was blown away. But I still felt like it was unfinished. Same sister said FINISH! This time I had another two weeks. And when I finished this time, I felt like it was really good. Like yes, I can present this. And it was a whopping 65k+ words too! I felt so satisfied. I sent it for two rounds of edits that really helped me tighten up the plot and here we are. "And She Lived!"

This is the first novel I have finished, but I have been writing stories, poems, halves and pieces of "books" since I could understand sentence structure. I finished this and it feels amazing! I'm grateful to God for this story that I pray will inspire and free those who read it to live in their full truth no matter what life has to say about it.

To my sweet children we are finishers and we are great! Mommy did this for me, but for you too. You can do great things. You can do really hard things. No matter what happens, we can do great things when we keep God first. I looooooove you CeeCee and my sweet son! Y'all are the best kids OUT here!

I am grateful for my mom who loved me and taught me so much. I know she's smiling down. This is for you mommy! You always pushed me to do great and be great and I will keep it going. I know you're laughing at some of the antics in this story. Thank you for giving me your joy and your silliness on top of everything else you unselfishly poured into me. I carry your strength, determination, grit, kindness, and expensive, elegant taste in everything with me. I'm trying to adopt your feminine and elegant style of dress and your ladylike demeanor but it's still loading! Thank you for every sacrifice and your unwavering love. I will continuously honor your legacy with my life!

Daddy, I love you and Jody. Thank you both for all the prayers, encouragement, support, guidance, love and example of faith, determination, and strength. Thank you for showing me how to persevere and walk in God's strength while wounded. Thank you for your faith and belief for the supernatural and all the books you've blessed me with on my journey to sure up my faith.

This is a work of fiction but I want to acknowledge the journey that caused me to even have the ammunition to write this story. Yes, I am grateful for the journey. I am the best I have ever been in my life and it feels amazing.

Now here's where it's about to get tricky. I have 262 people I want to thank and I want to write something for each of you in this book but I feel like I will miss someone so I'm going to be brief.

Cherise, my big sister, we been down like two peas in a pod since I turned 18 and we stopped having petty fights lol. I love you!

Grateful for my little sisters Olivia and Joy. You are beautiful inside and out just like your beautiful mom Rita and this book is for you too. Evan and Miles, I love you little bros. Our whole family is great and will continue to accomplish great things.

Dad Flanagan and Mama Lydia, thank you for genuinely loving me and accepting me into your family and home. You're stuck with me forever. You too Justin, Jeremiah, and Jor'Dyn. I LOVE y'all.

Thank you, Mama Denise, for the prayers, words of encouragement and love. Thank you for always accepting me as daughter. And thank you for accepting me as sister Terrance, Monise, Angelique, Angel, and Cry.

Thank you, Big Mama, Auntie Delores, Auntie Sheila, and Cousins Markisha and Gerald, for always showing me I'm family and loved.

I'm grateful for my whole Anderson, Hackney, Wallace, Robinson, Flanagan, Ware and King family. Family is important to God.

Qiana Nicole. That's the whole line. Those that know, know. More of the world will soon, and it's exciting.

Amber, thank you for believing in me, affirming me, getting me, and pushing me. Thank you for investing in me. Thank you for crying with me! You are a jewel.

Erika, thank you for your friendship and support. I love you! Thank you for warring with me in prayer and helping me see my worth. Thank you for encouraging me and keeping me steady.

Tasha, "And She Lived!" You spoke words that planted a seed. And God confirmed it. And now it is OUR time to live and make it do what it do! You've always had it. I'm glad you're shaking the dirt of life off. People better get ready!

Tanae, thank you for lifting my head and changing the trajectory of this story. It was different before you tag teamed me into the confident woman of God mindset from the broken one, I hadn't realized I slipped into. Whatever mindset you're in will inevitably show up in your writing. Thanks for reaching down and getting me when I couldn't see truth.

Rondell, brother, thank you for seeing the truth and not letting me believe a lie! Your perspective helped change the story and the narrative. I am grateful for you and for giving me your wife lol.

God Mama Pat, thank you for lovingly shepherding me since I was 15 years old! Thank you for giving me the special family holiday memories I will cherish forever. Thank you for sharing your family with me! Thank you for continuing to be there for me when my mommy passed. Thank you for pushing me to not crumble and to write and create. I love you!

Thank you Mama Tiny for teaching me and helping equip me with the spiritual tools I have used to make it through the years and had to tap into to birth this book! I love you! Thank you for affirming me and lovingly correcting me.

Thank you, Auntie Delores for the words of encouragement to do this and go hard for my dreams and for the prayers! You are the G.O.A.T.

Alexandria, this is our book! Lol. Thank you for walking with me dear friend. Partnering with me, and investing in me!

Angelica! Man. I just love you. Thank you for editing and guiding me on how to make the story better! Thank you for being there. THANK YOU! Thank you… bye because I'm tearing up!

Eman, thank you so much for your edits and guidance! You helped make this story so much better. I appreciate your input and time and effort. I'm so grateful!

Thank you JZ for mentoring me, helping me overcome my writers block, and remaining a friend after I quit my only ever real job working for you lol! You and Monica are beautiful souls that I cherish.

Tammi, you've become my friend during this process and I'm grateful for your input and guidance in my realization of me as I have produced this book! Thanks for telling me all the things to do to POP! Lol. I'm excited for you too!

To Tanya DeFreitas, author, publisher, and speaker/teacher. Thank you for teaching, training, helping, taking a chance on and loving a stranger. You're so dope! She has the whole package available if you're ready to get your book out! Hit her up at lovewinspub.com

Nathaly! You are so amazing. I told you my vision and you created this cover in ONE day when I found myself in a bind. I hope you get countless bookings for your beautiful work! You are the truth!
Hit her up for your book covers, website designs, and more at her site: theevans. group

I love all my family and friends and while I can't mention each and every name, I wanted to acknowledge Sheena, Charneice, Erica, Nnamdi, Kelvin, Tamara and Dru, Rondell, Eric, Mama Karen and Papa Ced, and Mama Darlene. Y'all have special spaces in my heart forever. This book is for you too! Thank you!

There are many people I can and want to thank! So even if your name isn't mentioned above, THANK YOU!!!! I LOVE YOU and you can do great things. I'm either rooting for what you've already released or eagerly awaiting it because everyone attached to me is great! And we are setting this world on fire!

Love,
Camile Jené

www.ingramcontent.com/pod-product-compliance
Lightning Source LLC
LaVergne TN
LVHW091117080826
845145LV00008B/1949

* 9 7 8 0 5 7 8 8 0 2 5 7 2 *